Suppose

I0654204

Drabbles, Flash Fiction, and Short Stories

By Kathy Steinemann

Print Edition
ISBN 978-1-927830-12-3

Cover by Kathy Steinemann
With some graphic elements from
PublicDomainPictures.net

Contributing Authors
Amber Hayward
A. L. Kaplan
Donna Milward

Foreword
Barbara Galler-Smith

Dedicated

To my husband,
my first and best beta reader.

And to Brad and Peggy,
inspirations and role models.

Table of Contents

Foreword

Barbara Galler-Smith

Short is good.

I love short fiction. One of the best things about short fiction is that it lends itself to our super-busy lives. We can have a satisfying read for fifteen minutes, pack a few stories together for a quiet lunch hour, or read a super-short while we wait in line somewhere.

This collection, *Suppose*, provides all of that.

Suppose you saw something you couldn't explain. And then suppose it turned out to be something far stranger, or funnier, or more horrifying than you ever expected. That element of surprise, and a different way of looking at things, is what this anthology is all about.

You're in for some rewarding twists and turns and smiles.

Most of the short stories take less than fifteen minutes to read, and the drabbles (exactly one hundred words long) are clever and engaging and take less than thirty seconds.

Kathy Steinemann has provided us with an assortment of creepy, quirky, and wonderfully fun tales. Along with contributing authors, Amber Hayward, A. L. Kaplan, and Donna Milward, she's put together an anthology that *rocks*.

Even the busiest person can read a couple of drabbles while waiting for the barista to make coffee. So, I suppose you should order coffee, sit down, and be charmed.

Introduction

Not only is the universe stranger than we imagine, it is stranger than we can imagine. ~ Sir Arthur Eddington

Suppose your imagination were bursting with ideas, dreams, and fantasies. Suppose you had life experiences imprinted on your brain, experiences so strange that nobody could ever imagine them to be true. Suppose you were able to share what was tumbling about inside your head.

Would you?

Kathy, Amber, Amy, and Donna do just that in this book of drabbles, flash fiction, and short stories.

Immerse your imagination in tales that embrace an eclectic mix of humor, horror, fantasy, sci-fi, romance, and life experiences so unbelievable they have been disguised as fiction.

Twisted endings. Horror that turns into comedy. Romance in unexpected places. Will you see the clues, or will you be surprised?

Buckle your seatbelt and read carefully, my friend.

Anonymous Artist

Kathy Steinemann

This story is based on a tale penned by a young woman who identified herself as Ada. She created it from her recollection of events, assisted by entries in her mother's diary. Could it be true? How would you know if it were?

Marianne cradled Heinrich's emaciated hand in hers and gazed at his yellowish-grey skin. His tortured breathing, a rattle interspersed with bubbling, was almost inaudible among the beeps of monitoring equipment. His weak exhalations barely stirred his bedraggled mustache. Tubes fed him and drained him. He floated in and out of consciousness.

Less than a week. The doctors said he'd be dead in less than a week. I'm going to paint him. I want something to remember him by.

The nurse checked Heinrich's vitals. "Your brother's fortunate to have a dedicated sister like you. You should go home for a while and get some sleep. He's stable for now. We'll call you if his condition deteriorates."

Marianne opened her mouth to protest, but realized the nurse was right. She stroked Heinrich's hand just one more time before she left his room.

As she plodded home, contemplating the watery sidewalk cracks through the rain, she recalled how he had looked when he was well. The hospital staff had believed her when she told them that Heinrich was her brother. But he was an aging, homeless man with partial amnesia, whom she had rescued from the street.

By the time she had walked the five blocks to her apartment, her blonde-streaked auburn hair was plastered to her brow. She toweled off and hurried straight to her easel.

She painted Heinrich healthy. Handsome. Happy.

It was the painting that changed her life.

It was the moment that changed the world.

~*~

The unit clerk at the nursing station gaped, unable to speak. She pointed in the direction of Heinrich's ward. Marianne rushed toward his room. *No. Am I too late?*

Heinrich was sitting up in bed. He was healthy. Handsome. Happy.

She hyperventilated. The bright lights blurred before her eyes. … She passed out.

~*~

Nobody believed it at first, but Heinrich's brain tumor was indeed gone. He remembered Marianne. He remembered his surname. His family, delighted to find him after searching for so many years, took him home.

Nothing in Marianne's world seemed real anymore. For several weeks, she teetered in a daydream, or maybe a nightmare, hovering on the brink of insanity. Lights appeared brighter. Darkness appeared blacker. She often found herself staring at nothing. She entertained a fleeting urge to dye her auburn hair cobalt-blue like her daughter's, but she decided it wouldn't befit a woman her age. As most humans do, Marianne adjusted. The months marched by, and life continued.

Then, her daughter fell ill.

Ada had leukemia, the doctors said. Poor prognosis, the specialists agreed. Ada quit her classes at the university, and she asked Marianne to paint her portrait before it was too late, before she was too skinny.

"Please, Mom. It'll give me something nice to look at when I can't get out of bed anymore."

Marianne hugged her. The words she wanted to say to her only child lodged in her throat, blocked by a profound sadness she refused to release. *She's so thin I can feel her shoulder blades through her sweater. I can't lose her. She's everything to me.*

Ada squeezed her mother. "Thanks for everything, Mom. For raising me all by yourself. For everything you've taught me." She sobbed. "I don't want to die. I'm not ready."

Marianne bit her lip and resolved not to let Ada see her weep. She'd cry later. For now, she had to be strong.

Ada was stoic for the entire portrait sitting, managing to smile in spite of her anguish. Her smile deepened when she stood back to look at her likeness. The painting was flattering, with exactly the right tints of cobalt-blue in her hair.

Ada's next checkup showed complete remission of her disease.

~*~

Marianne was a religious woman, yet she didn't feel like a saint. Did she truly have the power to heal through her art? *There's only one way to be sure.*

During frequent visits to the hospital, she photographed terminal patients and talked with them, trying to put them at ease. Then she returned home, and she painted. She painted them healthy and happy. The hospital gained worldwide recognition for its unprecedented cure statistics.

Finally, the inevitable day dawned. Ulrike, one of the nurses, recognized Marianne's talent. Ulrike's cervical cancer had spread to her uterus and metastasized. She cornered Marianne in an empty patient room. "You're my only hope. I know what you can do. I don't know how, but you're a miracle worker: a healing angel. Please. I'll keep your secret."

Marianne painted Ulrike, and the nurse became another one of the hospital's success stories.

However, neither miracles nor saints can be kept under a bushel or hidden from social media. The news spread, and people came from all over the world to sit for their portraits. They camped outside Marianne's building, lining up for blocks.

She switched from oils to acrylics to speed drying. Her brushstrokes grew faster and more accurate. In order to keep up with demand, she quit her job at the museum. All she asked in return was for people to bring her takeout food and fresh art supplies, to pay her bills, and to read to her while she worked. Rowling. Hemingway. Austen. Anything that didn't contain gore or porn.

She often toiled until she could no longer hold a brush. When that happened, Ada would put her to bed and turn off the light before returning to her own apartment.

Unfortunately, Marianne couldn't save everyone. Some of the sick died while they waited in line. She lost weight. Her skin turned sallow, and she developed severe back pain from so many hours of bending over the easel.

Then, the government intervened.

They assigned handlers. They sent away the sick. They transported Marianne and Ada to a secret facility where ailing senators, oil magnates, and presidents were treated.

Marianne's health continued to fade.

Ada argued with the government handlers. "Look, if you don't treat her better, she'll get sick and die. If you want her to continue doing this, you have to give her regular hours, exercise facilities, and healthy food."

The government met Ada's demands. A personal trainer set up individualized fitness programs. Audio books were piped through the sound system. Daily shipments of fresh fruit and vegetables were arranged.

Soon, Marianne realized that some of the people she was painting were villains: drug-cartel kingpins, dishonest dictators, and weapons smugglers. Roiling with indignation, she ground her teeth so hard she needed a dentist to repair the damage. Still, she kept painting.

One night, she slouched in front of her easel. *I'm so tired. Why am I doing this? Who am I helping?* She wept. Then she painted: a beautiful beach sunset on a planet with two moons, fruit trees, and waterfalls. *I hope Ada will understand.*

~*~

When Ada woke from her nap in the rocking chair, her mother had vanished. Ada's initial reaction was panic. Where could Marianne have gone? Government goons still stood guard in the hallway. The windows had bars on them. She checked the adjoining suite and the bathrooms. There was no sign of her mother, but Marianne's clothing, painting supplies, and possessions were intact.

She noticed Marianne's final work of art. *A new painting, but it's not a portrait.* Ada scrutinized it for a few moments. Then her expression turned from puzzlement to exhilaration. She pulled a magnifying glass out of the art supplies and examined the canvas.

Ah. Right there, just as she suspected. A tiny woman with blonde-streaked auburn hair walking on the beach and clutching a solar-powered e-reader. *Mom painted herself into the scene! She'll have peace now.*

Ada frowned, and her exhilaration transformed into sorrow.

She paced. *Can the world live with the knowledge of such power? With the knowledge that it even exists? And that it might be gone forever?*

Ada tied her blue hair into a knot at the nape of her neck and painted until dawn. She painted the Earth: a serene Earth where nobody knew about Marianne. Then she walked out the door past bewildered handlers, who couldn't remember why they were there.

Ada never spoke of the talent she had inherited from her mother.

~*~

Dear Reader,

I suppose I should tell you how I came in possession of Ada's story.

One afternoon last year while I was browsing through the *arts & crafts* category at *Craigslist,* I saw a painting advertised:

Painting, acrylic, by anonymous artist - $500

I clicked on the photo. It showed a beautiful beach sunset on a planet with two moons. A planet with fruit trees and waterfalls. It was gorgeous. I had to have it. I bought it without dickering over the price or worrying about overnight shipping costs.

When it arrived, I removed it from the battered frame in order to send it out for reframing. In the backing material, I found several pages containing a preposterous tale that nobody would ever believe. The story was accompanied by a note of explanation. I chuckled.

Then, I grabbed a magnifying glass. When I inspected the painting, I did indeed find a tiny woman with blonde-streaked auburn hair strolling on the beach. But there was also a second woman. With cobalt-blue hair. Both women clutched solar-powered e-readers in their hands.

As I write this, I look across the screen of my laptop and see the painting hanging on the wall. I can't decide whether it's mocking me, or perhaps inspiring my writing.

8

Is this fiction? Or is it so unbelievable that it could be true? You must judge for yourself.

MUDD

Kathy Steinemann

Beauty products come in a wide range of prices, but quality is always more expensive. Would you be willing to pay for the best mud treatment in the county?

August is the best month: the month after local creeks and rivers overflow, depositing generous accumulations of sediment. Mallory, co-proprietor of Mallory and Ursula's Dirty Delights Spa, a.k.a. MUDD, loves the feel of mud on her fingers. Her hands are always smooth and soft, her fingernails long and strong. She and her harvesters haul the mud from Sludge Flats to the spa. There they add volcanic ash, seaweed, clay, mineral water, and an essential-oil mixture that neutralizes the unusual smell.

Clients luxuriate in 102° MUDD-baths, cucumber slices over their eyelids, ecstatic to discover the improvement in their skin and muscle tone. Over the years, the price for a MUDD-bath has doubled, tripled, quadrupled. And nobody complains. The price is worth it, everyone says.

Mallory and Ursula's bank accounts continue to bulge, and they wallow in the good life.

~*~

Every summer, retired plumber Jed Rentner watches birds and hikers from the creaky rocking chair on the porch of his retirement cabin in the woods. The wizened geezer is always happy to talk to strangers. Nobody can tell whether his stories are true, but his visitors sit around him on wooden chairs, sometimes for hours. His favorite tale is about his flush outhouse. The only one in the county, he claims.

"Yep. I kid you not. Happens every year. My outhouse is just yonder, over there beside the road into town. In June when the runoff's high, muddy water floods everythin' out here. It raises the water table and fills my outhouse to ground level. By August, the crapper's clean and empty. Just a little silt and mud in the hole. Even smells good."

He cracks a toothy grin and pokes at his teeth with a toothpick. "Yep. Sweet smellin' and maintenance-free."

Today's rapt listener is Sonja, a frequent customer of Mallory and Ursula's Dirty Delights Spa. She scowls. "But your cabin is right above Sludge Flats, isn't it?"

"Now that you mention it, s'ppose it is."

"You don't mean—" She recoils.

"Sure do. I s'ppose one of these days I should tell those girls where their mud comes from. Maybe old Jed should be gettin' a royalty."

Pablo's Pain
Kathy Steinemann

And ever has it been known that love knows not its own depth until the hour of separation. ~ Khalil Gibran

Pablo shivered.

A fog of pale shadows and shapes surrounded him. He strained to hear, but all he could distinguish were occasional fragments of Kirsten's distant sobs, partially muffled by the sounds of a windstorm and the squawks of nearby birds.

Kirsten spoke to Leslie, a friendly woman Pablo had met a few minutes previously. "I hate to leave him like this, but it's for the best. In his condition, he needs special care. I feel so guilty, though."

Pablo moaned to the empty room.

A door slammed, and the sobbing stopped.

The radio diverted his attention with a faint melody, resurrecting images from better days.

Sharing breakfast toast smeared with peanut butter. Waiting in anticipation for Kirsten to get home from work. Dancing to their favorite tunes. Sitting together while they watched TV.

He swayed, and closed his eyes. The images drifted further back in time.

Hot, humid days. Watching birds from a lofty vantage point above the valley. The insistent cries of the young ones demanding food. Playful spats and reconciliations with his sister.

He envisioned the men who had shackled him along with his siblings and neighbors. And relived the desperation he felt while watching most of the prisoners suffer and die. He re-experienced the anxiety that consumed him when his tormenters separated him from the few sad captives who managed to survive.

A violent tremble shook him.

More scenes fluttered into his isolated world: insistent, repugnant memories.

Lonely existence in a cell. Separation from the other inmates. Scars from his ordeal. Lingering pain. Pining for lost companions.

But Kirsten had rescued him, taken him into her home.

And he had fallen in love with her.

A pleasant sensation flew down his spine as he remembered her tender touch.

He scrutinized the room. Unfamiliar scents floated through the air. His universe was a terrifying, alien landscape fraught with unseen perils. He focused through a semi-opaque veil to examine a confusing assemblage of indistinct forms and colors, and he flinched as an unfamiliar object from above brushed his head.

Pablo shuffled to the side, step by step. If he moved too far, he might walk into something, or he might fall. And Kirsten wasn't there to protect him.

Another woman came near. He concentrated and recognized Leslie's sympathetic voice. But many of the words were foreign. Where was Kirsten? He ached for her, not this person he barely knew.

Leslie continued to murmur. When she reached for him, he lunged forward. But she evaded him. Her silken voice became a perpetual thrum emanating from somewhere in his gloomy twilight. After several minutes, she vanished.

An eternity passed before the door reopened and announced the approach of Kirsten's comforting scent. Pablo peered in her direction, and his face grew warm as he blushed. "Kirsten."

"Hello, Pablo." She cuddled him. "It's time for me to leave. Leslie's going to take care of you. I love you. If there was any other way, I'd do it. I'm so sorry, but I can't take care of you anymore."

Pablo felt a tear splash onto his cheek. He kissed her. "See you later."

"Bye, bye, Pablo. I'll miss you, baby. Oh, I'll miss you so much."

As she trudged toward the exit, he said bye-bye several times, and she answered in kind.

The door closed with an almost inaudible click.

Pablo listened while Kirsten scraped the windshield. She cursed at the frightful cold and slammed the car door. Then the scrunch of tires on frozen snow faded into silence.

He wailed a sorrowful, throaty lamentation for the person he adored. Kirsten had explained her intentions to him, but until this moment, he had never truly understood. He tried to break out of his enclosure. Cold metal greeted him no matter where he moved. It trapped him in another prison reminiscent of the one that had confined him so many years ago. And he couldn't escape this one either.

He uttered a raspy sob. Exhaustion consumed him.

Pablo was jolted awake by the clatter of Leslie unlocking the cell. "Come here, Pablo. Everything's going to be all right. This is your new home."

His peripheral vision revealed the presence of a hand held out in a gesture of encouragement. He ruffled his feathers as he groped with his beak to find a secure foothold. He sniffed at her skin. Leslie smelled like unfamiliar birds, perhaps the flock that Pablo had been listening to since his arrival.

Leslie patted him. "You stepped up. You're a good boy. Would you like to see the other birds?"

"Yeah."

"Kirsten has to go to the hospital, and she can't care for you anymore, but you'll meet lots of new friends here, and I'll talk to the vet about fixing your eyes."

The bird sounds became a welcoming melody that increased in volume as Leslie neared the aviary. Pablo could distinguish the shapes of manzanita playstands and fluttering wings. He leaned into Leslie's chest and laid his head against her. Then he ran his cheek over the texture of her sweater. The calls of the other birds, although foreign to him, were comforting. He relaxed his stranglehold on her wrist.

She scratched beneath one of his wings. "Good boy. You'll like it here, I promise."

He clicked his beak. "Good Pablo. Ohhhh, good bird, Pablo. Pretty bird, Pablo. Good boy."

Leslie placed him on a perch.

He gurgled a purring chuckle from deep within his throat. This was his perch. He had memorized every groove and bump in the manzanita. He knew where the food and water dishes sat, where the barriers blocked the edges. And it smelled like Kirsten.

He strutted and pranced, comforted by the sudden discovery of a familiar object in his environment.

Aromas wafted through the air: bananas, oranges, his favorite bird pellets. But what was that? A scent from the past. He swiveled his head from left to right, trying to discern its source. A flash of red wings from another scarlet macaw crossed his field of vision. He stretched toward her … farther … farther …

Leslie's voice warned, "Pablo, be careful. Do you want to go and sit with Sherry?"

"Yeah!"

She picked him up, and his claws dug into her arm as he extended his body as far as he could. She placed him on the other bird's perch.

Pablo bobbed several times. Then he filled his crop with partially digested food for the sister from his first life. Sherry licked his cheek, preened his feathers, and whispered soft coos while she groomed him. Pablo unfurled one wing to pull her close.

Her scent tugged him into the past, to a world that existed long before his eyes had betrayed him, to the nestlings and their home at the roof of a verdant jungle. He recalled joyful hours in the nest with his mother and two siblings while they waited for his father to return with food.

But the memories soured.

Metal monsters destroying ancient trees on the hillside. Poachers with noisy chain saws. Shrieks of terror from nestlings as their homes plummeted to the floor of the forest. Thunderous bangs that stilled the adult birds when they swooped down to protect their babies. A dark, constricting box. Young birds struggling and trampling one another as they shared the blackness with the trophy tail feathers that had been wrenched from their parents' still-twitching bodies.

Pablo shivered.

How to Tell if Your Human Worships You

Donna Milward

This story is by Donna Milward's cat, Spartacus. He emulates his talented author mamma and her fantastic sense of humor as he shares his feline philosophy with you.

Psst … She's asleep.

My writer needs a nap. She's been working hard at looking for a job, writing, and spring cleaning. We'll let her sleep, and I, Spartacus will point out to all you felines the various ways you can tell when your human is a little too obsessed with you. This will help you learn the train-ability of your human and allow you to determine their place in the event of the global cat domination.

1. That flashy thing. If you have a human, chances are your human has one of those annoying flashy things. They point it at you constantly, no matter what you are doing and will spare you no decorum or dignity. This is an unfortunate thing that cat-obsessed humans do, and cannot be avoided. Be adorable whenever possible. It will lead to expensive toys and treats once you master "The Cuteness". Which leads us to …

2. Insufferable Cutesy Nicknames. It is the absurd habit of people to give you one name, but call you by a variety of others. These include, but are not limited to: Sweetie-kitty, Handsome-boy, Little-Man, Sweet-boy, Baby, etc., fill-in-your-humiliating-moniker-here. The good news is you can pick and choose which one, if any, you will respond to. I myself only respond to Baby. You would too, with a name like Spartacus Thomas Jones Milward.

3. They will share their noms. Once you have mastered "The Cuteness", stealing noms becomes easy. This also works on forbidden surfaces like counter tops. The worst that can happen is being "shooed", and the rewards outweigh the possibility of needing to execute a hasty landing.

4. *The Constant Cuddle.* Obsessed humans always feel the need to pick you up and cuddle you. I suspect it is due to their lack of fur. They covet the soft warmness that we have and feel the need to rub it upon themselves. This too can be used to your advantage, and for training. How, you ask?

5. *They will remain motionless for your benefit.* The devoted human will endure extended minutes of discomfort to avoid disturbing you. It is the true indicator of gauging your human's commitment. Feel free to perch on whichever body part you find comfortable. A worthy human will suppress tingling nerves, hunger, and even the need to urinate in order to maintain your happiness. Feel free to nap. Feel free to interrupt THEIR time on their poo-pond. If they are willing to sit on their wet white seat, in the dark, while you enjoy a siesta in their lap, you have an obsessed human, and therefore a dedicated minion when cats take over the world.

These are but five reliable indicators of fanatical behaviors in the species Homo sapiens. If you are lucky enough to find such a human, congratulations. If you are not, don't worry. Humans are highly susceptible to cuteness and easily trained. Maybe sometime soon I will tell you the finer points of "The Cuteness", and how to use it.

Shades of Red

Kathy Steinemann

Mix one part passion and one part flattery. Sprinkle with red. What do you get? Titillation? Or something else? Our mild-mannered accountant is about to discover the answer.

Drew's eyebrows arched above the frames of his glasses. Three envelopes in three days. Each one had included a short message.

Day one: *My favorite color is red. What's yours?*

Day two: *Are you going to the sci-fi museum again today?*

Day three: *You like Bradbury. So do I.*

Today's note was the fourth: *You have a nice smile.*

He didn't know whether to feel flattered or apprehensive.

Either way, Drew Gordon experienced a rush of adrenaline.

The fifth day dawned in Drew's one-bedroom apartment on the fourth floor of Baker Block Suites.

A breakfast of coffee and two pieces of brown-sugar toast sprinkled with cinnamon; social media feeds; a check for responses at Compati-Date; a quick browse through sci-fi forums.

He checked the clock. Time to set out for his boring job at Blanchard & Brown Chartered Accountants.

The super nodded at him as he sauntered down the hall.

Drew studied the woman who smiled at him in the elevator: dark hair, calm blue eyes, well-dressed, a quick remark about the weather.

Could it be her? Maybe someday he'd find the courage to ask her out. She was good-looking, cheerful. She always chatted and smiled at him. It would be easy for her to slip a letter under his door. *Or maybe it's a guy.*

He shuddered.

Drew picked up a paper at the newsstand around the corner. The girl who operated it greeted him with a cheerful grin. Did she brush his hand a little too long when she gave him his change? *Do I know her from somewhere?*

When he got to work, he watched the people in the office. He didn't notice anyone spying on him.

Noon: The server at Cinnamon's Cafe was friendly. She seemed to spend more time at Drew's table than she needed to.

After lunch: Normal office routine punctuated by frustration, constant side-glances, and errors.

Shortly before quitting time, the boss reprimanded him. "Where's your head today? You've been making mistakes."

"Sorry, sir. I'll try harder."

But it's difficult to try harder when you feel as though you're being watched, when every stranger you meet is a potential suspect. He eyed the pedestrians on the sidewalk. He scrutinized the salesman in the men's clothing store.

When he returned to his apartment, he found the fifth note: *Nice shirt you bought today. Black goes with everything, even red.*

~*~

Over the ensuing days, the notes took on a sinister twist.

Day six: *Playing games is so much fun, don't you think?*

Day seven: *Are you nervous? Isn't this exciting?*

Day eight: *Where's that winning smile?*

Day nine: *Red, red, the color of dead.*

Drew called the police.

Two bored-looking officers put in an appearance. They asked a few questions. The taller one rolled his eyes and said he'd pass the information along to one of the detectives. The shorter one smirked. "Right. It's not as if they don't have enough trivial things like murders to keep them busy."

Drew waited for hours, but nobody from the police department contacted him.

He didn't sleep well, and when he did, he dreamt.

... A nebulous woman in a red cloak materialized in the bedroom. When she came almost near enough for him to remove the veil from her face, she laughed a sinister laugh and broke into shards of glass. He looked down to see his terrified reflection mirrored in the splinters ...

~*~

On Saturday, Drew decided to go out for breakfast. The notes always showed up late in the afternoon, but he couldn't stick around just waiting.

Cinnamon's Cafe was quiet. Unusual for a Saturday morning. His favorite server asked him what he'd like to drink.

He pushed up his glasses. "Coffee, please, Arlene."

She fetched a menu and the coffee pot, and sat across from him. "You're here pretty early for lunch."

"Yeah. Didn't feel much like sticking around my apartment."

She passed him a menu. "You look worried. Need someone to confide in? I'm a good listener."

"I shouldn't keep you from your other customers."

"Do you see anyone else in my section? Besides, the boss is away, so I can sit for a while."

He could see by the ripples in his coffee that he was shaking. He set his cup on the table. "Just a rough patch at work. I've been making a few mistakes, but I'll be okay." He changed the subject. "What do you do when you're not slaving away here at Cinnamon's?"

"I'm taking computer courses at night. I want to get out of this hole and do something interesting. Waitressing's boring. I enjoy the occasional break when I can talk to someone and not rush my butt off."

He grinned. "You gonna turn into a computer hacker?"

"No. Just trying to better myself. I enjoy challenge and stimulation. Computers are the future." She pushed her bangs off her forehead. "So, what kind of work do you do? It's Andrew, right? You were in here one day with one of your co-workers, and I think that's what he called you. Everyone knows me. The beauty of name-tags. But you're not wearing one."

"I prefer Drew. Sorry, I should have introduced myself. I'm an accountant, so accuracy is important. That's why my boss is on my case." His expression turned pensive as he looked at the tattoo on her arm: the word *Red* in an arrow. "Hey, I never noticed that before. Is Red someone's name, or are you a closet communist?"

She rolled up her sleeve to show it off. "I got it last week. Red's my boyfriend. He likes archery." She scratched around the tattoo. "I've got to stop doing that. Don't want to get it infected."

Three customers slid into the next booth. Arlene shrugged. "Guess my break's over. It was nice talking to you again."

~*~

After breakfast, Drew bought a paper. He nodded at the girl who ran the newsstand. "Hi, I'm Drew Gordon. Nice weather today if you ignore the smog, right?"

She frowned.

Drew squinted. Scrutinized. Where had he met her before? "I can't recall a day when I haven't seen you here. Don't you ever get time off?"

Her dark eyes flared. "I'm Nellie. Don't you remember me?"

"Nellie?" He craned his neck. "Nerdy Nellie? Is it really you?"

Her face flushed. Embarrassment? Anger? He tried to read her expression.

She played with the ruby pendant around her neck. "You come here every day for weeks, and you never look me in the eye. And no, I don't get time off. I work mornings, and I paint in the afternoons."

"I'm sorry. You've changed since high school. Your hair is darker and …"

"Say it. I've lost weight."

"Well, yeah, but you're pretty. You always were. I'm sorry if you took offense at the nickname. Everyone envied you because you were so smart." He swallowed. Floundered for appropriate small-talk. "You said you paint. Do you work for a construction company?"

"No, I'm an artist. You've probably seen my work at the Schattner Sci-Fi Museum. Redscapes. You know the ones. Skyscapes on alien worlds."

"Redscapes? Yeah, I remember. They're good. Really good." He contemplated his feet. "When do you get off?"

"One o'clock."

"Would you like to join me for lunch? There's a nice little cafe just down the block. Cinnamon's."

She straightened a couple of magazines. "Are you asking me out on a date?"

"Well, not really. … Yeah, I suppose you could call it a date. I'd like to catch up on what's happened between high school and now."

She peered into his face with a contemplative expression. "Fine. You're not a total stranger or anything. Here's your paper."

Drew took the proffered newspaper. She seemed harmless enough. Could she still be holding a grudge after all these years? *It's not like we bullied her or anything.*

~*~

Drew roamed. Looked in store windows. Wandered through a shopping mall.

At 12:55 he approached the newsstand and watched Nellie as she waited for her replacement to arrive. She blushed as soon as she saw him, an endearing pink that made her seem sweet and vulnerable.

However, the moment soured when a magazine cover with a photo of Al Pacino made him flash back to Michael Corleone's voice in *The Godfather Part II*: "Keep your friends close, but your enemies closer."

The hairs on his neck prickled.

~*~

While Drew and Nellie strolled to the cafe, they chatted about old school chums.

He ushered her to his usual booth. Arlene appraised her with raised eyebrows. "What tasty treat would you like to order off our delicious *gourmet* menu?"

They all laughed.

He observed both women during lunch. Arlene acted snippy with Nellie. Nellie stumbled over her tongue and giggled even when his jokes weren't funny. After he walked her home, he puzzled over the encounter. He couldn't remember hardly anything she had said, but he didn't get any bad vibes.

He took a roundabout route back to Baker Street, delaying his homecoming as long as possible. Weekends alone made time drag, and he liked to get out in the fresh air.

Lost in thought and fantasizing about a faceless beauty jumping his bones, he almost collided with the super in the entryway. Drew wrinkled his nose at the man's nicotine breath and pungent, sweaty odor.

The stench lingered in his nostrils during his elevator ride to the fourth floor. He hesitated at the entrance to his apartment. His heart pumped faster, and his stomach rolled as he eased the door open. No note.

The breath he'd been holding hostage escaped in a noisy hiss. With trembling hands, he gathered his clothes hamper and headed for the coin laundry in the basement.

~*~

The well-dressed woman with the dark hair and calm blue eyes rode the elevator down with him. His pulse galloped. "On your way to do your washing too?"

She nodded. "Every Saturday, rain or shine. I'm Rosie, by the way." She offered her hand, and her cheeks reddened. "I work in the same building you do. On the main floor. TeleTours Travel Bureau."

"Glad to meet you, Rosie. I'm Drew. Strange the way things are, right? How many times have we been in the elevator together, and how many times have we talked? But we never introduced ourselves." A tingling warmth flooded every one of his extremities.

They exchanged pleasantries and safe conversation while they sorted laundry and started their machines.

Rosie revealed that she did a lot of reading. Business was slow at the travel bureau. Her favorite author was Ray Bradbury. And she loved jelly doughnuts with a generous sprinkling of icing sugar.

Drew scrutinized her neatly folded laundry and cocked his head. "You sure have a lot of red clothes."

"My favorite color. What's yours?"

"Blue, I guess."

"I'm a winter. Red, shocking pink, navy blue, white, and black all suit me, but I really like red. My mom says it matches my outgoing personality."

"Winter?"

"It's the color profile for my complexion and hair."

"Oh." He looked at the floor. "You have a boyfriend?"

"Not right now."

He fumbled with his hamper.

Rosie narrowed her eyes. Then she spoke. "Do you want to join me for homemade lasagna? I've got some in the oven. I know it's a bit early for supper, but we have to wait for the wash to go through. That gives us at least an hour."

Good-looking woman, homemade food. What's not to like? "Sure."

They shared a meal, political views, opinions on eco-tourism, likes and dislikes, and a bottle of wine. It was more than two hours later when they finally returned to the laundry room.

With clothes washed, dried, and folded, they exited the elevator at the fourth floor. Drew was unprepared when Rosie dropped her hamper and pulled his face to hers. The kiss was long, arousing, spicy.

Without a word, she pulled away and walked down the hall.

His blank gawp followed her hips until she disappeared behind her door. He stood, dazed, and blinked several times before plodding to his apartment. He had almost forgotten the notes.

Almost.

He hesitated at his door. Then he unlocked it and flung it open. Another envelope lay on the floor. He swallowed hard, and held his breath while he broke the seal.

Another note: *Arlene. Nellie. Rosie. You're getting far too cozy.*

He slammed the door and yelled at the walls. "Who are you? What do you want?"

Drew's cell phone rang.

UNKNOWN NUMBER

"Hello?"

Nobody spoke, but he heard heavy breathing.

"Who is this? What do you want?"

More breathing. A television in the background. Some horror show with a screaming woman. Maybe the opening scene from *Jaws*? Or was it a real woman? Someone spoke. The words were like a twanging guitar reverberating through a long tube. *"Who I am is my business, and I want you, Drew. Andrew. Drewdeedrew."* The voice could have been either male or female.

He yelled, "I don't understand! What do you want with me? What have I done to you? Why are you tormenting me?"

Short silence was followed by a loud click.

Pounding on the door.

His breath came hard, as though he had just finished a marathon. He edged toward the entrance and pressed his body tight to the wall. If someone shot through the door, he didn't intend to be in the line of fire.

Rosie's voice: "Drew? Drew? Let me in. It's Rosie."

He opened the door.

She frowned and pressed her fingers to her mouth. "You look terrible. What's wrong? I thought someone was here with you. I came over to apologize for … before. I've been watching you for weeks and hoping you'd make a move, but …"

He pulled her inside; looked both ways down the hall; closed and locked the door.

She touched his shoulder. "Drew?"

He explained what had happened over the past several days.

Her eyes grew progressively wider. "And you must have figured I was behind it, what with all my red clothes."

"The thought had crossed my mind, but you were with me when the last note arrived. So I knew it couldn't be you. Right? It's not you? Say it isn't you!"

Rosie gazed around the room. Then she drew his head down and whispered in his ear. "Do you always leave your laptop on with the lid up?" She put a finger to her lips.

He whispered back, "Yes."

She circled the room, came up behind the computer, and closed the lid before pressing her lips to his ear again. "Where's your cell phone?"

He pointed.

She turned it off. Then she spoke at normal volume. "I had a stalker who monitored everything I did. He installed software somehow. RAT: remote administration tools. He used it to control the webcam on my computer, and he hacked my cell phone. He knew everything I said and did."

"I thought the light had to be on when the webcam was working."

"So did I, but someone can rat without triggering the light."

"Now I'm getting shivers up my spine. This is really disturbing."

She shuddered. "There's nothing worse than finding out someone has been watching every private detail of your life."

"I assume your stalker was a guy. Did they catch him?"

"Sort of. But all they had was a bit of circumstantial evidence that couldn't prove anything. I think the police kind of dismissed it, like it wasn't serious. But it was serious to me."

He sighed. "No need to apologize for before. I've been thinking about you for weeks. You sorta remind me of Sandra

Bullock. I enjoy all the conversations I have with you, and I was trying to work up the courage to ask you out."

"You remind me of a young George Clooney with glasses. And you can hold an intelligent conversation with a woman without …" She looked at him with a passionate spark that fanned the slow fire she had started with her kiss in the hallway.

He sat on the sofa and patted the cushion beside him. She smiled. And she stayed the night.

~*~

Drew stretched. He heard breathing beside him. His eyes shot open, and his heart pounded. Until he remembered. Rosie. Sweet-smelling, passionate, voracious Rosie. He threw off his half of the blanket and looked down. *Pity to waste this.* He reached for her.

Her lashes flickered. "Mm. Okay, but no kissing. Morning breath."

What a way to begin a Sunday!

~*~

Neither of them spoke much in the shower. If the stalker had been watching, he might have thought they looked as though they were in a haze of dreams and private ponderings, maybe wondering where this was going, Drew perhaps still suspicious of Rosie and her motives.

Their reticence continued over coffee.

Drew put his hand on her shoulder. "Rosie, what is this? I mean, is this just a one-night stand or …?"

"Is that what you want? A one-night stand? I want you, Drew. I thought I was clear about that. I'm not a one-night woman."

His shoulders relaxed. "I—"

"Just so you know, I've never done this before. I mean, I've never kissed someone and then hopped into bed with him on the same day. I don't want you to think I'm easy. I can count the number of guys I've slept with on one hand."

"Me too. I mean, I want to keep seeing you, and I don't believe in one-night stands."

She blushed as she walked toward the door. "See you soon."

He pushed her against the wall and stroked her neck with his lips. "When?"

"My place. Six o'clock. Supper." She sucked his lower lip into her mouth. Her tongue was hot and moist. Drew pressed against her. She pushed him away and giggled. "No. Later."

The door latched behind her with a quiet clunk.

Did he dare open his laptop? He rummaged for a roll of masking tape and covered the camera lens as soon as he opened the lid. Should he do a virus scan? How would he know if it cleaned his system? It always found something.

He decided to leave the masking tape in place and go for breakfast while the scan worked its magic. What about his cell phone? If he turned it on, the stalker would know what he was doing. He left it off and stuffed it into a pocket.

~*~

The outside air was chilly. He shivered as he walked to Cinnamon's.

Arlene wasn't on shift. Drew scanned the cafe customers. He made special note of anyone wearing red, and one man reading a book with a red cover. Nobody seemed to notice him.

After breakfast, he wandered to the newsstand. Strangers in the street brushed by as they always did: in a hurry, texting, talking on cell phones, chatting with friends.

He waited until Nellie was finished with her customers before he asked, "Hi. How are things with you?"

She crossed her arms and glowered at him. "Fine."

He paid for his newspaper. "Are you okay? You look mad."

"I've decided not to go out with you anymore."

"We weren't— It wasn't— Did I do something wrong?"

She ignored his question and busied herself with paperwork.

He twisted his bottom lip. "Fine. Be like that. I just came here to tell you I'm seeing someone, but you already seem to know. How'd you find out?"

"Rosie's one of my customers. She couldn't shut up about you when she picked up her paper this morning. Didn't mention your name, but I knew who she was talking about. You haven't changed. You're still the same inconsiderate lout you always were."

"I'm sorry, Nellie. I didn't mean for you to think …"

"Just go. Leave me alone."

He hung his head. He'd heard guys at the office brag about stringing along several "chicks" at once, chortling about how good it felt, and how stupid the women were. Drew didn't feel good. Two women were interested in him, and he felt like crap.

He mumbled an apology to Nellie and trudged to the nearest strip mall, shoulders slouched, newspaper turning soggy in a rainsquall. He window-shopped while he dried off. Then he had a coffee and tried to read the still-damp paper.

After leaving his cell phone at the telephone kiosk for a wipe and reinstall, he wandered back to Cinnamon's Cafe. Rubber hamburger. Crispy fries. Dishwater coffee. He chewed every mouthful until it was the consistency of toothpaste, to could draw out the meal as long as possible.

But he couldn't sit in the booth all afternoon.

~*~

Drew eased the door open a few inches and peeked inside. No envelope. His breathing slowed as he pushed the door farther. It caught on something.

A harder push created a trail of dark red where the door had been. He stopped. With heartbeat drumming in his ears, he pushed his toe against the door.

Partially mashed into the carpet was a heap of raw liver.

By now, Drew's suspicions had progressed beyond the point of thinking a woman could be involved. It was too ... unladylike. *How'd he get in?*

He called the cops. Sunday, short-staffed, the woman said. She asked if it was an emergency. No, he said. Well, give me your number then, and I'll have someone call you. He gave her both his and Rosie's numbers.

Drew donned a pair of gloves, pulled his camera out of a dresser drawer, and photographed the pile of bloody meat from several angles. Then he remembered his computer.

The screen saver had activated. He pressed the space bar. Instead of the expected display of icons and shortcuts, a message appeared: *You won't get rid of me this easily.*

He vomited.

~*~

Drew swabbed at his pukey mess with paper towels. Then he called the super.

The repulsive little jerk seemed unimpressed with the shoddy cleanup job. He chewed at the cigarette drooping from the corner of his mouth. "You'll need to scrub that if you want your deposit returned when you leave. And what's the red muck by the door? If the blood isn't removed while it's still wet, it'll stain. We'll have to replace the carpet."

As if Drew didn't have enough to worry about already.

He apologized; said someone had entered without permission; asked the super to change the locks.

"It'll cost."

"I'll pay."

The super eyed the room, gawking as though he were trying to make a mental record of everything. "You leave your keys somewhere? Give one to a girlfriend, maybe? Or leave a copy at the office?"

Drew mused. A few weeks ago he had forgotten his keys at Cinnamon's, but they were there when he went back. He looked over the super's shoulder. "No, I don't think so. But somebody broke in, and I need to keep them from breaking in again."

"Did they pinch anything?"

"Not as far I can see."

The super grumbled and left.

Stupid, creepy-looking squirt. I wonder how often the guy showers. His hair is so greasy I could use it to make French fries.

Drew called Rosie. She told him to come right over.

He gargled to clear the vile taste from his mouth. No need for his breath to reek when he kissed her. Despite his anxiety, his pants grew tight at the thought of being near her again.

~*~

The mouthwatering smell of chicken stew filled the hallway outside Rosie's apartment. Worries about the stalker evaporated. But when she opened the door, he goggled like an awestruck teenager.

She dragged him inside and ran her tongue over one of his earlobes. They made it as far as the sofa.

After a few breaths, he froze and pulled away.

Rosie gasped. "What's wrong?"

"Where's your laptop?"

"In the bedroom. With the lid closed. Don't worry, nobody's watching us. Unless you want me to make a video." She giggled as she pressed close. "That's better. Come to Rosie, baby. Come to Rosie."

~*~

An hour later, Drew was startled by a strident buzzing noise. His exposed butt was cold, and the short nap had made him groggy. "What's that?"

"The buzzer on the stove. Playtime's over. That's supper calling." She threw on her crimson T-shirt and padded to the kitchen. Then she screamed.

He dashed toward the scream and stared at the mess on the table. Another bloody pile of raw liver.

Rosie retreated several steps. "Stuff it! I'm calling the cops. With two of us hounding them, maybe they'll do something about this nutcase."

~*~

Ten minutes. Two officers. No snide remarks.

Sure. It takes a complaint from a female *to get any action from the police. What am I? Chopped liver? That's not even funny.*

The officers asked Rosie questions. They wrote down the details. And this time they took a full statement from Drew as well.

~*~

The cops dusted for prints, but they didn't find anything.

They requested the video feeds for the hallway security cameras. The super said the system was broken. They told him to get it fixed.

In the interim, they set up surveillance. No point in cameras, they said. This guy's too smart, and he'd see us installing the equipment.

There was always a strange person lurking in the hall, whether it was a supposed cleaning lady, casual visitor, or courier.

Drew avoided the newsstand on Monday, and he stayed away from Rosie's.

His suspicious nature morphed into a state bordering on paranoia. He told himself he was safe among people on the street and in his office. But loud noises made him flinch. A stranger asking for directions set his heart racing. And his spine tingled when a vehicle slowed down while the driver reached for something on the passenger seat. He couldn't shake the feeling that someone was watching him, following his every move, and deliberately making his life miserable.

It was quiet at home and at the office: no notes, no liver, no phone calls on his newly restored cell phone. But his desires and doubts disturbed his sleep. He fantasized about Rosie. And he dreamed of a faceless male stalker in red carrying a blood-covered scythe.

He called Rosie at two a.m. She wasn't sleeping either. She came to his apartment, and they made love.

Once.

Rosie sighed as she lay in his arms. "I feel better now."

"Me too. No more tension. You're here with me, and the cops are near …"

She was already asleep.

~*~

When Drew picked up his newspaper on the way to work Tuesday morning, Nellie's voice was cold but civil. "Here's your change, sir."

"C'mon. It's me. I'm sorry. I didn't mean to hurt you."

"You didn't mean to hurt me in high school either, but you did. You ignored me. You made fun of me. And I'll bet you're making fun of me now when you're in private with your new girlfriend."

"I can't change what I did in high school. I apologized for then, and I apologized for now. Look, I didn't try to lead you on. I treated you with respect, and this is what I get in return?"

She sucked in her cheeks and sighed. "You're right. It's just that I used to have a crush on you, and all of a sudden I figured … Well, I was wrong. Friends?"

"Friends."

He felt better. The sun shone, the air smelled fresh, and the street performers were surprisingly good on this fine September day. However, his optimism was still tempered by worry.

~*~

Shortly before lunch, the boss took him aside. "Drew, what's going on?"

"I've got personal issues, sir, but the police seem to have the matter under control."

"You have two weeks of unused vacation left over from last year. No time like the present. After lunch, show Shelby what you're working on, and she can take over for you. You need to get your private affairs in order."

"Yes, sir."

The boss patted him on the shoulder. "If you need more than two weeks, let me know."

~*~

Drew walked to Cinnamon's.

Arlene smiled when she spotted him. "Hey, Drew. I saved you a piece of lemon-meringue pie. Too busy to talk, but if you stick around until after the rush dies down, I have a couple of questions for you."

He ordered, then tapped on his cell phone while he ate; sent flowers to Rosie; checked social media feeds; deactivated his Compati-Date profile; deleted old messages.

It was almost 12:45 before Arlene got a minute to chat. She dropped into the seat across from him. "I wanted to ask you what qualifications someone needs to work for your company. Do they have to be accountants?"

Caked-on makeup couldn't camouflage the swelling caused by a bruise on the right side of her face, and her mouth didn't move as freely as it should have.

Drew tried not to stare at the injury. "No, we have entry-level positions in the IT department, but the jobs would probably pay less than what you get here at Cinnamon's after you add in tips."

"Not everyone tips as well as you."

He smirked. "You're not a hacker yet?"

"No. That would be my boyfriend. He sees every computer system as a challenge. He claims he's hacked some pretty big guys. I can't say if it's true or not, but I guess I have to believe him."

Crap. How do I ask her? Just come out and do it. "Are you all right? You have a big bruise there."

Her hand flew to her cheek. She blinked. "It's nothing. Red can't ... I mean, I uh, it's nothing."

She hurried away.

He paid his bill. Then he spent the afternoon wondering about Arlene and Red. He didn't even know the guy. Could Red be the stalker? And if so, why?

~*~

Drew couldn't force himself to go to his own apartment. He knocked on Rosie's door instead.

The door opened a few inches. "Rrruf. Rrruf. RRRUF."

Rosie was gripping a leash with a Doberman pinscher straining at the other end. "Thank you for the roses." She ordered the dog to sit.

"You're welcome. Roses for Rosie. You deserve them for putting up with me. What's with the Doberman?"

"I took the day off and went to Rent-A-Dobie. We can keep Sushi for as long as we need to. She's really quite tame and easy to handle. Just looks mean. She'll bark and scare off intruders, but you can pet her."

Drew slipped through the door, and Sushi ran her nose from his feet to his crotch. "Whoa, girl!"

Rosie snickered, pulling back on the leash. "The trainer made her sniff the T-shirt you left here. Then he gave her a command that let her know you're a good guy. Here, you can pat her head."

Sushi's hindquarters swayed, and her stumpy tail wiggled as he scratched behind her ears. He grinned. "Hello, good girl. Can you speak?"

"Rrruf. Rrruf."

The corners of his eyes creased. "She'd make a good bed partner. Warm. Speaks when spoken to."

Rosie swatted his shoulder. "I want to discuss that with you. The bed-partner thing. Why don't you stay here for a while? My place is bigger than yours."

"Stay with you? You snore. You might keep me up all night."

"I'll keep you up, but not with my snoring."

"Promise?"

"It's settled then. Why don't you pack some things while I make supper? Take Sushi with you. By the way, I cleared her with the super."

~*~

With Sushi pulling at the leash, Drew headed for his apartment.

He talked to the undercover cop in the hall. She said that nothing eventful had happened.

He unlocked his door and smiled. No note.

Socks, underwear, shirts, pants, e-reader, laptop …

He headed for the bathroom. And recoiled at the sight of a lipstick-inscribed note on the mirror: *I'm still here.*

His jaw dropped. Sushi whined.

Drew stuck his head into the hallway and motioned for the cop to come in. With a puzzled expression, she inspected the mirror. "Nobody did this during my shift. Only two people entered your apartment: the locksmith and the super. Are your windows locked?"

"Always."

The officer checked. "The patio door isn't completely secure. He could've got in here."

"But—"

"I know. You keep it locked, but the last time he entered, he could have left himself another way in. It's secure now. We'll check for prints again, but I doubt if we'll find anything. This guy knows how to stay off the radar."

~*~

A dim room; a bright computer screen; a dark form silhouetted against the shifting display of bedrooms, living rooms, bathrooms. His left hand manipulated a mouse. He pressed a key that zoomed in on a woman. She was naked except for a ruby pendant. She ogled Drew's photo on her computer screen as one of her hands fondled her breasts and the other hand massaged, stroked. He zoomed in even closer. He rewound. He watched again … and again.

He sobbed.

~*~

Drew and Rosie didn't sleep well. Any passionate notions had been squelched by the fresh intrusion into his apartment. They threw off the blankets. Covered up again. Rolled from one side to the other. Scrutinized the ceiling.

An hour passed. Then Rosie whispered into the darkness. "Who do you think it is?"

He adjusted his pillow and checked the time on the alarm clock. "It has to be somebody who knows us, not some random stranger."

"I've never felt so violated in my life."

"Could it be the guy who stalked you before?"

"No, he moved to California."

"But he could still be watching you via computer."

She pondered for several seconds. "But he wouldn't have left notes or liver."

"Yeah, you're right. I keep trying to figure it out. It doesn't make sense."

"I have to get some sleep. I can't call in sick again."

He sighed. "You go to sleep. Sushi will bark if someone tries to get in."

~*~

When the alarm went off, they were both in such a stupor that they almost didn't hear it. Neither of them climbed out of bed. Drew mumbled, "I'm exhausted."

The phone rang. Rosie groped for it on the nightstand and pressed the *Speaker* button. "Hello."

Heavy breathing crackled over a staticky connection.

"The police are monitoring this number. Quit tormenting us."

The line went dead.

She rolled into Drew's arms, and she cried.

He stroked her hair. "Maybe I should go back to my own apartment so he'll leave you alone."

"No. I feel better with you here. I've watched you for so long and hoped you'd notice me. I think I fell for you the first day I moved in, and I'm not a big believer in love at first sight."

His arms stiffened.

She sighed. "Blast! I broke the cardinal rule. Never tell a guy you love him unless you know he loves you back."

"Rosie, I … I watched you for weeks too, but I've never told a woman I love her, except my mom." He ran his lips over her eyebrows, her nose. He sought her mouth, pulled her close in a greedy embrace. Her softness pushed against his chest. Her hips pressed, invited. He gasped. "Ahhrrrr. Woman. You'll be late."

~*~

No time for breakfast. Drew walked Rosie to work. He had the feeling they were being followed, but several inconspicuous glances over his shoulder revealed nothing suspicious. If somebody was there, he was adept at the game of stalker vs. prey.

The feeling persisted as he strode to the apartment.

His cell phone rang. It was the police. *"Arlene Simpson has been hospitalized. She asked us to get in touch with you. She'd like you to stop in and see her as soon as possible."*

He grabbed a handful of granola bars from a convenience store and caught a taxi to the hospital.

~*~

Drew padded to Arlene's room on the balls of his feet.

He flinched and drew back a pace. She looked as though she had endured a battle with a garbage compactor. Her face, especially on the right, was a mass of bruises and contusions, and she had a bandage wrapped around her head.

A single tear trickled to her chin when she noticed him in the doorway. "I don't feel as bad as I look." She moaned when she

41

attempted to prop herself on her elbows. "I withdraw that statement."

He sat beside her bed. "What happened?"

"Red happened. It's embarrassing to talk about, but I guess I should. I um … sometimes Red can't perform, if you know what I mean."

Drew bit his lip. "Yeah."

"He's been trying, but whenever it happens, he gets mad and says it's my fault. He's hit me before. Never like this though. The reason I asked you to visit is something he said. I think you might be in danger. Or the girl you brought into Cinnamon's on Saturday."

Drew's throat constricted. "Danger?"

"He muttered something about a woman named Ruby and how she was all hot for Drew. I think he might've been talking about you and that girl."

Arlene continued, "Red took off somewhere. The police are trying to find him, but they need to warn her. You need to be careful too. I haven't told the police yet. I wasn't sure, and I guess with everything Red's done, I still hoped he'd … well I don't know what I hoped."

She drew her upper lip between her teeth. "I don't know why I stayed with him for so long. After I had a chance to think about it, I realized he's not going to change."

Drew clenched his fists. "I don't know a Ruby, just a Nellie. She wears a ruby necklace." He cursed. "When I find him, I'll clean his clock."

"The police have already searched the Baker Block. He's not there."

"Baker Block Suites? That's where I live."

Arlene pulled at her sheets and frowned. "Red's the super there."

Drew took a taxi home and didn't notice when the vehicle stopped.

"Sir? We're here."

He opened his wallet, offered the driver a fifty, and exited the cab without the change.

He moved mechanically; pressed the elevator buttons; shuffled down the hall; realized he was daydreaming outside Rosie's apartment, but didn't remember how he got there.

Drew unlocked the door and slipped inside, then dropped onto the sofa and leaned back.

A faint smell hung in the air: cigarette smoke mixed with bad body odor. *Crap. Either he's here, or he's been here. Where did Rosie put her gun? And where's Sushi?* He held his breath and listened.

Somebody in the upstairs apartment was vacuuming the floor and moving furniture. A stereo in a nearby unit was playing music a little too loud.

No barking. No breathing. No sinister voice.

He scanned the room, trying not to move his head any more than necessary, then pushed off the sofa. *Find the gun. In Rosie's nightstand. It's in the nightstand.* His breath came in short bursts, his heart pounding like a fist trying to punch its way through his chest.

The chill of foreboding filled him with terror when he reached the bedroom door. But he squeaked it open.

Two bodies lay on the carpet: Sushi's and Red's. Were they breathing? Yes. Sushi's muzzle was pillowed on what was left of a pile of raw liver. Red had a goose-egg on his forehead. He was bound and gagged. Drew reached for the nightstand …

~*~

He regained consciousness spread-eagled on top of the bed, his wrists and ankles tied to the bedposts. A sock had been stuffed into his mouth and secured with his belt. A cast-iron frying pan, probably the weapon that had knocked him unconscious, lay in the doorway.

Someone spoke in a sing-song tone from just out of view. "Drewdeedrew. I got you, and *I* got the *gu*-un."

He recognized the voice.

"Drewdeedrew. You thought it was Red, didn't you? He's too stupid. Likes to watch, but doesn't know enough about hacking. He's so stupid he gave me his pass key when I came on to him. Even led the cops on a wild goose chase for me."

Drew struggled to break free.

Nellie cackled. "Pooooooooor Red. He has a crush on me. Follows me around like a little puppy. All I ever wanted was you, Drew, but you ignored me. Then I thought … when you asked me out, I thought maybe I had a chance. But you picked *her* instead."

A picture frame containing Rosie's graduation photo crashed into view. A glass splinter landed on his nose.

Nellie's hysterical sob became another cackle. "She'll never know what hit her. We'll wait for her to come home, and then you'll stay tied up while I kill her and Red. I'll keep the dog, though. I like dogs. But after Rosie's dead, I intend to strip you and take what I want."

She cackled again. "Maybe I'll help myself right now. If Red wakes up, he can watch." Her voice sank to a quiet purr. "You'll enjoy this." She stepped into view and began a strip tease that would have been a delight to watch under more favorable circumstances. She moved closer. Closer. She caressed herself with the pistol and watched with amusement as Drew's face contorted in fear.

She didn't hear Rosie or see the meat tenderizer when it clubbed her over the head. Nellie fell forward and slumped across Drew's torso.

~*~

The police carted Nellie and Red away in cuffs. The vet pronounced Sushi healthy: The ketamine Nellie had administered wasn't a lethal dose. An ER physician informed Drew he had a mild concussion, gave him an informational leaflet, and told him to see his family doctor for follow-up.

~*~

Drew and Rosie sat on her sofa after supper and watched the news. She started flipping channels. He finally broke the awkward silence. "I guess now the danger's over, I should get my things and move back to my own apartment."

She straddled his lap; teased his lips with her teeth. "Or you could stay here at least one more night."

"Woman, I'm in love with you. You hear that? I was too dense to realize it. But tonight, I have a headache from that bonk on the noggin. Do you think you could trade your cast-iron frying pans for something a little softer?"

Her breath was moist on his neck. "I'm soft, and you *really* should stay here. I can't let you loose in the building with that snake. You might attract another secret admirer."

Jilted
Kathy Steinemann

This piece was featured in Weird Year, December 2014.

A hard object hit Doreen's dive mask. Momentarily disoriented in the icy depths of the mountain lake, she reseated her mask and tapped her dive buddy's elbow. Ken twisted, his fins churning up sediment from the wreck. She gestured to explain what had happened, and they peered through the murky water.

A cinder block with a canvas bag attached to it lay in the silt. They checked their dive computers: only two minutes left. They hurried to free the bag from the block.

During their ascent into the warmth of the shallows, they scanned the surface. No boat and no noise except for the sound of their bubbles.

Ken towed their burden ashore. Doreen, exhausted from the strenuous surface swim and high-altitude air, trailed behind with their dive flag. They stripped off their equipment and hacked with their knives at waterlogged ropes and knots until they were able to open the bag.

Doreen screamed. Ken vomited.

They laid their scuba gear under a tree and stood several feet away, staring at their gruesome discovery.

Hoof-beats pounded nearer. Two horseback riders called the police and stayed to help. One of the animals raised its tail, depositing a smelly pile on Doreen's fins. But she didn't notice. She knuckled her fists to her temples and rocked, rocked, rocked.

Scents of vomit, horse manure, and pine trees mingled in the air. Ken sniffed, moved closer to the bag, sniffed again. Then he let out the breath he'd been holding prisoner and laughed. The laugh became hysterical. He wiped the tears from his cheeks. Then he turned silent as everyone glared at him in hushed horror.

A horse snorted. A squirrel scolded. A faraway train whistled a warning at a traffic crossing ... and the waiting continued.

The police finally arrived. And they snickered when they examined the contents of the bag.

~*~

On the opposite shore of the lake, a small cabin with a private boat launch lay nestled among the trees. Its owner, Betty, stood in the small living room with scalpel in hand. She was tired of being jilted, and none of her ex-boyfriends was beyond the reach of her revenge.

Vapid eyeballs, pale faces, blood-stained necks. Those guys couldn't jilt anyone without heads now, could they?

William had been the first. What joy she had experienced as she stroked his lifeless cheeks and felt the red goo slide between her fingers. He hadn't taken long. The others? Well, once she realized how much she enjoyed it, she started to prolong the pleasure; and each time, the disbelief and pain etched on their faces grew progressively more horrific.

A canvas sack full of body parts. It was grotesque. It was fulfilling. It was art.

Ted was Betty's latest victim. She stepped away to survey her work. He was almost ready for a watery burial. Dismembered. Submerged. Forgotten.

Only one more trip to the middle of the lake. One final, watery burial.

She smiled.

The wax sculpture looked just like the real Ted. It would rival the best of Madame Tussaud's creations. And it was excellent therapy.

The Relative Importance of Relativity

Kathy Steinemann

This piece appeared in Mash Stories, July 2014.

A pulsating thrum woke Trula. She stared into the darkness. "Is that you, Starr?" The thrum diminished. She threw off her blankets and groped for the touch lamp. A soft glow illuminated the room. Nothing appeared out of place: her clothing for tomorrow laid out on a chair, her wedding photo poking out of the wastebasket, thyroid medication on the dresser—

No. Wait. Were the curtains stirring?

"Starr, I'm not kidding around."

A little girl peeked out, cherry cheeks damp with tears. "I can't sleep, Mommy. When's Daddy coming home?"

"We've talked about that already, Monkey. Daddy has his own place now. You can visit him this weekend." *How am I supposed to explain to a five-year-old that Veryl's lab and ridiculous temporal theories are more important to him than his family?*

"Can I sleep with you, Mommy?"

"Hop up." Trula cuddled her. "Were you playing with your SynthOhSyzer?"

The thrum resumed and increased in volume. It became a crescendo that vibrated the box of tissues off the dresser and onto the floor. *Omigosh. It wasn't her Synth.* She pulled Starr tight to her chest.

The noise faded.

Starr whimpered. "Mommy, I'm scared."

"It's okay. There's nothing to be afraid of. Mommy will take care of it."

Trula searched about for a weapon. The only object within reach was a heavy, dog-eared copy of Veryl's latest book, *Einstein's Error: Relativity Debunked*. She picked it up. "You stay here, Monkey. I'm going to see what's making the weird noise."

Sparks of static popped from the carpet as she sidled toward the door. She eased it open, hesitated, and then looked back at the bed. Starr stared at her, wide-eyed, embracing a pillow. Trula squeezed through the partially open door, closed it with a gentle click, and crept toward the undulating light emanating from the kitchen. *Is this another one of Veryl's stupid attempts to get me back? It's too late. All the cajoling and pleading in the world won't make me change my mind.*

She inched closer. Closer. The light surrounded her ...

It was her wedding day. She was standing before the altar in St. Paul's Cathedral, with Veryl at her side, her tiny baby bump concealed by an empire waist. The wisp of a memory tickled at her brain: something important, but she couldn't quite access it.

Veryl took her in his arms and kissed her. Thoughts of their approaching honeymoon crowded out any efforts to find that elusive memory. Her body responded with fire to the lips of her new husband.

He whispered in her ear. "I meant every word of our nuptial vows, and I promise to throw away all my research. I've learned my lesson. You and Starr are more important to me than relativity, thought transference, and time travel."

She frowned. *Who's Starr?*

Paranoia

Kathy Steinemann

Insects, spiders, conspiracy theories, voices. Where does reality end and paranoia begin? Could you tell the difference?

The voice buzzed like an angry fly struggling to escape a sticky trap. *"I'll kill him."*

Kiefer Klein flinched. "Pardon? Who's there?" He squinted at every corner of the psychiatrist's waiting room while he scratched his arm and brushed imaginary ants from his brow. "I said, who's there?"

He hyperventilated and pressed his palm against his chest. *Easy now. Remember what the doc said. Breathe. Breathe. Slow and easy. That's it. Slow and easy. There's no bugs. No insects. No spiders. It's just someone playing a practical joke.*

He squeaked, "Whoever you are, that's not funny. Come out and face me."

Silence.

He peered around again, and an adrenaline quiver trembled through his body.

There's nobody here. Nobody here. Nobody.

He forced his attention back to the JFK wiki on his computer tablet, maintaining a vigilant watch in all directions with his peripheral vision.

Three university degrees and a cushy job as a researcher in a prestigious pharmaceutical company, and here he was, a delusional crybaby, reduced to spilling his guts in a shrink's office. *Maybe it's caused by the drugs I'm developing. Or maybe someone in the company is out to get me.*

He continued to press icons and swipe screens. His unease crawled to his fingertips. They shook as he pushed up his glasses. *Seven months of treatments, and I'm getting worse, not better. Now I'm hearing voices that aren't there.*

The office door opened, and Dr. Praxis stepped out: expensive suit, confident air, creepy eyes. He motioned to Kiefer. "Come on in."

The voice in Kiefer's brain escalated to a furious whine. *"Obnoxious little pimple head with all his pomposity and conspiracy theories. If I have to listen to any more of his drivel, I'll exterminate him."*

Kiefer tried to ignore the voice. And he didn't divulge his new symptom to the head-sucker. Instead, he ranted about a JFK conspiracy and government plans to sterilize the population with secret additives in the drinking water. He confided that aliens wanted to kill him. And he scraped at the ghostly gnats on his arms.

The usual soul-sucking session: "And how does that make you feel?" The doctor's bony fingers tapping a tattoo on his clipboard. His office transforming into a dimly lit cave filled with bats and giant spiders. The doctor morphing into a flickering praying mantis with Venus-flytrap claws. "I see. Tell me more." The doctor shuffling papers and continuing his click-click-clicking on the clipboard. "I suppose so, and what do *you* think?" The doctor staring at the clock and click-click-clicking with his tongue.

The timer beeped.

Dr. Praxis put down his pen. "I'm afraid the hour is up. See you next week, Kiefer."

Kiefer darted toward the door.

Praxis pulled a revolver from his desk drawer. "Obnoxious little pimple head." He shot Kiefer in the back.

Then he phoned his psychiatrist. "It's Praxis. I need to see you right away. I'm afraid I've exterminated another Earthling."

Undead

Kathy Steinemann

This flash fiction appeared in "Robbed of Sleep, Volume 2: Stories to Stay Up For".

Day one: He looks so innocent and young, but I can't let his tender youth deceive me. I feed him poison. Lots of it. At first he seems ecstatic, stretching and enjoying the sunny day. When he finally dies several hours later, I smile.

Day eight: No! It couldn't be the same one, could it? How? I wrestle with him and hack, hack, hack until I kill him. This time, my smile is tentative when I stand at the sink and scrub the stains from my hands.

Day eighteen: Can't be. Is it really him? He sways and smirks at me when I walk out the door. Why won't he stay dead? I flee for my car to escape his smug superiority. At work, I pace and plot and plan. I search the Internet and delete my browser history so the boss doesn't know I've been using company time for personal stuff.

Day nineteen: Predawn. The street is quiet. It's still dark outside, and everyone's asleep. Everyone except for me. I sneak into the yard. The security light switches on. I spray him with an acid solution I read about on the Net. Good. That's the end of him. I leave for holidays on an early flight and *try* not to think about him while I'm gone.

Day thirty-three: Now he's back. With several friends. Why are they haunting me? What are they? Zombies or something? I grit my teeth and grimace while I lop off their blond heads. I hope the neighbors won't hear me chortle as I complete the gruesome deed and watch the zombie intruders collapse. I'm sure I've killed them all for good this time.

Day forty: I realize they're here to stay. I peek through the kitchen window at the sea of yellow that used to be my lawn. Then I cruise the Internet seeking recipes for dandelion wine.

Hitchhiker

Kathy Steinemann

This piece placed in the top ten, WOW! Women on Writing,
December 2014.

How many will I find tonight? Dianne wonders.

She cruises Highway 16 until she finds one among all the backpackers with their thumbs held out. The amber display on her watch shows 8:55 p.m., and the indicator flashes a tiny number one. She stops and rolls down the window. Just a little. "How far are you heading?"

The muscular hitchhiker smiles at her with even, white teeth framed by perfect lips. "Jasper National Park. There is a hostel in that community."

Dianne's breath comes in small bursts as she looks into his eyes. She unlocks the doors. "Hop in. I'm going to Prince George, and I could use some company."

With a grunt, he hefts his pack into the van and climbs in. "Nice vehicle, ma'am."

Her smile masks her nervousness as she scrutinizes him. To say he was handsome or sexy would be an insult. "All the other minivans I took for test drives didn't fit me. I'm just shy of five feet, and this one has an eight-way power seat adjuster."

She offers her hand. "Dianne."

There's that sexy, overconfident smile again with the too-even teeth ... and those eyes with the blue that's too blue.

Perfection incarnate.

He takes her hand. "Pleased to make your acquaintance. John is my name."

She checks him out as she drives, trying not to be too obvious: just a quick, targeted glance his way now and then in the deepening dusk. She listens to his voice and inhales his scent.

Yes.

Dianne passes him a bottle of water from the side pocket of her door.

He gulps.

His head starts to droop and roll with every movement of the steering wheel. She waits until he slips into unconsciousness.

Then she drives down a secluded road, pulls onto the gravel shoulder, and raises one of his eyelids. She nods, presses the power button to lower the windows, and she listens. It's dark now. All she can hear is the sound of her own racing heartbeat, a distant coyote howl, and leaves rustling in the wind. She gazes at the stars for a long moment, wondering how many planets out there sustain humanoid life, and she tries to ignore the voices in her head.

C'mon, you know you like it, the element of danger, the rush you feel afterward.

No, I don't like it.

But you have to do it.

Hurry then, before somebody comes along.

She closes the windows, drags her prey into the back of the van, and removes his clothing, piece by piece, throwing everything into a tote box. She admires his body as she runs her fingers over his perfect torso.

Such a shame.

She takes a syringe from the small kit hidden beneath a blanket and administers an injection. She feels for the pulse in his neck several times … and waits. When the pulse disappears, she rolls his corpse under a tarp, next to the other body.

Dianne examines the display on her watch, now green instead of amber. The indicator flashes a tiny number two.

It'll be midnight soon, and no more in the vicinity. That's two tonight. How many aliens will I find tomorrow?

Code Contravention

Kathy Steinemann

Prepare yourself for a disturbing look into the future.

A curious osprey circled, watching, while a jogger clutched his chest and toppled to the ground. After the man lay silent, the bird glided to the trail. It cocked its head for a wing beat, and then soared away, startled by a nearby rustle. The photographer observing from a small copse of bushes smiled and hurried off to his next assignment.

When a woman found the jogger an hour later, his blank stare was fixed on the brown waters of the North Vanderlein River. She screamed, then with trembling fingers searched for his ID-chip and scanned it with her aeroPhone: *Blake Sadler, 146 years of age.*

She whispered, "Another one. So young," and notified Pharma-4-All EMT Services.

~*~

Harrison Hetherington, 150-year-old CEO of Stellar Systems, paced while he composed his thoughts. He peered out from his office at the vista of tall buildings and sooty haze of Edmopolis while he dictated into his wireless headset. "And when they reach Venus ..." He crumpled into the plush carpeting and fell forward. The photographer watching from the shadows inched into the hallway.

Assignment #175. A good month.

~*~

Richard S. Cain, enforcer and phony freelance photographer, filled out the form on his encrypted aeroPhone app, sent it to headquarters, and assessed his ampoules. Enough to last for at least another month. Three brain aneurysms, two heart attacks, one DVT, and four strokes.

He wasn't sure how they worked. Some technical gibberish about nanocrystals that clotted blood corpuscles. He had two varieties: remote-activated and regulated-release. The bosses left the decision up to him. As long as he produced results, they didn't care about his modus operandi.

Richard wasn't sure who deposited the lavish credits into his account, but he spent many hours in speculation.

Voters had elected the Pharma-4-All Party twelve years previously. Their platform: free health care and pharmaceuticals for all citizens, with no tax increases. However, the current system would collapse without intervention. People who lived too long became a drain on public funds. Perhaps the government was attempting to balance the books by eliminating those who utilized life-prolonging technologies like nano-rejuvenators.

But then it began to happen worldwide, so Richard decided it couldn't be the federal government.

Maybe it was the Planetary Pension Plan. Nobody had ever envisioned pensioners living 200 years or more. Or could it be Supremo-Sweepstakes? Winners received $1000 per week for life. The Fuel-Forever Lotto perhaps? Or a conglomerate of several groups?

Waiting for the old to die apparently wasn't an option for an unknown entity or organization. Once a person reached 130, all bets were off.

Richard was paid well. That's what counted.

Although he employed other methods, his favorite approach was to converse with his targets in a coffee bistro. He would add a few undetectable drops of death to their lattes. It took a few days of waiting and watching for the opportune moment, but he was patient.

"Mind if I take another headshot, Mrs. Nixon?"

"Not at all. But isn't it about time you called me Olyvia? I hate being addressed by my ex-husband's last name."

"Okay, Olyvia, and please call me Richard."

They sipped on their StellarKups CinnaChokolatto, an aromatic blend of coffee, faux chocolate, and cinnamon. She inhaled the scent. "I miss real chocolate. This just isn't the same."

"But it's cultured from the best DNA. It should have the exact same taste and aroma."

She harrumphed. "Malarkey. It's different."

Richard watched her lips as she spoke. They were full, moist, kissable. She didn't look a minute over thirty, and her eyes … well, they made him feel something he hadn't felt in a long while. Olyvia was different. She was real. A woman you could talk to for hours that seemed like mere minutes.

She passed him her 3D-Micro. "Have you seen the latest news-vid?"

… and reports continue to filter in from around the world. Healthy seniors are dying for no apparent reason. Scientists are unable to explain the untimely deaths. Autopsies show nothing unusual. Those affected are fit individuals with no history of medical problems or disease …

He perused the display, nodding and altering his facial expressions long enough for her to believe he had watched the entire story. Finally, he spoke. "But you don't have to worry. You're a long way from being a senior."

"No. My 130th was in August. I feel healthier than I've ever been, but every day, I wonder if it'll be my last."

Richard looked into her inviting caramel eyes and made a decision. No matter what the cost, she would *not* join his growing list of victims.

He patted her hand. The electric excitement was instantaneous. "Shall we go for a stroll? The pollution index is low this afternoon." Her enthusiastic nod made him hopeful she had feelings for him.

They wandered to the river.

Reconstruction artists had proved their proficiency in a manicured walking path with a view of the murky waterway. Fertile soil had been hauled in to provide an arable medium for trees that transformed the putrid landscape into a piece de resistance. It made the metropolis more palatable for the few who ventured onto its paths.

He led Olyvia by the hand, his arousal growing by the heartbeat. He faced her and drew her close, his lips seeking hers in an ardent expression of desire. Her response was as earnest as his demand. With ragged breath, he whispered, "I want you. All of you."

She gasped. "My place is nearby."

~*~

Richard's affair with Olyvia became a consuming obsession. She was all he could think of or dream about whenever he was away on assignment. Their lovemaking changed color and mood with every rendezvous. It was a dynamic kaleidoscope of fiery passion that surprised him at every turn.

Sometimes they squeezed into the confines of her nano-rejuvenator and giggled at the tingle that crept through their bodies. They found an antiquated vid-version of the *Kama Sutra* and experimented. Then they invented a few of their own positions.

~*~

Early spring announced its arrival with a few migratory birds that ventured into the grey gloom of Edmopolis. Richard and

Olyvia discussed marriage, an old-fashioned ritual still practiced by many.

Olyvia beamed. "It's settled then. On June 30th. Just a few friends. But first, there's your birthday. I want a big shindig with all the trimmings."

"I haven't celebrated my birthday for decades. Why start now?"

"Nonsense." She paced while she planned. "We'll have a pseudo-chocolate cake with electronic candles, lots of presents, and some of our close friends."

"Lyv …" He sighed. "All right."

~*~

Richard accepted the birthday greetings and gag presents with good-natured comebacks.

"An elephant clock with a cracked display? Really? Come to think of it, the trunk looks a bit like your nose. I'll remember you whenever I check the time."

"Two tickets to last year's Lasers 'N Roses concert? Gee, thanks. Do you have a time machine to go with it?"

"A pair of stinky socks: exactly what I needed. They look just like the pair I put in the laundry basket this morning."

Several times as the evening progressed, Richard caught one of the invitees, a nano-rejuv tech named Callum, watching him. Whenever Richard looked his way, the tech shifted his gaze elsewhere.

After everyone else had left the apartment, Callum asked if he could speak to Richard in private. "Want to take a stroll? I need to consult with you about a new assignment." He winked. "I don't want to discuss business in Olyvia's presence."

Richard's eyes widened. It was forbidden for enforcers to reveal their identities to anyone. He scowled. Was Callum one of the bosses? Best to go along. For now, at least.

Olyvia gave him a puzzled frown when he hugged her good-bye.

He armed the PenLaser in his pocket. The two men made their way through the rain to the nearest path, trying to conserve energy so they wouldn't have to breathe any more of the smog than necessary.

The air by the river was brisk and fresh.

Hidden from view by a small copse of bushes, Callum placed his hand on Richard's shoulder. "You've broken Primary Rule."

Richard fingered the PenLaser, hand quivering, fearful he might fire it by accident. "I couldn't help it. She's my only violation. I do good work. Everyone knows that."

"Yeah, you do. But the bosses are bent out of shape. She's my new assignment. I figured I should tell you."

Richard's stomach churned. "Please don't do it. She's the only thing that makes life worth living. I'll do anything. I'll give you anything. You can say you completed your assignment, and nobody'll be around to dispute your claim. Just let us disappear."

Callum's face sank into an expression of regret. "My hands are tied. If I don't do it, I'll have to pay the penalty."

"But—"

"Sorry, Richard." Callum checked his wrist display and pushed the activator on the remote detonator. "She just died from a cerebral aneurysm."

Richard moaned. He dropped to his knees, held his head in his hands, and retched.

Callum whispered, "Surely you didn't think they'd make an exception for you. The Code is clear, and so is the penalty for contravention."

Richard clutched his chest and collapsed to the ground. His face sank into the vomit-soaked mud.

The rain stopped. A curious cliff swallow twittered from atop a nearby branch. The live human removed a shiny object from the wrist of the dead one and sauntered away. The swallow fluttered to the path beside the corpse, harvested a beakful of mud for the nest she was building, and flitted off in the breeze.

Dirty

Kathy Steinemann

A beta version of this piece won the "Indies Unlimited Flash Fiction Challenge" of November 23, 2013.

A cop in the woods is tracking someone. He has just heard the unmistakable cocking of a pistol behind him. What does he do? Can he escape the inevitable? Or is his fate already sealed?

I dove into the underbrush as a bullet whizzed past my ear. *This dude's good. Crap, my Glock is jammed.* I slid out my SIG, and I waited.

Get your breathing under control. C'mon. You can do this.

Boots crackled on dry leaves. A branch broke. The silhouette of my pursuer passed by my hiding place. I heard noisy panting, along with footfalls and splashes in the water. The baying of the hounds diminished as they disappeared into the distance.

Just you and me, bub.

I rolled onto the path. Then I paused. *I don't think he heard me.*

I inched forward, every nerve and muscle twitching with excitement. *No way. You're turned on, aren't you? Get a grip.* I could see the guy's back about twenty feet away from me. He crouched down with his weapon aimed forward, scanning from side to side as he stalked like a panther on the prowl.

It's Billy! I moved as only a well-trained cop can, alert for danger, senses in hyper drive, ready to react. And I didn't notice the sinkhole until I was up to my chin in it. A pistol cocked behind me.

I suppose this is it. Billy wins. With a rueful grin, I raised my hands above my head and tossed my SIG onto the creek bank. I could feel the mud and dirt dripping from my hair onto my face. "You got me, dirty duds and all."

Billy's toothy sneer reflected the little bit of sunlight squeezing through the branches. "You're under arrest. There's no room on the force for dirty cops."

The Guardian's Angel

Donna Milward

Even immortals have weaknesses.

Tazminn's breath came in sputters. Sweat dripped into his eyes. *I must stop him before he leaves.*

The boy, no more than five, toddled toward the exit. "Mommy?"

Tazminn quickened his steps and grasped the child's shoulder. "Your mother is at Spencer's." *Buying grown-up stocking stuffers for your father.* "She is looking for you, Johnny, and she is worried." She would not be difficult to locate. Tazminn experienced her distress telepathically from across Sea Lion Rock.

Johnny shot him a suspicious glower. "How do you know my name?"

"Can you keep a secret?" he asked. Johnny nodded. "My name is Taz and I am an angel. I am here to take care of lost children like you."

Johnny studied Tazminn's face. Long seconds passed before he took Tazminn's hand and allowed himself to be led away from the heavy doors, and Tazminn's tension waned. *That was close. What would I have done if he got out?*

He and Johnny made their way past the hat store and the decorative pirate ship that dominated Phase Three. Johnny stared at Taz as he walked.

"Are you a Christmas angel?" Johnny asked.

"I am here every day."

"If you're an angel, where are your wings?"

Taz smiled. "I left them in Heaven."

"Why?"

"Because they are too big," Tazminn said. "And sometimes I trip on them." *Not to mention how difficult it would be to blend in with a bright, white wingspan in a sea of mortals.* He winked, and Johnny giggled.

They were close enough now that Johnny's desperate mother could be heard calling for him.

"Oh my God, there you are!" She rushed over and dropped to her knees. "Johnny, you scared me."

Johnny pooched his quivering bottom lip. "I'm sorry, Mommy."

"It's okay, Baby." Johnny's mom folded him into her arms. "It's okay." She glanced up at Tazminn and mouthed the words, *thank you.* He grinned and nodded before leaving them to their reunion.

Her emotions were that odd mix of relief, anger, and guilt he often experienced from the mothers of misplaced offspring. The gratitude in her eyes reminded Tazminn that he had the most interesting and satisfying post on this entire planet.

True, the foliage smelled like plastic, and the skylights let in only the palest rays of sunshine, but where else could he experience so much of this world in a warm pocket of shelter? Everything he could ever need lay within a stroll's length.

He liked the ever-changing clothing stores, especially the ones with pretty pink, purple, and red lingerie. He could spend hours watching all the lovely women peruse the bits of lace and satin. He could savor the exotic scents of David's Tea in Phase Three, the floral and fruit perfumes from The Rocky Mountain Soap Company in Phase One, and everything in between. He took pleasure in the screaming laughter of children as they rode the waterslides in Phase Two, or sometimes the sparkling bumper cars in Galaxyland. He enjoyed the multitude of delicious offerings from around the world, all sheltered in kiosks and restaurants and food courts.

Tazminn rubbed the softening belly he had grown during his years as the West Edmonton Mall guardian. Maybe he enjoyed the fare a little too much. If he still had wings, could they lift the extra two inches of his girth? *No matter.*

He did not need wings to mingle among the mortals. Earthlings from every walk of life—every race, every age, every color and creed—roamed this tiled ground. Tazminn loved them all.

And Christmas Eve. Tazminn *loved* Christmas Eve. True, he still needed to patrol for shoplifters and lost children, more so than the rest of the year, but the mood seemed different today … brighter, friendlier. It meant cramped space, but he did not mind. He savored the earthy musk of human and the crackle of their frenzied energy.

"Hi, Tazminn!"

Tazminn startled, realizing he had stopped in front of his favorite fast-food vendor. "Hello, Elaine. How are you?"

"Same old, same old," she said. "What can I get you?"

Tazminn's stomach responded to the question loudly, and he obeyed the command for food. "Chili dog and a large Strawberry Julius, please."

"Right away." Elaine set up the blender with his drink and dressed his hot dog with a generous spoonful of meaty tomato deliciousness. She said nothing, but Tazminn could hear her thoughts. *She is going to ask again.* She filled his order and punched it up at the register.

"So Tazminn …"

"You may still call me Taz."

"Taz." Elaine gave him a distracted smile. "What are the chances of you coming back to work for me?"

"I will come back," he handed her the very currency he had earned at this Orange Julius, "when I need the money again."

Elaine chuckled. Apparently he had said something amusing. He accepted his meal and sought a suitable location to consume his food while he listened to the cacophony of life. *So many busy thoughts to sift through.*

And yet in all the chaos, her heartbeat called to him, like birdsong, not far from him. A mirrored pillar let him check his hair, and he pushed a stray black curl behind his ear. His eyes reflected more confidence than he felt.

He let his senses seek her loneliness, and he followed them across Gourmet World to Freshii. The location did not surprise him. She wanted to eat healthier. Her weight concerned her, despite her tiny waist and slender frame. Sure as the Energy was Love Incarnate, she sat by herself, picking at a salad and twirling ribbons of black hair around her fingers with the longing misery of someone wishing for Crepeworks. Her thoughts were sad and distracted.

"Hello, Tina," Tazminn said. The way her face lit up when she saw him brought a tickle to his stomach. "May I sit with you?"

"Hi, Taz!" The smile spreading across her face made it impossible not to grin back. So pretty when she smiled. … He had been drawn to her ever since she began her employment at a well-known jewelry kiosk months ago. He could not pass by without soaking up her sweetness like … sunshine. Her soul was as beautiful as her face. "How are you? Ready for Christmas?"

"Christmas. Ah, yes." He never knew what to say whenever humans asked him such questions. Are you ready for Christmas? Are you finished shopping? He discovered the best answer came in two words. "Almost. You?"

"Pretty much. I guess." Tina sipped at her water, and Tazminn experienced rare discomfort. He was not the only one

70

avoiding questions with vague answers. Her thoughts were of home, a place hundreds of miles from here. She could not get time off to visit. Even if she could, she could not afford a ticket to fly. Tazminn wanted to apologize, but he knew Tina would not understand why. And she did *not* wish to discuss it.

"You must be on Christmas Break," Tina said. He nodded in agreement. Everyone believed him to be a foreign exchange student. "Must be nice." Her giggle sounded as false as her cheer. "Are you going home for the holidays?"

Tazminn shook his head and swallowed a bite. "Home is too far." He took another spicy mouthful to discourage more questions. He would not leave the Mall. Not even to return to the heavens whence he came. West Edmonton Mall had become home long ago. *When did* that *happen?*

"I know how you feel." Her mood worsened, and Tazminn switched the subject. It would not do to be so unhappy on Christmas Eve. He wanted to cheer, not depress her.

"I like your necklace," he said. "Did you purchase that at work?"

She peered downward and pressed her hand to her chest. "This?" She grasped the green stone between her fingers. "Yes. It's peridot. My birthstone."

"August?" He could never be sure with human months. Time did not have the same meaning where he came from. "It is lovely. Like you."

Her blush he did not expect. "I like it too," she said. Her gaze became intense, flirtatious. "It matches your eyes."

His turn to be embarrassed. *Why do I experience giddiness in her presence?*

He glanced away, slurping at his Julius until the buzz of other conversations replaced the strangeness between them. Her thoughts were of a city by the ocean. She longed to hike the coast without the heavy clothing of winter.

Tina stood abruptly. "I have to go," she said. "Nice seeing you again, Taz."

Tazminn struggled to respond around a mouthful of frothy strawberries. "Umph! Moo-ooh!" By the time he had swallowed, he saw nothing but her ebony hair trailing behind her like a comet as she melded with the crowd.

"You too. ..." he said to no one.

Her dreams made Tazminn shudder. He rarely ventured from the Mall, never made it farther than the sheltered parkade. He never even ventured to the top parking lot with its endless expanse of sky that reminded him of his insignificance in the vast Realms of Life. Even if he could still fly, he would not, *could not,* take her home.

As the afternoon passed, the oppressive heat of panicking, last-minute shoppers made Tazminn's skin clammy. Their musk stank of frustration and impatience. Their rushed thoughts made him dizzy. He perched, invisible to human eyes, atop the bronze shoulders of the oil-patch workers statue in Phase One, like a shepherd tending his sheep. He found it more peaceful there.

He spied three young men sauntering past the shops with the unhurried gait of those who are trying, with great effort, to seem casual. If their thoughts of robbery had not alerted Tazminn, their darting eyes would have. He descended from his vantage point and stalked them.

He could smell the cloying scent of their body spray, all three of them coated in the stuff as though they bathed in nothing else. It itched Tazminn's nose and caused his eyes to weep. He shadowed them from one end of the Mall to the other, slipping into stores where staff judged them with as much suspicion as he did.

After all, wearing matching black hoodies with the hoods pulled up inspired paranoia.

The young men meandered their way to Phase Three, where Tina worked.

The Metalsmiths kiosk had some security precautions, with all their merchandise behind glass showcases. Nothing to steal.

"Hey." The leader of the trio smiled at Tina. His pale, crooked nose stuck out from his hood. Tazminn caught sight of his blondish, unshaven chin. "How's it goin'?"

She saw the false charm in his demeanor, and his friendly mannerisms were met with a tense grimace. "Can I help you?"

"Maybe," the man said. "I'm ah, looking for a gift, …" He gawked at the name tag on her breast with a wide smirk. "Tina."

"I see," she said, not returning the smile. "For your girlfriend?"

"No, ah …" He cast a quick glance at his friends. His blue eyes narrowed. "For my mom." His lackeys snickered.

Tina's lips tightened. She did not want to serve them; any fool could see her trepidation. Now would be a good time for Tazminn to make his presence known. He willed himself visible and approached the counter.

"Everything all right here?" Tina jumped, and the men swiveled their heads in his direction so fast that Tazminn heard at least one neck crackle. His senses were awash in their instant animosity, like cold prickles on his skin. "Is everything okay here?"

They studied him, eying the bulk beneath the Canadian tuxedo. As though of one mind, the group retreated, blending into the human current.

Tina's audible relief filled Tazminn's ears. "You've got fantastic timing. Thanks, Taz."

"It was my pleasure." Indeed, his assurance was as profound as hers. "Are you okay? Why are you working alone?" Worry coiled around his heart. "Should I stick around?"

Tina ducked her head and tucked her palms into her sleeves. "Vicki is on a break. She'll be back soon."

"Oh. Okay." The heat of his blush encompassed his entire face. "As long as you are all right."

"I am." Her voice sounded soothed. "Thanks so much for your help. I appreciate it." Another customer approached the Italia charms. "I have to go," she said. "Thanks again."

"Bye." Tazminn nodded. *I also have work to do.* Someone on the skating rink in Phase Two was about to pass out from heat exhaustion, thanks to a vigorous game of ice tag in a bulky winter coat. The grandfather would require attention and possibly a defibrillator. Tazminn let Tina slip from his thoughts. For the time being.

He spent the rest of the afternoon pining for wings again. *So many mortals.* Despite his talents, he could not be everywhere at once.

The hours passed in the usual blur that had become Tazminn's existence. When one has been alive for millennia, one hardly notices the mere hours mortals endure. Before long the multitude thinned and disappeared, but for a few lingering souls.

Tazminn gravitated toward Phase Three, past Gourmet World. Closing time had come. This day, as all others, he could not permit Tina to see him trailing her.

She made the deposit each night across from the Casino. He always waited until the day's profits passed from her tiny hands to the armored lockbox of the CIBC bank.

Tonight felt different. Tazminn disliked the energy. The anger and resentment.

His stomach churned. Tazminn scanned the corridor. Someone, something caused this unease he experienced now. *Where is it coming from?*

They crept from the corner of the Casino. Had Tina seen them? The three thugs from the afternoon? *Tina, turn around. Turn around!* Her thoughts were preoccupied with a reluctance to return to her empty apartment. She made the deposit and closed the box with a bang.

"Aw, did we miss the cash?"

Tina whirled around, and Tazminn saw dread on her face. They blocked her passage out.

The leader sneered at her as he shuffled forward, narrowing his icy eyes. "*Now* what are you going to give us for Christmas?"

"Maybe she has something in her purse," his buddy said. "Have you got some goodies in there, *Tina?*"

Tina tossed her bag at their feet. "Take it." She began to edge away, closer to the escalator.

Please, Lord, let her escape.

The lead thug let the purse drop before his feet. "Is that all?" he asked. "It *is* Christmas, y'know. Maybe there's a little something else you can give us? Hey, Tina?" His goons guffawed.

Tina spun on her heel. She sprinted for the escalator. The men gave chase.

Tazminn sprang. He tackled, then straddled the man who stooped to grab her purse. Two quick punches to the head. The man went limp and rolled his eyes shut. Tazminn found his footing and snagged Tina's purse by the strap. He had lost sight of his quarry, but Tina's screams for help reverberated downstairs.

He sprinted to the top step of the escalator and slid down the hand rail. Tina headed toward an empty exit, past the Dollarama, with both assailants in pursuit. Her wails of terror echoed. She ran for the glass doors, the closest way out. Her flat shoes clicked like a distress signal, but laughter drowned it out. One of them howled like a wolf.

"Come here, girl!"

"Why are you running? We just want to fill your stocking!"

Tazminn raised Tina's handbag above his head. He whipped it in a circle over his head until it reached the desired velocity. He calculated his aim and let it loose. The second man dropped to the ground like a meteor. Yet his partner gained on Tina. Tazminn hurried to grab the improvised weapon once more. He had to stop him before they left the—

Too late.

Tina fled into the darkness and driving snow, with her assailant right behind. Tazminn's heart plummeted. He should not have stopped to retrieve the bag.

She would not get free after all. The bastard would catch up to her in the frozen, concrete expanse of the sheltered parking lot. And she would …

She would scream, but no one would come to save her. No one would hear her cries.

Except for Tazminn. And he feared the outside.

Tazminn raced to the Mall doors, plastering his face to the glass. Tina darted for a small vehicle in a dim corner, but her stalker had almost caught up. Tazminn could almost taste her terror like blood in his mouth. *What do I do?*

His fingernails squealed against the glass. He had to do something. Or Tina would suffer the consequences of his inaction.

He opened the door. The winter wind screeched in his ears and moaned through the concrete pillars, lamenting Tina's plight and Tazminn's cowardice.

His breath came in aching gasps, and he tried not to see the black and endless sky beyond the reaches of the Mall, all the unfamiliar spaces on unknown horizons.

Tina gave another piteous scream. Tazminn glanced up to see her in the clutches of the last thug. He heard her clothing rip, heard the sick cackle of her attacker. Tina was out of time.

Now. Now or never again. Tazminn twisted his terror into action and let himself become visible as he charged. He would not sacrifice this human, *any* human, to his fear.

"Let her go!"

"What the f—"

Tazminn heard the muttered astonishment just before he delivered a kick to the would-be rapist's torso that launched him straight upward. He grabbed a handful of clothing and yanked the man away from her.

A song of groans played in the wind, bringing Tazminn satisfaction. He glanced over to check on Tina.

She huddled into herself, holding her torn blouse closed as tears trickled from her almond eyes.

"Are you all right, Tina?" He wanted to cradle her in his arms and make this night go away. But he heard his foe rise, and Tazminn's heart rate quickened. Sometimes his own violence shamed him, however necessary it seemed.

But not today. He would fight this creep again. Just for her.

Tazminn fixed the greasy man with a glare. "Are you certain you wish to pick on someone your own size?"

The murderous expression had disappeared, to be replaced by a cocky smirk. The creep glanced back and found himself solo. Tazminn lurched toward him with a hiss, faking an attack. The rapist slipped, landing on his ribs with a loud grunt. Tazminn observed the crawling retreat with unrepentant amusement, until Tina's shuddering whimpers brought him back.

He spun to face her, relieved that he could finally comfort her, that she lived so that he could do so. Tazminn dropped to his knees and covered her body with his. The frigid tweed of her coat scratched his face. He squeezed carefully, trying to warm her although he knew her shivers were not a result of the weather.

"Shhhh. ..." He stroked her silken hair. "It is over. They will never bother you again, I promise." He made no false platitudes. *If I ever see them again I will finish the task I started.*

"If you hadn't been here ..." She could not finish the sentence. Her breath came in hiccups as she hastened to do up her coat.

"I know," he said, enfolding her in his embrace. "It will be all right."

They huddled until the dank moisture of the parkade soaked through Tazminn's sleeves to chill his bones, and still he did not want to release her. He never wanted to let her go.

"Am I still shaking?" Tina asked, "Or is that you? You must be freezing." She squirmed to study his clothing. He looked down at himself. Small wonder he felt cold. He had stormed out here in nothing but denim.

He stole an extra squeeze as he helped her to her feet. "You should go home now. It *is* Christmas after all."

"Yes, it is." She gazed into his eyes, her ideas flickering fast as Christmas lights. "Do you have someplace to go tonight?"

"Tonight?" Tazminn had not given it any thought.

"I was thinking maybe since you and I don't have family here ..." Tina dropped her eyes. "You saved my life and it's Christmas and I have no one to spend it with and if you didn't have any plans maybe we could ..." She paused in her ramble and took a deep breath, lacing her fingers together. "Maybe you and I could celebrate Christmas together. I could make you dinner. To say thank you. It's the least I could do."

Tazminn's mind went blank. No one in all his years on this planet had asked. No one had ever even invited him to their home. *What would it be like to have a homemade supper?*

"You have plans," Tina said, mistaking his silence for rejection. "I understand."

"I do not," Tazminn said, "have plans. No one has ever invited me to Christmas."

"Is that a yes?"

He glanced back at the metal-and-glass doors. Sanctuary waited a brief sprint away. Security and routine beckoned him back to where he could sleep undisturbed in any number of secret nooks and hiding places. Alone. Suddenly the Mall did not feel like home anymore.

"You're shaking," Tina said. "You must be frozen." Tazminn peered into her inviting, brown eyes. If she only understood his dilemma. Mere cold could not cause him to tremble. Only fear of the unknown could do that.

Suppose he went with her? Suppose he challenged his phobia and stepped away from those secret spots for the first time since he had arrived at this world?

"Here." Tina put her arms around him. The gentle gesture was awkward but well meaning as she rubbed his back. "Maybe this will help?" He treasured her trust, the deep affection she had for him.

A lonely night in an empty Mall, or Christmas with a friend?

Tazminn made his choice. *Time for a change.*

He was a guardian in service of the Energy, with free will. Perhaps he had forgotten that. If he could brave these outdoors—if he could challenge three men to save the woman he loved—and win, he could do anything.

"I would be delighted to join you, Tina." He hugged her back. "Thank you."

"Great!" Her tension evaporated, even as she let him go. "Hop in. I have a nice turkey breast roast at home. Glad I don't have to eat it by myself!"

Tazminn tucked himself into Tina's car and willed his eyes to stay open, to take in a different world.

Now was not a time to run from new things. Now was a time to try all things new.

Tarnation with Decorum

Kathy Steinemann

This story won fourth place in the fall 2013 "WOW! Women on Writing Flash Fiction Contest".

The people in this piece are from Kathy's Sapphire Brigade series. The story is a sneak peek into the early life of two characters.

Emma sobbed as the chugging train jostled her from side to side. Sunlight played with her amber hair, creating a fluctuating halo of radiance around her head.

The stranger across the aisle doffed his hat. "Are you all right, ma'am?"

She shook her head.

"May I take the liberty of sitting with you?"

She squinted through her tears at the audacious young man. His bushy mustache that twitched as he grinned made her smile. "It wouldn't be proper for a strange man to sit with me."

"And what's proper about a young woman riding the train unaccompanied? May I introduce myself?" He bowed. "Roderick, at your service."

"Roderick who?"

"Just Roderick."

She peered in the opposite direction for a moment before she extended her hand. "And I'm just Emma."

Shivers crept down her spine when he lowered his lips to her fingers.

The train lurched. It pitched him so close that she felt the caress of his mustache on her forehead and smelled the sweet fragrance of pipe tobacco on his breath.

He righted himself.

Emma's face reddened. "Now that we've been introduced, I suppose we're not strangers anymore. I believe I would enjoy your company."

"May I ask why you were crying?" He offered her his handkerchief.

"My guardian arranged a marriage for me, and I'm on my way to meet my betrothed for the first time. But I intend to run away at the next station. I already abandoned my maid at the last stop."

"In my opinion, women should have the right to vote, preach, and choose their own mates. However, are you not beholden to reject him in person?"

She tucked her tongue into her cheek. "I suppose you're right."

"Eluded your maid, did you?" His eyes crinkled at the corners. "Reminds me of a story about a maid. The master says to her, 'Look, I've found a button in my salad.' And the maid replies, 'That's all right, sir. It's part of the dressing.' True story, I tell you."

"I hardly think so. I've heard that joke before."

"But at least now you're laughing. And you're beautiful, Emma, even with those puffy eyes."

She sighed. "I shouldn't have been crying. I admit that my future husband's correspondence makes him sound quite endearing, although a bit of a mischief-maker, I suppose. He plans to meet me at the New Salem station."

"Quite the pickle. The man could be as ugly as the hind end of a mule and as old as Methuselah." Roderick chuckled as he glanced at the open letter in her lap. The closing, "Yours with great affection, Lucas Ames", was scrawled prominently in a messy hand.

82

He pursed his lips. "I know a Mr. Ames in New Salem. He's a pleasant, older gentleman."

She looked out the window, her lower lip trembling. And she redirected the conversation.

The miles passed too quickly as the strangers conversed. She laughed at his silly jokes and blushed whenever his gaze lingered for too long. He gawked into her eyes with an expression that made him appear almost adolescent.

As they neared the Howard Tunnel, her animated demeanor disappeared.

But she maintained her composure.

It's 1840, in the United States of America, and I have no intention of letting a man determine my mood, especially a man I've never met.

When the darkness of the tunnel engulfed the train, Roderick muttered, "Tarnation with decorum!" He seized her and pulled her into his arms. She gasped as his mouth sought hers, and after a brief hesitation, she responded with an ardor so intense that she found it difficult to breathe.

A few moments later, they said their awkward farewells on the train platform, but her heart was still racing when she turned her back to him.

A middle-aged gentleman in a tailored suit approached her.

She bit her lip. "Mr. Ames?"

"Yes, my dear, at your service. You must be Miss Prospero."

"I'm afraid I can't marry you."

He guffawed until his face turned red.

She scowled. "Why are you—"

"My dear, I'm not your intended. It's my soon-to-be-doctor son. The rascal is sneaking up behind you."

She whirled around, into Roderick's arms.

Roderick smiled. Then his husky voice whispered in her ear. "May I properly introduce myself? Roderick Lucas Ames. My friends call me Lucas. Emma, will you be my wife?"

She pushed him away and propped her hands on her hips. "No!" But dimples appeared in her cheeks. "Not without another kiss."

Maternal Imperative

Kathy Steinemann

This piece won first place in the KTF Press Writing Contest, May 2014.

The sickening stench of burnt flesh filled the air.

Karla Cooper, orthopedic surgeon, squeezed her son close in a smothering grip that turned her knuckles white. *It's a miracle we survived.*

Four-year-old Cecil shivered in the damp air. He rubbed his sightless eyes. "Mommy, I'm scareded. And I have lots of owies."

He's had to suffer through olfactory meningioma, blindness, and now this. She slipped into her most reassuring bedside manner. "The plane had a teeny bit of trouble. We were off course, and we're in some high mountains. But someone'll find us. You lean up against this tree while I look around." *Someone* has *to find us. Thank God he can't see the carnage.*

Bodies black to the bone. Glowing embers. Hot air near the twisted wreckage. *I wonder how long I was out.* She limped through the crash site, favoring her left leg with its long gash from knee to ankle. *I can't tell him we're the only survivors.* She talked to her son as she moved him upwind and inventoried everything that might be useful. "We've got Mommy's doctor bag, three granola bars, blankets, hunting knife, water bottle, and lots of dried branches and wood. We'll be okay."

She built a fire. She sutured her leg. And they waited for rescue.

~*~

The nights were cool, and the morning dew chilled their bones.

Every day, for twelve days, Karla kept the flame going. She carried water from the stream, built a metal structure to protect them from wildlife, and searched for food. Mother and son weakened more with every desolate hour.

Day thirteen dawned.

"Mommy, I'm really hungry."

"I know. Those berries aren't very filling. I'm sorry I'm not a better outdoor person. I should have paid attention to my daddy when I was a little girl. He took me camping lots and lots. Let's pretend we're camping."

"What's that noise?"

"I'm carving some crutches. As soon as I've finished, I'll find food." She continued to prattle as she carved, keeping Cecil entertained with stories and idle chitchat. *Now or never, Karla, before you get too weak.*

She tousled his hair. "You stay in our metal tent until I get back."

~*~

The little boy was a stone statue waiting for his mommy to return. He heard strange, spooky sounds. In his dark world, the noises were extra special scary and big and menacing. But he was brave, and he didn't cry. He tried to remember pictures from happier days. The air turned warmer then cooler again as the sun moved across the sky.

Cecil heard a rustle. The rustle grew louder.

"Mommy?"

Karla sighed. "Yes, I'm back." Her voice was a weary whisper.

"I was scareded." He cocked his head. "Why are you crying?"

"My leg hurts, baby, but I'll be all right. Here, I've got some food for supper. It needs to cook over the fire."

Soon the savory smell of roasting meat made Cecil hungrier than he could ever remember. He stretched his mouth wide like a greedy robin each time Karla offered him a hot morsel.

"It's yummy, Mommy. What is it?"

"Rabbit."

He spit into the dirt. "Rabbits are cute and cuddly." He pinched his lips closed.

"You have to eat. If you don't eat, you'll die. And I'll be lonely."

Cecil resisted. But his hunger overcame his mental image of fluffy Easter bunnies. He ate. He ate until he couldn't eat any more.

Then he slept.

Karla's moans woke him several times during the night. And so did the droning mosquitoes that dive-bombed every exposed patch of skin. Early in the morning, she wept. It was a disconsolate wail.

Cecil reached for her. "I'm scareded, Mommy. You're all hot."

"My hand was too close to the fire. It's … okay."

They were both awake shortly after dawn when a search helicopter whirred over the crest of a nearby hill.

Within two hours, the mountain was teeming with EMTs and crash scene investigators.

~*~

Karla Cooper, devoted mother, watched the glaring parade of bright lights flicker by as she was wheeled into emergency surgery. Voices seeped into her medication-induced haze.

"Good thing she had her bag."

"Man, I couldn't've done that. Any sign of infection?"

"She has a fever, but she did a nice, clean job. Not much to debride."

"I wonder how she controlled the bleeding. If only she'd waited another day."

"What difference would that've made?"

"We could've saved her leg. She cut it off and fed it to her boy."

Fire Escape

Kathy Steinemann

Is this Good Samaritan a hero or a harebrain?

"EyeInfo12 NewsBeat now takes you live to Patsy Reasoner."

"Thanks, Bill. I'm here on Alder Avenue with a woman who would like to remain anonymous. She was just involved in a bizarre rescue by a Good Samaritan firefighter. Ma'am, what happened?"

"Well, I s'ppose I should start at the beginning. One of my neighbors invited me to a costume party. Like my zombie-bride outfit?"

"I must admit it looks authentic. When I first saw the bruises, I thought they were real. So, what happened, ma'am?"

"I was walking to the party when a young kid wiped out on a bike. Right over there. With my fake cast and these six-inch fingernails, I couldn't help. The fingernails are real, by the way. Took me months to grow them. Anyway, I couldn't help, so I called 911."

"I thought you were the person rescued."

"Lemme finish. This firefighter came running up outta nowhere like some kinda superhero. I shouted at him to help the boy. So he did. Lemme tell you, that kid wasn't very nice. He stole the firefighter's wallet. I tried to bean the little brat with my cast. But I missed. It threw me off balance and I hurt my ankle. The firefighter stayed to look after me instead of running off to get his wallet back."

"So, he's the hero?"

"Yeah. Strange thing, though. He had a beard and a mustache. Not allowed for firefighters, far as I know. So I figured he was a fake. But he looked kinda familiar. Then he started gyrating around and taking off his clothes. When the police showed up, they arrested him for indecent exposure."

"Really?"

"Turns out he was a college student doing male stripper stuff on the side, and he thought I was the bride-to-be for his next gig. Bit of a harebrain for doing it in public, but …"

"Oh, I'm so sorry you had to go through such a harrowing ordeal."

"Wasn't so bad. He put on a pretty good show before the cops arrived, and I gave him a generous tip. But I think he'll be really embarrassed when I show up to pay his bail."

"You're going to pay his bail?"

"That's my plan."

"And why would he be embarrassed?"

"I haven't seen him in years, but when he turned around, I recognized him by a birthmark on his butt."

"An ex-boyfriend?"

"Nope. I used to change his diapers. I'm his aunt."

Drowning in Guilt

Kathy Steinemann

What do you suppose you'd think about if you knew death was imminent?

Shawn stomped out of the dorm and tossed Troy's 1914-D wheat penny into the pond. *That'll be the last time stupid idiot Troy steals my beer.*

Sun glinted off the dirty water like shiny new pennies. Someone's hands pushed his back. Then he was falling … falling. He thrashed his arms to keep his head out of the murky water.

The coin sat on the snout of an alligator half submerged in the sludge near the bank.

Maybe it isn't an alligator. A crocodile, maybe?

As foul fluid rushed up Shawn's nose, he decided he didn't care what the beast was. A monster with fetid breath planned to devour him.

Its teeth were sharp.

Period.

Shawn's roommate, Troy Lincoln, was the undergrad who went along with the only dorm room left on campus. He was the kind of guy who had a reputation for torturing small animals and playing practical jokes that crossed the line from practical to downright dangerous.

Troy was a weirdo.

Period.

Now that I'm about to die, you'd think my mind would focus on something besides insignificant details.

Shawn pushed himself off the slimy bottom and broke the surface. The creature's guttural growl resounded like a roaring lion in an echo chamber.

Shawn smelled death.

His.

He gasped for air and swallowed a mouthful of brackish liquid.

This is like a slow-motion movie clip.

He realized that the pond was shallow enough for him to stand. Not that it would help. The monster was almost upon him.

Troy yelled at him. "Get out. Move." He pelted the creature with rocks. "Hurry."

Shawn's pants tangled on a branch. His efforts to dislodge them were futile. The creature grabbed his leg. He gasped as his lungs demanded more air. His heart raced. The water churned red.

"Shawn. Shawn. Wake up."

Someone was shaking his shoulders. His eyes adjusted to the semi-darkness of the dorm room. He blinked several times before feeling his legs to be sure they were still there.

Troy smirked. "A penny for your thoughts."

Shawn bit his lower lip. "Guess I was having a nightmare. Sorry I threw your collector's coin into the toilet this morning. I've been feeling guilty about it all day."

Troy shrugged. "It's all right."

"Then why are you chok—"

Crying Girl
Amber Hayward

*Suppose you could choose between reality and a dream. What
would you do? Would you recognize the difference between fact
and fantasy?*

Ama was dragged from an already-broken sleep by the
sound of someone softly crying. She tried to roll over and tunnel
back into the dream she'd been enjoying, a dream of lying on a
warm sunny beach, with surf sounds and bird cries the only
intrusion to the perfect peace. She hadn't been alone. She'd been
with someone wonderful. But the dream, which had recurred all
night in short bursts between unpleasant spells of insomnia, ebbed
away, and she was forced to open her eyes.

A crying girl hovered at the ceiling, staring down at Ama,
reaching toward her beseechingly. Her tears dripped down, but
Ama didn't feel them fall on her. In fact, the tears weren't falling
toward her, they were falling away from her.

Ama was the girl on the ceiling, mourning a bloodied and
broken figure on the gurney below her, an unmoving statue in the
midst of a chaos of purposeful activity—doctors, nurses, beeping
electronic devices.

Ama was the figure on the gurney.

On the gurney, she felt the dream of the beach seductively
near. At the ceiling, she felt it recede in the face of her impotent
desire to help her injured self below.

But suppose the dream were true? Suppose this, in fact, was
the dream?

Ama ignored the crying girl. She held tight to herself on the gurney, enduring the pain and the approaching blackness. She willed herself toward the dream.

She opened her eyes to brilliant sunshine.

"Hello, darling," Benjamin said, rolling toward her on their shared towel. "You were moaning. Were you having a nightmare?"

Fly on the Wall

Kathy Steinemann

None of God's Creatures absolutely consider'd are in their own Nature Contemptible; the meanest Fly, the poorest Insect has its Use and Vertue. ~ *Mary Astell*

But there's a fly in the ointment, dear reader.

A fly swooped and flitted out of the Oval Office. It whirred away from the White House, unnoticed by security cameras, as the President smoothed the silken fabric of her blouse and finished her vid call.

Willa Washington, President of The United States of America, paused while she lowered her lashes and pictured her mood soft and smooth: like the fabric beneath her fingers. She inhaled the calming scent of lavender wafting from the aroma-simulator on her desk, and rose from her chair. "Gentlemen, shall we?"

Secret Service agents escorted her to the Bingham Briefing Room.

She waited for calmness to prevail. The frantic buzzing in the room lowered to a murmur. She glared at the noisiest reporters.

Cemetery silence.

"Ladies and gentlemen of the press, the Intergalactic Health Organization has quarantined Earth. They have devoted all their resources to locate Patient Zero. They're optimistic they'll find said person and rapidly produce a vaccine: enough for every citizen of Earth. There's no need to worry or panic. As always, avoid physical contact with others."

She provided further details, ending the news conference without accepting any questions. Then she whispered to her press secretary as they walked back to her office, "Was I convincing?"

"Superb job, Madam President. I suppose I should go home and get my affairs in order." He swiped at his bloody nose with a tissue.

~*~

Kane Blasdell, microbiologist and geneticist, stood between a pair of vertical cylinders: two of hundreds set in row after gleaming row, connected by a shiny metal network of tubes. Towering above his head, they bubbled with blue liquid, nourishing young adult Kane-Klones with closed eyes and serene features. He ran his fingers over the smoothness of the glass exteriors. *I should have called the originals Adam and Eve instead of Ebner and Anja.* He pondered, his scrutiny focused on Anja's body. *She's perfect. Just like Jordana.*

He sighed and returned to his work station, where he grimaced at the unappetizing glop on his meal tray. Oh for the good old days when he could order a veggie burger coated with a generous slathering of McD's Secret Garlic Sauce. He set his aroma-simulator on hamburger and sniffed the plate. *Needs more garlic.* He sprinkled yellow powder over the blue paste. *Ah, that's better.* Even with the flavor improvement, he twisted his face in disgust as he spooned the concoction into his mouth.

Blasdell extracted the most recent DNA specimens that had been collected by the fly-bots, and placed them in preservative ampoules.

The walls flickered with refracted light from liquid in dozens of cloning tanks. Blue brightness bounced off his nearly bald head. He rubbed his hands together, admiring what he had created and marveling at his brilliance. He'd been able to set up this laboratory near Metropole City, deep under Mount Frei Wilderness Sanctuary, without anyone discovering his plan.

He leaned back and admired his work. Thanks to the fly-bots' communication systems, he knew about the current medical emergency that threatened to wipe out the human race. And he was sure *he* had the solution, that *he* was the savior of the world, that *he* could solve the population plight and the medical crisis.

They would owe him. Their fate was in his hands.

Interlacing his fingers across his chest, he contemplated the events that had brought him here.

~*~

Scientists couldn't agree on the cause of the population decline. The number of people on Earth had grown, multiplied, expanded, like a balloon about to burst. And then something happened. The urge to procreate fizzled.

Governments offered subsidies for couples who had children, but almost everyone was too busy, too self-absorbed, too disinterested. Most people couldn't force themselves to perform the disgusting act that would guarantee survival of the species.

Marriage? Why should they get married? Solitude was the new norm. Everyone could still interact on the Intergalactic CompuNet. They didn't need physical contact as long as they had virtual reality.

Then there were the bees. Most apian colonies had died. Causes of their demise were located. The endangered insects made a weak comeback. When they started to die again, all insecticides on the planet were banned.

Although the bees were decimated by mankind's folly, the flies were not. In some places, these irritating little demons became billowing blankets of black, transforming into a swarm of buzzing darkness that blocked the sun whenever they were disturbed. Gooey fly-traps hung everywhere. The traps droned and spun in the wind as though they were alive: buzzing with flies; shrieking with the occasional bird they lured into their lethal embrace.

Some so-called experts blamed the loss of human libido on fluoridation. Other pundits said it was chemical pollution from plastics, food additives, or smog. Still others were sure it had something to do with vaccinations or GMOs. A few argued it was God's way of saving the planet from the sins of His children.

Many scientists linked the human and bee problems, insisting they were triggered by the same factors. The world resorted to cloning. However, the procedure was imperfect. Each successive generation exhibited more genetic imperfections. Many clones perished shortly before harvest.

Kane Blasdell contended that the problem was a reliance on only one donor. He proposed a combination of male and female DNA from two primary donors, along with purified mitochondrial DNA from several secondary sources. His secret Kane-Klone technique would employ unique nutrients and procedures that produced only the best results. He avowed that his system would filter out disease as well as genetic abnormalities.

Scientists scoffed at his foolishness. They ridiculed him and rendered him an outcast: someone no reputable company would hire.

But Blasdell was adamant.

He was a smart man with talents and resources in many sectors. He developed a system that would funnel embezzled financial credits into secret bank accounts. He amalgamated funds, made purchases, and developed fly-bots. Then, he recruited a few well-qualified believers.

After he set up the lab, Blasdell sent bots to collect DNA from the smartest, most artistic, most talented people left in the diminishing gene pool.

Unable to travel extreme distances, his fly-bots hitched rides via aero-rail, transporter, or sonic-taxi, and brought the specimens to Mount Frei. There, Blasdell and his associates extracted the DNA and sent the fly-bots out for more.

~*~

Blasdell roused himself from his arrogant introspection and yelled at the nearest Klone cylinders. "Someday those charlatans will respect my work. They'll have to respect it when I save mankind. My children will overcome." He laughed an eerie laugh.

~*~

Kane-Klone Ebner concentrated on the music, literature, and lessons relayed to his brain via wireless transmission. Today was his Harvest Day. He would wake and enter the world beyond his tank as a young man of nineteen. He yearned to see, but something held his eyes closed. He longed to breathe, but his body was not yet ready. *Soon.*

He waited. He scanned the sadness of the outside world and the minds of everyone nearby. His telepathic abilities grew by the hour.

~*~

Kane-Klone Anja was bored with the music, novels, and endless lessons relayed via wireless. Today, her Harvest Day, she would wake in her new world as a young woman of nineteen. She could already see, but not with her eyes. She longed to breathe, but her lungs were not yet functional. *Soon.*

She waited, and she scanned Ebner's mind as she lingered. Although weak, her telepathic abilities were also growing.

~*~

When the first two Kane-Klones left their tanks, they were fully formed adults with the emotional maturity of children. They coughed up copious globules of blue phlegm from their lungs.

They donned the uniforms given to them by tank tenders, ate their first solid food, vomited, and ate again.

The cycle continued until their digestive systems were able to cope with the new source of nourishment. Their legs were weak, but the Klones were eager to work. As soon as they were capable of using their vocal chords, they asked their tenders to lead them to their stations.

After their first week of duties, Anja found a linen storage room hidden away from the purview of tenders, security cameras, and fly-bots. "Ebner, come with me. I have something to show you."

She led him to the room, pulled her uniform off her shoulders, and stood, exposed to the waist, her breasts heaving as her breathing rate accelerated.

Ebner's gaze fixed on her bare skin and moved down to her nipples. She circled them with her fingertips and moved slowly backward, passing her tongue over her lips.

He zipped out of his uniform. "My lessons explained this, but they didn't explain how powerful the feeling would be."

They learned the pleasures of copulation. Authors had extolled its virtues in fiction. However, this wasn't fiction. It felt good. It was real.

Yet it was a realness that nobody else within telepathic range seemed to care about. Anja and Ebner were shy, embarrassed. So they kept their amorous activities hidden.

If one of the fly-bots had been programmed to follow them, it would have found them several times a day, pushing and giggling and gasping as they savored the euphoria of this blissful experience.

But the flies had more important tasks in their programming.

~*~

Blasdell reviewed his files.

The first Kane-Klones were functioning as expected. Tank-trained in microbiology, genetics, parthenogenetics, chemistry, physics … He examined the endless list of sciences and qualifications. His creations were outstanding specimens of beauty with their perfect bodies, tank-blue eyes, fair skin, and tawny-blond hair.

Ebner and Anja would be invaluable in his research, and a great aid in orienting the second group of 200 Kane-Klones due for harvesting in a few months.

A sudden spasm scrunched one side of his wizened face for a blink. Then a second blink. The spasm pulled at his sparse grey eyebrows. He waited until his facial muscles relaxed before he ventured out into the cloning chamber.

~*~

Ebner discovered that his ability to sense thoughts from the world beyond Mount Frei wasn't normal by human standards. He searched Anja's mind. He explored the minds of Blasdell and his associates. His was a talent that nobody in the compound, including Anja, possessed.

Anja embraced her ability to scan the people in her proximity. She didn't need to play coy games with Ebner, although she sometimes did just for fun. She liked scanning his mind, and she appreciated how gentle he was with her.

They both delighted in playing pranks.

One morning they built their own fly-bot: a rudimentary model without DNA-collection or long-range capabilities.

The conspirators giggled like little children when they guided it up Blasdell's nasal passages. He swatted at the fly and gave himself a bloody nose. They didn't understand why his annoyance was so funny, but they snickered about it again when they saw him later with tissues shoved up his nostrils.

Anja whispered to Ebner, "Meet me at our place in five minutes."

"Mmm. Gladly."

"Not for that. Well, maybe after. I want to talk to you."

"What are you blocking in that devious mind of yours?"

Ebner grinned and drummed his fingers while he waited for the time to pass. Then he hurried to the linen storage room.

Anja pulled him inside. "I was doing a random scan of Blasdell's mind this morning, and I found something I don't like."

"You were serious about—"

"Yes!" She slapped his hand away. "His thoughts were sad. Some kind of dark secret I couldn't access. And he keeps thinking about my naked body. Or someone who looks like me. And he fantasizes about copulation."

Ebner scowled. "He'd better not touch you. You're mine."

"I never sense any thoughts like that when he's near me. I think it might be someone named Jordana. He becomes agitated and morose whenever he thinks about her. And there's something dark he keeps buried beyond my reach. Maybe it has something to do with the Outsiders."

"*He's* an Outsider. Everyone here, except you and I, is an Outsider."

"Not the Outsiders in here. The ones out there. Beyond the mountain. What do they think about?"

Ebner stared at the opposite wall. "Mostly about themselves. They don't seem to care much about others, and they don't copulate. At least, most of them don't. They're sad and afraid. All I get are vague impressions. But they have a great fear. All the Outsiders share a great fear."

She shuddered. "Blasdell is afraid too. We need to find out why."

Ebner pulled her uniform partway down, wrapped his lips around one of her nipples, and mumbled with his mouth full. "I'll listen to the Outsiders. Maybe I can find out more." He unzipped his uniform. "Now stop being so serious, and let's have some fun."

~*~

Blasdell now had sufficient DNA to keep his project alive for decades. In an isolated corner of the compound, he deactivated the last of the fly-bots.

A sudden tic forced his face into a lopsided scrunch for a blink. Then a second blink. A third. He rubbed his eye. A thin dribble of red trickled from his nose. He dabbed with a tissue, then threw it in the trash.

A fly on the wall readjusted its lenses, relaying its video feed to Anja and Ebner. They watched and waited until Blasdell left the room. Then they extracted his DNA from the tissue in the trash.

They analyzed, computed, and hypothesized as they continued their work over the ensuing weeks.

On the appointed day, the next 200 Kane-Klones left their tanks. They shouldered their various duties and performed as expected under Blasdell's supervision.

Anja and Ebner monitored the Klones' progress.

Within three months, they recognized the same facial tic in their Klone companions that they had seen on Blasdell's face. They discussed their suspicions and hypotheses, and performed confirmation tests.

All the Klones except for Anja and Ebner had the same primary male-DNA contributor: Kane Blasdell. And they were all infected with the same fatal virus as their father. Preliminary experiments indicated that everyone in the compound except for Anja and Ebner would be dead within six months.

~*~

Anja pulled Ebner into a quiet corner and asked, "Why did Blasdell use different primary donors for us? Have you been able to find anything?"

Ebner's face pulled into a lopsided frown. "He's almost as good at hiding secrets as you are. I can't determine his reasoning, and I'm pretty sure he knows nothing about our abilities. We must be mutations. Or unanticipated variations from the norm. He altered the process and donors after he created us."

They scanned Kane Blasdell's mind together. He hadn't known about his condition until recently, and he didn't realize he had transmitted it to his biological creations. His foolproof process for avoiding disease and genetic abnormalities had failed.

Ebner stared at bank after bank of cloning cylinders. "We can't let him know what he's done. Imagine how much torment it would cause him."

They re-analyzed their tests. The results didn't vary from their initial evaluations.

And something else perplexed them. Ebner seemed to have lost his ability to sense the thoughts of the Outsiders. Except for one distant imprint from someone named Jaxxon.

~*~

The first deaths occurred earlier than predicted. Blasdell conducted emergency autopsies. He discovered his failure and realized that his creations were imperfect.

He couldn't bear to have them suffer, so he decided to set the auto-destruct sequence for late one night when everyone was asleep. The radiation would destroy all biological matter in the compound, including him and the virus. But it would leave his files intact; it would leave his machinery in working order; and it would allow future scientists to continue his research after he was gone.

He enabled a communications drone with a message for President Washington, and programmed it for the fastest route to the White House.

~*~

Ebner paced while he discussed the options with Anja. "I feel duty-bound to stay, but I want to live. I want you to live."

"We can't do anything here. What purpose would it serve for us to die? We should take our chances in the upper world among the Outsiders. I'll locate the exit codes in Blasdell's memory."

His eyes moistened. "This is our home."

"Do we have a choice?" She squeezed his hand. "We have to leave. Maybe there's something we can do on the outside."

He pulled her close and remained silent for several seconds. "All right. Let's gather as many provisions as possible."

~*~

They tiptoed through the muted light to the elevator shaft, entered the security codes, and rode to the surface.

After walking for several minutes, they discovered a Mount Frei Wilderness Sanctuary maintenance vehicle with its driver slumped lifeless over the navigation controls. They pulled his body from the seat, laid him to rest a few feet from the road, and covered him with rocks.

The lights of Metropole City beckoned like a distant beacon in the darkness. Anja and Ebner climbed into the front seat and initiated the control system. While the vehicle hummed to their destination, they sat silently, sharing despondent thoughts.

They reached the outskirts shortly before dawn. They embraced. And they cried.

Corpses littered the streets. Remnants of tattered clothing hung from bodies picked clean to the bone. Flies swarmed and hummed: an undulating whine of pests that flew into mouths and ears, buzzed up noses, and tangled in hair. And the dogs. So many dogs: ravenous former pets that chased after cats and other small animals.

Ebner now understood why he had lost the thoughts of the Outsiders. There were no Outsiders left to scan.

A canine pack circled them, teeth bared, saliva hanging from emaciated faces. The Klones concentrated and stared until the dogs ran away with tails tucked between their legs.

Anja leaned against a light standard and wiped the sweat from her forehead.

Ebner collapsed onto a bench. "Why didn't Blasdell know about this? I thought he maintained some kind of contact with the outside world."

Anja sighed, a sob catching in her throat. "This must be the dark secret he tried not to think about."

"It looks like the same disease that infected the compound. The fly-bots must have transmitted it."

She closed her eyes to block the glare from the rising sun. "We're probably the only humans left on the planet. Except for Jaxxon and his kind, whoever he is, wherever he is."

Anja and Ebner found a bountiful supply of provisions. Outsiders' dwellings were fascinating lodgings with solar-powered appliances and canned, frozen, and dried food. The sustenance was ambrosia compared to the blue paste they had eaten in the lab. They estimated they could stay in one area for several weeks, until they used up their food supply, and then move on.

Marauding packs of dogs haunted them wherever they went. Anja and Ebner traveled with whatever weapons they could find. They buried bodies, but during daylight hours only. Mind control over the dogs seemed to work best when the Klones could see what they were trying to influence.

The hungry canines clung to shadows during the day. When the sun was high, Metropole City remained silent except for the wind and strange, faraway sounds.

Dusk erupted with yips and yowls, growls, and the sounds of dying dogs as the strong overcame the weak. Many nights it was difficult to sleep. Anja and Ebner lay in bed until late morning to compensate.

Their skin tanned to demerara-brown, and their tawny-blond hair lightened to buttercup-yellow. They developed muscular arms and legs. They spent every minute together, working in unison, never needing to express their thoughts. But they couldn't bear the silence. So they talked. And they sang songs from their tank libraries; songs they had heard over the lab's sound system; new songs they composed as they toiled.

Regret tempered their happiness to be alive. They found it difficult to reconcile their good fortune with the death and horror that surrounded them. Although they missed the mental stimulation of their work in the lab, they retired every evening with a feeling of accomplishment. Their efforts were gradually restoring the streets and domiciles. They were transforming death and decay into life and beauty.

~*~

One night in July, Anja sniffed at Ebner. "You stink. You should put aroma-sims in your armpits."

He pulled her close and nuzzled his nose in her hair. "You smell like fresh air. There's no aroma-sim for that. I promise I'll have a shower in the morning."

She murmured into his chest. "I remember classic novels, and the authors' devotion to love and passion. I love you. Just like in those books. I feel as if we were created for this, like the being they call God put us here for a purpose. If I didn't have you, I wouldn't want to live. Life would be unbearable."

She closed her eyes and recited from a 19th-century poem:

"How do I love thee? Let me count the ways.
I love thee to the depth and breadth and height
My soul can reach, when feeling out of sight
For the ends of being and ideal grace."

He kissed her and replied:

"I love thee to the level of every day's
Most quiet need, by sun and candle-light.
I love thee freely, as men strive for right.
I love thee purely, as they turn from praise."

He sighed. "I should feel sad, knowing we're surrounded by such desolation and death. But what I feel for you can't be explained by logic. You make me happy."

As she stroked her belly, she remembered more stories, and the lessons about reproduction and birth.

He scanned her mind and smiled a sad smile. The world was theirs. They would have their child, and they would search for the few survivors of the Homo sapiens race. He patted her abdomen. "I'll look after you and the baby. I'll protect you, no matter what. But we must find Jaxxon and the other Outsiders beyond the range of my mind."

~*~

Near dusk on a day in October, Anja felt a whoosh of water at her ankles. "Our baby is coming, and I feel pain. It hurts. Ohhhh, it hurts so much."

Ebner picked her up in his arms and stumbled toward their living quarters. Dogs circled, seeking an opening. He yelled at them. "Go away. Leave us alone."

The animals sensed his weakness, his lack of a weapon, his inability to repel so many of them. They attacked his ankles.

He kicked at the frenzied creatures. "Too many. I can't control all of them. Too … many." His legs filled with bloody gashes as the fangs tore at him. He staggered and dropped Anja. The pack closed in on her.

Anja scanned their minds and found one friend in the pack: a snarling dog with a huge belly. The dog bared her fangs. She chased attacker after attacker away and stood guard over the two Klones. The pack retreated, except for one resolute dissenter that leapt at Ebner, sank its teeth into his abdomen, and hung on, legs dangling in the air. When the friendly dog tore into the attacker's hind end, it relented and slunk away.

Anja dragged Ebner inside. The pregnant dog followed. She licked his wounds while Anja locked the door and collapsed in pain. As soon as her contraction was over, she tended to his injuries as best she could with the materials at hand.

Many hours passed while dogs howled and scratched at the door. They jumped into the air to peer through windows. Even in her escalating pain, Anja could sense their hunger and desperation. Ebner's thoughts worried her. They faded in and out. When they were at their strongest, his mind registered pain and terror.

She strove to comfort him. She soothed him with her thoughts and gentle words of encouragement. Between contractions, she offered him water to sip and laid cold cloths on his brow.

Her pain intensified. "Oh, Ebner. If the survival of humans depends on having more babies, we'll become extinct. Now I realize why women refused to copulate and reproduce. Giving birth hurts."

He lay prone, unable to do anything except squeeze her wrist. "Soon, my love. The baby will be here … soon."

"It's coming. Now!"

Ebner inched closer. "I love you."

Anja tried to remember her lessons. She was in so much pain that she couldn't do anything to help Ebner. She needed to deliver their baby first. After using her teeth to rip two pieces of fabric from her shirt, she sat against a wall and pushed … pushed … pushed.

A wail. Two quick, breathy sobs. Another wail. She tied off the umbilical cord and held her son to her breasts, then grunted as the placenta arrived.

Now she could relax, just for a moment. She slouched back, limp with exhaustion. "The pain is gone. It feels so good that the pain is gone."

The pregnant dog seemed to know what to do. She bit through the cord, gnawed on the placenta, and slurped blood from the floor.

Anja watched in horror.

Ebner's eyes fluttered open. "It's … all right. She's starving. Puppies … need nourishment."

Anja laid the baby down and stroked Ebner's brow. "Soon you'll get better, and we'll find another place. A place without dogs. Except this one here. I like her."

Ebner focused on Anja's face. "The baby? You?"

"He's healthy, and I'm all right."

"A boy?"

"Yes, and he's perfect, just like you."

"He needs a name." His breathing turned into a cough. He gulped. "Gulliver. Like … in the book." He coughed again. Blood-flecked spittle spewed from his lips. "Let me see him."

She propped a cushion behind his shoulders and held baby Gulliver to his chest.

A wan smile ghosted Ebner's lips. "Gulliver. Our son. Give me … your hand."

She placed her hand in his.

"Concentrate. Don't say anything. Jaxxon is … aware of our location. Good man. Can you see him …?"

A shimmering apparition took shape before her eyes: a man wearing a beekeeper's hat. He removed it to reveal a rustic face with dark whiskers, brown eyes, and determined jaw. She saw rows of beehives and clover fields near the banks of a river. "I see him."

"Wait here. Remember. Think about … his face." Ebner's breathing grew more labored. "You. Baby Gulliver. Jaxxon. Will find … other Outsiders. You will be … the new human race."

"But what about you?"

His halting words became a weak whisper. "I love you. But I cannot stay. I …" His body convulsed. He opened his eyes wide. "I love …" He lurched and stiffened with one final convulsion. Then he lay silent, his vacant stare devoid of life.

Anja lay across his chest and cried. "No. No! Please don't leave us." Gasping sobs wracked her body. Rivers of tears flowed from her eyes onto his bloody shirt, drenching it in a horrible pattern of red and wetness. Never in her short life had she felt such pain. Not even the birth of her baby had hurt this much. She lamented until she had no more tears.

Then she heard the sounds of the female dog giving birth.

As Ebner's body grew cool, the first puppy whimpered against its mother's warm tummy. The bitch licked it. Kept licking until it was dry. Nudged it with her nose toward her mammillae.

The soft suckling sounds and whines of the little whelp interrupted Anja's distant thoughts. She squinted through swollen eyelids and kissed her baby's forehead. "Baby boy, I think we'll name this puppy Lemuel, from the book your daddy liked."

~*~

Six-year-old Gulliver threw a rock into the creek. His two-year-old half-sister, Swift, threw a bigger rock. Gulliver swatted her.

Anja laughed. "You two stop fighting."

Jaxxon warned, "Listen to your mother." Juice from a fresh tomato dribbled down his chin.

She kissed him and slurped the juice from his lips. "Give me some of that tomato." She bit a huge chunk out of the juicy red fruit and stared at Mount Frei. "So it was the bees. That's what all my experiments show. The only people who survived were beekeepers and apiologists. It's something in the venom. Ironic. Humans almost killed the bees, and in the end the bees saved them."

Jaxxon stood behind her, massaged her swollen abdomen, and kissed her hair. "Someday, other survivors will find us and the commune, or we can go look for them after the baby's born and you're strong enough."

"Not until I develop a vaccine. I hypothesize, given what I know at present, that the first generation inherits immunity and passes the protection along to the children. Beyond that, I have no data on which to base any speculations. Ebner and I survived. Gulliver and Swift survived. But ..."

"You said you discovered something about your parents when you were reviewing Kane Blasdell's files?"

She stretched her arms up to encircle his neck. "My father was Blasdell's associate, an apiologist. My mother was Blasdell's fiancée, Jordana. Ebner's primary donors were one of my father's associates and a friend of Jordana's. No more details yet, but I'm sure I'll figure it out with time."

She watched the other members of the commune working in the gardens, and the children playing with Lemuel. Her eyes veiled with tears for a moment as she remembered Ebner's last moments. *He would be so proud.*

She gazed, unfocused, at the cows in the meadow and the hives in the field, and murmured, "Are you still alive, mother and father?"

Wanted

Kathy Steinemann

This flash fiction appeared in Saturday Night Reader, January 2015.

LOVING HOME WANTED for umbrella cockatoo named Lionel. Three years old. Excellent disposition and health. Good appetite. Doesn't shriek much and talks well. Loves cuddle time. Goes to bed without making a fuss. A bit of a wood chewer, but he plays quietly when nobody is around. Includes cage and toys. This parrot must go by January 15 to make room for a new scarlet macaw. Seeking a reputable family with prior parrot experience. $1000. Contact JDoe388@mail.com to set up an interview.

GOOD HOME WANTED for scarlet macaw named Bella. Eight months old. Excellent disposition and health. Not a fussy eater. Doesn't talk much yet, but she's bright and learns quickly. Only squawks when wanting attention. Plays happily with her toys when nobody is around. Steps up willingly. A bit nippy. This bird must go by May 30 to make room for the hyacinth macaw we just purchased. Only seriously interested parties, please. $1000 OBO. Contact JDoe388@mail.com.

QUICK SALE WANTED for hyacinth macaw. Two years old. Excellent disposition and health. Not a picky eater. Talks lots and loves to say its name. Requires minimal attention. Goes poop on command. Comes with huge cage, toys, dishes, etc. We have to get rid of this bird within two weeks because we're going to Europe. Contact soonest, JDoe388@mail.com.

PARROT WANTED. Couple with prior parrot experience seeks parrot that can talk and do tricks. No feather pickers, please.

Must be well behaved, quiet, and in excellent health. Prefer a macaw, but will consider other breeds. Contact JDoe388@mail.com ASAP.

Herman's Dilemma

Kathy Steinemann

*Why do you suppose Herman is so afraid the EMTs might tell
someone how he got hurt? It seems he has a rather surprising
reason for his reticence.*

Herman's eyelids fluttered open as he was loaded onto the
stretcher. "What ... where?"

"You've had an accident, sir. Bit of a bump on the head.
Do you remember your name?"

"Herman. Herman Washburn. Where are you taking me?"

"To the hospital, Herman. One of your neighbors called
911 when he heard you yell." The EMT assessed the bruise on
Herman's brow. "Can you tell me what day this is?"

"The day after yesterday and the day before tomorrow. The
last time I checked the calendar, that was Wednesday. Hump day."

The EMT chuckled. "You seem to have full use of your
mental faculties. Can you tell me what happened?"

"Yes. But please don't tell anyone. ... I poured myself a
glass of wine."

"So you overindulged, got tipsy, and lost your balance?"

"No, I didn't drink a drop. I was texting my girlfriend and
not paying attention when I grabbed a bottle off the counter."

"You dropped the bottle and bumped your head trying to
retrieve it?"

"No, I picked up the mouthwash by mistake."

"You keep mouthwash in the kitchen?"

"Not usually. I was using it to soak my socks. Works great,
by the way. Gets rid of foot odor and germs."

"You wash your socks in the kitchen sink?" The EMT choked as though he were trying to suppress a laugh. "So … you swallowed mouthwash. What does that have to do with your accident?"

"I was emptying the glass in the sink when I received a reply to my text."

The EMT's face scrunched into a scowl. "And …"

"My girlfriend told me we're pregnant. But I had a vasectomy last year."

"And that's when you yelled? How did you bump your head?"

"No. Let me finish. I didn't yell when I got her text. And I didn't yell when one of my coworkers sent me a naked photo of his date for last night, who just happens to be my girlfriend. Needless to say, I was furious. Sick-to-the-stomach furious."

The EMT raised his eyebrows. "Tough luck. But I still don't understand how you got the goose egg."

"I received a text telling me my last book just hit the *New York Times* Bestseller List. I was so excited and distracted I didn't watch where I was going, and I tripped over a loose carpet. Please don't tell anyone."

The EMT's eyes crinkled. "Why?"

"My book is *The Ultimate Guide to Safe Texting*."

Blood Money

A. L. Kaplan

Ain't nobody coming after this money.

I backed deeper into Dad's half-collapsed toolshed and prayed Augie would stop counting long enough to turn around. My body screamed for oxygen, but my asthmatic lungs refused to comply. The man stepped with me, keeping the pistol inches from my head. Blood oozed from a gash across his neck. Bright and red, just like the blood on the bag of money Augie and I found on the tracks. I knew we should have left it, but money was tight and that bag had a lot of it.

"Ain't nobody coming after this money, Wyatt," said Augie. "There's way too much blood."

A crooked grin split the man's face. "I guess my name is Ain't Nobody, kid." His raspy voice sounded like the chain-smoking guy at the station.

Augie's voice shook. "Please don't hurt my brother, mister. Take the money. We won't tell. I swear."

A flicker of sadness crossed the man's face. "Just pack it up." He pulled out a bottle. "Slow breaths, Wyatt. Drink this."

I swallowed the liquid he poured into my mouth without thinking. It burned my throat, but by the time Augie packed up all the cash, my molasses-filled lungs had cleared. The man took the bloodstained bag from Augie and tossed a thick wad of twenties on the ground.

"For your troubles." He tousled my hair and smiled. "Slow easy breaths and a shot of whiskey, Wyatt. Worked for my brother every time. Remember, if anyone asks, Ain't Nobody been here."

Auld Lang Syne
Kathy Steinemann

Emmett avoids social occasions that require small-talk, and he detests fancy dinners with mysterious vegetables. But his wife, Megan, has planned a surprise retirement party.

Emmett dropped his keys after unlocking the front door. While he was fumbling to return them to his pocket, his wife switched on the lights. Several people shouted, "Surprise!"

He turned toward Megan and grumbled in an almost inaudible voice, "You know how much I hate surprise parties."

Plastering a fake smile on his face, he shook hands and listened to a barrage of "happy retirement" congratulations.

His grumbling continued during dinner. "Vegetables. Blech! Are you trying to kill me for the insurance? And what's this organic dreck?"

After supper, everyone sang "Auld Lang Syne". He responded with a grimace.

A frown swept over his face after Megan lit the sparkler on his retirement cake. An errant spark set the curtains ablaze, and the room erupted into a frantic burst of chaos.

Derek dropped his drink in his lap and swatted a fleck of ash from his hair. Aldona stumbled over Derek's feet as she ran from the fire. She tripped face-first into a piece of cake that had flown onto the floor.

The smoke alarm shrieked. The sprinkler system activated, soaking everything and everyone in the room.

Sabrina, their Siamese cat, clawed up the sofa, yowling her displeasure at the sudden wetness.

The sprinkler spluttered, hissed … and failed.

Kathy careened into Lorraine. Lorraine fell against Keith, knocking off his glasses. Bruno grabbed Kat's cane and started yanking down curtains. A flying ember landed in Al's mustache. He slapped at it and gave himself a nosebleed.

One empty ABC extinguisher later, the fire and festivities had been snuffed out like a trampled cigar butt. John put down the extinguisher to rub at the soot on his chin.

Smoke and steam hung in the air. The sickening smell of burnt mustache tickled Emmett's throat. He coughed.

Then he looked at the dour expressions and chuckled. His chuckle escalated into raucous laughter. He doubled over, face red, tears streaming down his face. "Megan, this is absolutely the best party I've ever had."

Where's the Evidence?

Kathy Steinemann

Who murdered Bill? Will you see the clues?

When Detective Dick Copeland reached the crime scene on the third floor of Citadel Apartments, it was swarming with EMTs, CSIs, and patrol officers. Neighbors loitered in the hallway or gawked through partially open doors to eavesdrop. The air reeked with sweaty excitement and overcooked suppers, overlaid by a bouquet of fresh paint and new carpeting.

Dick walked through the foyer toward the kitchen, where the victim's girlfriend, Wendy Wilson, awaited him. Before he could enter, his new partner rushed in from the hallway, elbowed him aside, and squeezed through.

Dick frowned. *Late twice in one week. Another doctor's appointment?*

PJ apologized. "Sorry. The doctor's office was running late."

Ms. Wilson smiled at Dick through her tears, but she addressed her remarks to PJ. "Patrick, uh, Detective Johnson. So nice to see you again." Her greeting transformed into violent sobs. She was young, probably twenty-five or so, petite, and pretty.

PJ's face reddened. He placed a hand on her shoulder, and his bushy eyebrows knit into a continuous caterpillar of dark hair. He waited for the sobbing to stop, then spoke with a nasal stammer. "Wendy, um, this is my partner, Detective Dick Copeland. Dick, Ms. Wilson."

Wendy pointed. "He's in there."

Dick and PJ walked into the living room.

The stench of urine, evacuated bowel contents, and fresh blood assaulted their nostrils. Dick held a hand over his nose. TV dramas never showed this part of a crime scene. In the throes of death, muscles relaxed, and excretions escaped.

The lifeless body of the girl's boyfriend sprawled face up on the floor near the sofa. A heavy lamp, its base broken and stained with blood, lay about two feet away. A feathery ornament fluttered in the open window. It was missing a feather, presumably the one in the victim's fist.

An empty box of cheap wine sat next to an overturned glass. The trash contained two flattened wine boxes, covered by a wad of pay stubs and a *World's Greatest Accountant* mug.

Dick's controlled, assertive voice stilled the other conversations in the room. "No signs of a struggle and no discernable defensive wounds. Unless the medical examiner finds something else, it appears as though the victim died from a single blow to the skull, apparently administered by the lamp. I suspect he saw it coming, and he probably knew his killer."

The medical examiner concurred. "No visible trauma except the obvious abrasion on his forehead. However, I reserve judgment until I get the victim onto my table for a proper autopsy."

PJ cleared his throat and whispered to Dick through the side of his mouth. "Ms. Wilson's first name is Wendy. Her boyfriend's name is, rather, was Bill Trenton. She's gorgeous, don't you think?"

"Watch those hormones, PJ. They could get you into trouble."

"It's not like that. I just think she's cute."

Dick contemplated, chin on knuckles.

PJ jabbed him in the ribs. "Cut it out, fella. You've watched one too many episodes of the *Murdoch Mysteries*. Crap, with that suit and tie, you could pass for William Murdoch on the street. It's

2014, not 1895. Get the stick out of your butt, c'mon down to Earth, and breathe my air."

Dick ignored the barb. When he finally spoke, it was in a decisive tone. "We have to assume the girl had something to do with it."

"No way. Wendy's a sweet kid. I'll vouch for her character." He sneezed into his baseball cap. "C'mon. We can't do anything more with this mess until we get the lab results." He adjusted the crotch of his too-tight blue jeans before he lumbered toward the kitchen.

The girl was talking on her cell phone. "But I can't. Not now." She glanced at the detectives and lowered her voice. "I have to go. Okay. … I will. … Me too."

Her almond-brown hair was fused to her face by the rivulets of tears still dripping into her cleavage. She stared at nothing as she laid the cell phone on the table. "That was my brother."

PJ extended a hand. Rather than take it, Wendy embraced him. He flinched as he drew his arms up to shoulder height, and his eyes grew so wide they resembled billiard balls. He blinked. He teetered toward the wall. Then he administered a few tentative pats as he blushed.

She extricated herself and lowered her gaze.

Seeing them together, Dick realized more than ever how short and stocky his partner was. His attention strayed to the girl's breasts. *I wonder if those are real.*

PJ coughed. "Wendy, would you, um, please answer a few questions?" He shuffled his feet and stuttered over a few more words.

Dick cupped a hand to PJ's ear. "What's the matter? Where are the customary quips and jokes that usually spew out of your mouth? And why did she hug you?"

"It's Wendy," he whispered. "I can't think straight when she's around."

Dick waited for further explanation. When it didn't come, he waved PJ aside and took control of the interview.

His scrutiny wandered around the kitchen as he conducted the interrogation. A refrigerator magnet partially obscured a snapshot of the girl, her boyfriend, and a parrot. She appeared happy in the photo. Her boyfriend, however, did not.

The sink overflowed with dirty dishes. A half-eaten bag of potato chips lay on the counter next to a bowl of fruit. Dick picked up a life insurance application from beside the bowl and perused it as he spoke.

After a routine battery of inquiries, he steered his questioning toward the bird. "I see a photo of you, the victim, and a parrot. Where's the parrot now?"

"That's Pepper, my blue and gold macaw. I got him from a bird-rescue sanctuary. He's just like a baby to me. Bill wasn't keen on him, though. Said he was too noisy."

"I see no evidence of a bird in your living quarters."

"He flew away when Bill forgot to close the window one day in June. I've been looking for Pepper ever since. He's probably still alive. Somewhere."

She sniffled. "My mom said I should put his cage away, so last week I finally took it apart and stored it in the hall closet, along with his toys and food. But maybe he'll come back now the weather's getting colder. I keep the window open just in case."

"Did the window incident make you mad at Bill?"

"Yes. But certainly not mad enough to kill him." She scowled. "All I have left of Pepper now are the feathers in the dreamcatcher. ... And my photos."

"The dreamcatcher is the window ornament?"

"Yes." Wendy began to cry again.

After a lengthy, uncomfortable silence, Dick arranged for a female officer to accompany the girl to her mother's house. A complete inspection of the apartment didn't reveal anything of significance.

~*~

The following afternoon, Dick and PJ reviewed their findings at the precinct, hoping to spot something they'd missed.

Dick paced in front of his desk with one finger against his lips and the other hand behind his back. "The feather belonged to the species Ara ararauna, commonly known as the blue and gold macaw. All the blood at the scene was Mr. Trenton's. Cause of death was blunt force trauma to the skull. The medical examiner's further findings are inconclusive at present."

PJ chewed on a lump of phlegm. "Bill's blood alcohol level was 0.17. That's high enough to cause staggering, slurred speech, and impaired reactions. Preliminary results indicate no suspicious particulates, fingerprints, or DNA at the scene. And nobody in the building saw or heard anything unusual."

Dick laughed in a sardonic tone. "If a man dies and nobody sees or hears it, is he really dead?"

"Hey, I'm supposed to be the funny man here."

"That wasn't humor. It was sarcasm. Regardless, according to witnesses, the couple didn't have any relationship problems. Although there was gossip that Mr. Trenton suspected Ms. Wilson of having an affair. Perhaps her 'brother' is really her lover. We need to continue our follow-up on that angle by getting a subpoena for phone records."

PJ's face flushed. "Um … Wendy wasn't aware Bill had been laid off by his accounting firm three weeks prior to his murder." He snuffled. "And she can't have kids."

Dick paused. *How would PJ know that?* He frowned. "Would you please blow your nose?"

125

PJ jumped to attention, responding with a sneer and a sloppy salute. "Yessireedick."

Dick continued without comment. "Financial records indicate the victim made regular payments to a finance company for an engagement ring, but we were unable to locate said ring in the apartment. The million-dollar life insurance application named Ms. Wilson as beneficiary. Both facts appear to confirm the couple's healthy relationship. Or are they inconsistencies?"

"I tell you, Wendy's innocent. The policy was never issued, because Bill couldn't afford the premiums. So she didn't have a financial motive. And video surveillance showed nobody entering or leaving the apartment near the time of death."

Dick continued to pace, fingertips pressed together. "But did Ms. Wilson realize the policy wasn't in effect? And I have to address the obvious. How did you meet the young woman?"

"At the Midtown Parrot Association. Every Wednesday night I take Joey. And she used to take Pepper. She still goes to play with the birds and hang out with the other owners."

"Joey?"

"My African grey parrot."

"Ah. That explains why you're always in such an elevated mood on Thursday mornings. And her love for the parrot gives us a possible motive. Some people become obsessively attached to their pets."

PJ horked. "Don't pigeonhole her. Wendy would never do anything as vile as commit murder."

"Perhaps a physical altercation with Wendy caused Mr. Trenton's demise. He was drunk, and he would have been unable to defend himself from an unexpected attack."

"But video surveillance shows her getting home at least an hour after time of death." PJ glowered. "There's no way Wendy did it."

126

"What about you? You obviously feel something for Ms. Wilson. As a police officer, you'd be capable of destroying or concealing evidence."

"No way. She's cute, and she makes me all tongue-tied, but she's outta my league. I'd never commit murder for a woman."

Dick scrutinized him. How well did PJ really know the girl? And how well did Dick know PJ? They had only been partners for a month.

~*~

Dick decided to work on the case alone in his free time. Something about PJ's behavior didn't ring true. But he wasn't ready to confront him.

Yet.

The brother-lover angle proved to be a false lead. Wendy's phone records confirmed that she talked to her brother several times on the day of the murder. In further interviews, nobody except the owner of a nearby pet shop could provide anything of relevance.

The proprietor of the shop called out to Dick from the reptile section. "May I help you, sir?"

Dick displayed his credentials and identified himself. "Do you recognize anyone in this photo?"

"Sure. That's Wendy Wilson, Bill Trenton, and Pepper. Sometimes Wendy brought Pepper into the store with her. I heard about the murder on TV."

The shopkeeper continued to volunteer details. "Pepper had one swear word, but he couldn't pronounce it very well. I always figured he was saying apple, until Wendy corrected my mistake. Came in every day at first to see if anyone had found him. She cried a lot."

He pointed to the front counter. "Bill was here the morning of the murder, looking for another macaw to cheer Wendy up. But he couldn't afford it. Left some stuff behind. I intended to return it next time he and Wendy came into the store. Forgot all about it until just now. Wait a sec while I get it from under the till."

Dick sorted through the coupons and credit card offers. The only thing he deemed important was a ticket stuck between two of the coupons.

Bill had pawned the engagement ring.

~*~

PJ cleared his throat. Then he coughed and rustled the papers he was holding. He cleared his throat again, adjusted his blue jeans, and twirled his baseball cap around an index finger.

Dick continued to feign busyness while he swiped at the computer tablet on his desk.

PJ jiggled Dick's chair. "We need to talk."

Dick glared at him. "You really should do something about that frog in your throat. If I have to visit one more crime scene with you and that infernal horking, I swear I'll go insane."

"I um, I have a confession to make. I consoled Wendy one night after Pepper went missing, and she was very thankful, if you get my drift. Bill saw me leaving the apartment, but I don't think he suspected anything. It was only once, I swear. She was crying. I felt sorry for her, and it just … happened."

Dick slammed his fist into the wall. "I knew there was more than what you were telling me." He swore. "Now you're a suspect. You know this means you're off the case?"

"Yeah."

"I can't believe you didn't tell me sooner. If I find anything, anything at all, I'll have to arrest you. Get out of here. I need room to think." He slumped over his keyboard. *PJ had means, motive, and opportunity, and as a cop, I have to hold him to a higher standard.*

Dick's expletive could be heard several cubicles away.

He discussed his dilemma with the Captain. Cap was quick to reply. "Where's the evidence? If you plan to accuse him, you need more than a suspicion. I can't suspend him based on what you've got. I'll put PJ on desk duty. Find some proof. For now, Paulson's your partner."

~*~

Dick's reflection in his bathroom mirror reminded him of a specter he'd seen on TV the week before. He rubbed at the dark circles under his eyes and splashed cold water over his face. *I wonder how much sleep I got last night.* He adjusted his tie and ran his fingers over his eyebrows to tame a few stragglers.

His extra-strong coffee was bitter. He killed the taste with a cinnamon-raisin bagel while he drove to the crime scene.

Yellow tape still crisscrossed the entrance, but he thought he heard movements in the apartment. He pulled the tape away, unlocked the door, and drew his revolver. Quietly, slowly, he inched inside.

The dreamcatcher rotated wildly in the open window. Chewed books littered the floor. The fruit in the bowl was now a pile of peels and pits. And the potato-chip bag was empty.

With a chuckle, Dick holstered his revolver, tiptoed through the obstacle course of debris, and closed the window. "Pepper? Are you still here? Are you trying to find Wendy? Here boy. Come here."

A voice squawked from somewhere behind him. "Hello. Apple. Pepper hungry. Hello. Wennnndy."

Dick fetched a coffee mug and filled it with water. Then he rummaged through the closet to find the bird food. As soon as he set it on the kitchen counter, Pepper flew over and sank his beak into the pellets. The bird made a cooing noise deep in his gullet.

Dick nodded. "That's a good boy. You fill yourself up while I look around." *Where do I begin in all this clutter?*

He inspected the hall closet, pulling out the contents and knocking on wood paneling while listening for hollow sounds. *Nothing anomalous. What in the world am I searching for? Would I even recognize it if I saw it?*

He opened kitchen cupboards, removed dishes, poked his head inside.

The living room came next. He lifted objects, looked behind picture frames, and tried to pull up a throw rug. It was fastened to the floor. *Guess I should sort through the mess.* He picked up an armful of bird-chewed books and dropped them on the sofa.

"What's this, Pepper?" On the middle shelf, in a space formerly occupied by one of the books, a USB cable protruded from the wall. He pulled out several volumes and exposed a panel. Behind it sat an external hard drive. He inspected the books on the sofa. One of the hardcovers contained a tiny spy cam.

It seems there's video surveillance after all. Ms. Wilson wasn't aware of this, so Mr. Trenton must have installed it.

Dick connected his tablet to the drive and reviewed the video footage time-stamped near the hour of the murder. After several minutes, he raised his eyebrows. *Now I have evidence. But Cap will never believe this.*

~*~

Everyone in the precinct gathered around the screen to watch. PJ popped a pill for his newly diagnosed allergy to feathers.

The back of Bill Trenton's head was visible as he sat on the sofa with a full glass of wine. The dreamcatcher dipped and twirled with each gust of wind wafting through the open window.

Pepper flew into the room and perched on the lampshade. The lamp wobbled and threatened to overturn. The bird flapped toward the kitchen. Bill stood, swaying and weaving.

A few seconds later, wings fluttered into view. Pepper flew toward the window. Bill staggered in the macaw's direction and tripped. He reached for Pepper's tail, but grabbed a dreamcatcher feather instead. Then he fell forward, breaking the lamp base with his skull.

He pushed away from the end table, teetered, and dropped to the floor.

Dick stopped the video. "You don't need to see the rest."

The room was silent except for a muffled snicker from somewhere behind the Captain.

Dick took off his new baseball cap and extended his hand to PJ. "Sorry to doubt you, partner. I apologize."

PJ shrugged and pulled him in for a thump on the shoulders. "No hard feelings. You were just doing your job." He smirked. "We should file this case away as 'Finis Most Fowl'."

Fourteen
Kathy Steinemann

The 1954 Pontiac had gone through thirteen owners, and all thirteen had died. Now my friend insisted on buying her, even though I tried to talk him out of it.

Eric's response to my disapproval of the new-to-him '54 Pontiac was a jeer. "You don't s'ppose I'm gonna be victim number fourteen, do you? No way. As a matter of fact, I called her Fourteen, 'cause today's Valentine's Day. She and me are gonna go all the way to the top in the Concours d'Elegance classic car competition."

"You better get life insurance and name me as beneficiary, then. Every guy who's ever owned this junker has ended up dead." I pulled out my cell phone and brought up an Internet blog I'd bookmarked. "This is why you got it so cheap. Let's see ... Three heart attacks, two muggings, seven 'unknown causes', and one suicide."

He snorted and turned away. "Pffft. Don't be a wet blanket. You can't believe everything you read online. She's over sixty. Of course a bunch of her owners would have died. Heart attacks? Everybody smoked back then. You can still smell the cigarettes in her upholstery. Muggings? Coincidence. Does that blog say anything about the increasing crime rate? And one suicide? Hey, I know people with friends who committed suicide."

"And the unknown causes? C'mon. You're trying to rationalize."

"Nah. Look at her. She just needs someone to love." He rubbed at a spot of rust on the right fender and didn't seem to notice when the red paint flicked off. The passenger side leaned at least two inches lower than the driver's side. The front fender listed in the opposite direction, making the monster look like a hag with lopsided boobs.

I shuddered.

Eric fondled the car the same way he once fondled a girl's butt in the bar. The girl slapped him. But I swear Fourteen leaned against his hand, and the engine started to purr instead of clunking like an ancient washing machine full of nuts and bolts.

He tossed his jacket into the trunk. "C'mon, I'll take you for a quick spin."

I tugged at the passenger door. It wouldn't budge.

He pouted. "Tsk, tsk, Fourteen. Is that any way to treat one of my friends? He'll love you too when he gets to know you. Just wait and see." The door gave way with a harsh groan.

I hesitated, a sense of foreboding slithering up my spine. But I told myself I was being stupid, and I crawled in.

A spring in the seat stabbed my thigh. The frayed seatbelt cut across my neck. The heat vent blasted frigid air into my face: frigid air that smelled like sulfur.

But Eric figured the old guzzler was perfect. He floored the gas pedal. Fourteen vibrated and rumbled like rolling thunder as she sped over the gravel.

Crap! I bit my tongue when I realized I had fallen for Eric's spiel. Now I thought of the damned thing as *female*.

Scenery whipped by faster and faster. Dust wafted up from the dirty dashboard. One of the windshield wipers flew off. The other wiper engaged and stopped halfway up, cutting into my view like a knife.

Eric coaxed her up to eighty-five mph on Todeskurven Road, careening around every curve as though he were a NASCAR driver. The scream from her engine grew louder. The smell of burning oil was so strong I could taste it at the back of my throat. Blue smoke burnt my eyes.

I yelled, "Let me out. I'll hitch a ride. You're a frigging lunatic."

He shrugged and skidded to a stop. I got out of that clunker faster than you can say "deathtrap".

The stench of scorched rubber mingled with the smell of burning oil as she sped away, leaking brake fluid like a blood trail from a wounded deer. He raced up the switchback, a scrambling beetle against the rocky bluff, until he reached the dead end at Lover's Leap.

The last I saw of Eric, he was piloting Fourteen over the cliff into the river, locked in the evil rattletrap's embrace.

Searchers abandoned the hunt for Eric and Fourteen after two weeks.

And when I spotted her in a used car lot the following month, I swear the accursed crate was smiling.

Accidental Allies

Kathy Steinemann

An ancient bull buffalo and an old female wolf shiver in the winery cold. Will they live through the night? Or will starvation and freezing take them before morning?

The old farmer shuffled back a step and dropped his armload of wood. "Sixty winters I been livin' on this land, and I ain't never seen nothin' like this."

An aging she-wolf lay against the ribs of a grizzled buffalo in the snow next to the barn. Both animals quivered.

"You two scared? Cold? Heh heh. Prob'ly both. I won't hurt you, I promise. At least you got each other to keep warm. But you look like you're about ready to turn into ice cubes. I'll go fetch some stuff. You two keep cuddlin'."

~*~

The farmer reappeared towing a toboggan laden with an assortment of blanket-covered bulges. He peeled back one of the blankets and threw several handfuls of hay to the buffalo. Then he set a dish of dog food a few inches away from the nose of the wolf.

"How 'bout I do somethin' to warm you up a bit? Hope you don't mind if I talk while I work." He covered both animals with blankets. "I'll just start a fire over here. S'ppose you two could try eatin' some of that chow?"

The buffalo tossed its head. The wolf cowered. He pushed the dog food and hay closer with one boot, careful to watch for any signs of aggression. "You look too weak to run off on me. Not that you'd get very far in this weather." They seemed more afraid of him than he was of them, wide eyes following every move he made.

"Nice and warm? Good. I'm Abraham, by the way. Folks just call me Abe. Awful gettin' on in years, ain't it? Here it is Christmas. Just the three of us. Alone and freezin'. The wife is dead, and Aaron ain't comin' to visit. Aaron's my son. Good boy, but busy. Always so busy."

His eyes glistened. "No farm critters to keep me company no more. Had to get rid of them." His voice broke. "Old Abe is dyin'. Doc says it's cancer. Only got a few months, he says. Haven't told no one. They don't got time for me. But you'll listen, won't you?" Abe's tears sparkled in his mustache.

The wolf's eyes brightened as she chewed. The buffalo snorted and then stood, gaining vigor with every mouthful.

"That's it. You just keep chawin'." He sat, propping himself against the barn while he watched predator and prey. "Does a soul good to help someone."

The buffalo pawed at the ground and snorted snow away with its muzzle. Soon it worked its way to the fistful of hay in Abe's fingers. The wolf yipped. Then she lay at Abe's side and whimpered.

He sighed. "Yup. Does a soul good." He rested his hand on the wolf's head. His shoulders relaxed, and his chin dropped to his chest.

~*~

Aaron rapped on the front door of the farmhouse. "Surprise! It's me."

Frosty crystals on a biting wind drove into every crevice on the porch. Aaron's throat stung as the bitter chill burned its way into his lungs.

"Dad?" He rapped again. "Dad, it's Aaron." He waited a few moments, lowered the giftwrapped parcel he was carrying, and fumbled in his pocket for his key.

A frown crept to his face as he pushed the door open. "Dad, what happened to the heat? It's as cold as the North Pole in here. Dad?" He searched through the house, his apprehension and anxiety escalating with every room.

Aaron hurried outside. There: three shapes against the barn.

He lowered his head and pushed against the wind.

Past the garden fence.

Past the well.

A sob caught in his throat.

His father now slept his last sleep, a smile frozen on his face. A grizzled buffalo and an aging she-wolf stood guard over his corpse, statues of ice in the blistering cold.

Dog Diary of an Old Man

Amber Hayward

The average dog is a nicer person than the average person. ~ *Andy Rooney*

Mar. 29 - Walked the dog.

Mar. 30 - Walked the dog.

Mar. 31 - Walked the dog. Got all the way to the river.

Apr. 1 - Walked the dog. Old Mrs. Watson caught me in the condo's foyer, asked if I liked the casseroles she sent after Helen's funeral. Asked how I was doing, if I wanted to come over to her suite for dinner some night. Told her I didn't feel up to socializing. Asked what I was doing. Dog leash and dog and warm jacket didn't seem to have given her a clue, but I know for a fact she has four cats, no dog.

Apr. 2 - Walked the dog. Mrs. Watson asked if she could walk with me today. Told her I'm training for a marathon, so I have to go fast. She's too tubby to go fast. Then I had to go fast until I got around the corner, in case she was watching. Then I leaned against a fence and wheezed for five minutes. Didn't get as far as the river today.

Apr. 3 - Walked the dog. Mrs. Watson in the foyer again, hovering. Pretended to have a coughing fit. She said I'd better get over the cough before the marathon.

Apr. 4 - Walked the dog. Marie Stratton waiting in the foyer. She said Mrs. Watson told her I needed a walking partner for my training. Said I supposed she could come with me. She sure walks fast. But she likes to stop for coffee half way through, knew a cafe with outside tables and a water dish for dogs.

Apr. 5 - Walked the dog. Marie is thinking about getting a dog herself, asked me for advice. Over to her place in the evening to check out kennels on the internet. She's going to help me get set up on the internet so I can stay in touch with the kids more easily. Helen was the one who knew all that stuff.

Apr. 6 - Walked the dog.

Apr. 7 - Walked the dog.

Apr. 20 - I see I've missed quite a bit of time. Pretty busy these days. Marie and I walked the dogs. They're getting along well.

Transported
Amber Hayward

This is a reprint of Amber's story that appeared in "Penumbra Magazine" in June 2014.

Three years alone can make you forget the things you need the most ...

It's time. I don't think I have anything to worry about. My cat's been transported a dozen times and she's just fine. I've jumped twice with no ill effects.

I wonder what they'll say when I appear in the lab back on earth? To tell the truth, I wonder if the lab will be there. There must be some reason Philip's replacement didn't show up. The corporation must know what spending three years alone would do to me.

Thank God for the cat.

When the prototype machine was ready, I had strong misgivings about transporting the cat. She's my sanity, honestly. But it became increasingly obvious that short of developing the machine I was sent here to develop, I would never get home. And, of course, I have often wondered if that's exactly why they left me here alone. If Philip really had a heart problem ...

I sent the cat to a storage shed not far from the base. I went and got her, terrified when I opened the door, but she was fine. After a few more short jumps, I sent her to the mine site. It took me an hour to get there. She was fine. I sent her to the far side. It took me six hours to get there. She was hungry, but fine.

Before I transported myself to the storage shed, I watched her for three days to see if there were any changes. I examined her as thoroughly as I could. She seemed to be healthy.

I positioned myself in the disintegration chamber. My head ached so badly, I considered putting the experiment off, but I knew it was just an excuse. I pushed the button. Immediately I was inside the shed. That my head still ached came as a wonderful relief.

This morning, I sent myself to the mine site. It was a long walk back, but I how real it felt to me as I walked.

I can be home this afternoon. I can see my parents, my friends, my co-workers. And Tracy, who agreed to wait.

I'm in the chamber now, my longing to hear another human voice nearly overwhelming. I know now that I've been in denial about how lonely I've been. One push of the button and I'll be home.

I reach toward the button, a strange nostalgia for this stark landscape and monastic life welling up within, a caution that I'll regret this, but I follow through. I push the button.

The lab looks exactly as it always did. As Philip turns toward me in amazement, I think—*oh shit, the cat.*

Impossible Passage

Kathy Steinemann

There are things known and there are things unknown, and in between are the doors of perception. ~ Aldous Huxley

Eddie Duval grabbed ... lost his grip ... scraped his knuckles as he slipped down the slime-covered rocks into the dark pool at the bottom of the cave. Murky water closed over him. He sank, and when his butt touched the silt below, he pushed himself into a standing position. He gasped as his head broke the surface.

They'll never find me in here. He inched forward, testing each step, watching, sniffing, feeling for vibrations. He needed to move away from the opening before they figured out where he was, and he had to be quiet. But all he could do was hope. He couldn't tell if he was making any noise. Eddie's world was nothing but sensations and silent forms.

He slid his fingers into his pocket and groped for his cell phone. The screen was cracked. He pushed buttons. Pulled the battery and reseated it. Pushed more buttons. No life. Just water and shards. He set it on a rock above water level and waded farther into the passage.

Two of the biggest bullies at school, Zack and Bronson, were pursuing him. *I could take either one of those guys by myself. But not two at once. Idiots. Now I'm gonna be late. I'm supposed to be home by four.* He looked over his shoulder to be sure no one was following him.

The roof of the passage closed in as he penetrated deeper into the gloom. His rapid breathing made him dizzy. He supported himself against the narrowing walls with both hands as he sloshed onward.

The water disappeared into a lower side passage. Dim light ahead. Narrow. Narrower. He crept on hands and knees, lowered to his belly, then snaked through the musty darkness and slithered out to the hillside beyond. A tingling sensation coursed through his body.

Noise filled his ears, as though he had slipped through a soundproof door into the pit of a philharmonic orchestra. He laughed. "I can hear." He yelled. "I can hear! I CAN HEAR." His words bounced from the rocks on the far wall of the canyon.

A quiet voice protested, "Do not yell. I can hear too."

He whipped around. Behind him stood a teenage boy. Eddie spoke in mumbled syllables that rolled over an awkward tongue. "Sorry. I just got my hearing back." A sudden dizziness struck him, followed by a wave of euphoria.

The boy twisted to throw a rock into the creek, revealing a tiny figure-of-eight tattoo on the left side of his neck. A sweet scent like honey wafted from his body. "It has been decades since anyone came through. Our healing is not meant to go to strangers." He made a clicking noise with his tongue. "I suppose you had better follow me."

Eddie stayed put, glancing around as though he could pull answers from the trees. He put his hands over his ears. Removed them. Stood with his mouth hanging open.

The boy's face flashed with an expression that could have been anger. "Well, what are you waiting for?" Unusual eyes. Amber with dark flecks.

Eddie followed like an obedient puppy for several strides. Finally, he spoke. "My name's Eddie. What's yours?"

The boy stopped short. "Alex. Of Alpha-Xonisis. Eddie is short for Edward, is it not?"

"Yes." His brow furrowed. "You talk kinda funny."

Alex retorted with a crooked grin. "So do you." He led Eddie along the creek to a dome-shaped building with two beings inside.

The translucent structure turned opaque as Eddie watched. He wondered for a moment if the occupants were humans or aliens. But the symphony of sounds, so long undetectable by his ears, sidetracked his speculation. He luxuriated in them: clicking, whirring, wind, birds chirping, water gurgling. It was an audio feast.

The beings inside the dome glanced up and nodded as though they were expecting him.

~*~

Eddie was back in the cave, this time behind Zack and Bronson. They seemed to be looking for him. The tingling sensation he had experienced when he passed through the portal coursed through his body again.

He felt strong. Invigorated. Invincible.

Eddie's eyes sparkled. He stared at his fingers. Did he dare? He held up his fists and called out to the bullies, "Whatcha lookin' for? Me?"

Zack snickered. "Weirdo dummy can talk now. How long you been scamming us? You think we're morons or something?" Both boys grabbed at him.

Eddie danced to the side, shielded his face with his left, and jabbed at Zack's temple with his right. Zack went down like a lead weight. Bronson's eyes widened. He made a feeble attempt at a right hook, but Eddie blocked him and connected with Bronson's nose. Bronson dropped to his knees.

Both boys scrambled to their feet and sprinted out of the cave.

I gotta find out what's going on. After blowing on his knuckles to relieve the stinging throb, he slid into the pool and

144

hastened through the passage to the hillside beyond. He yelled. "Alex. Alex!" No reply. *Doesn't matter. I remember the way.*

Alex intercepted Eddie about halfway to the dome. "You were not supposed to remember. What are you doing here? You have to return to your own people."

"Not until I find out what happened. And I never got the chance to thank you."

Alex shrugged. "Follow me."

"Why do you have a tattoo that looks like an eight?"

Alex touched his neck. "It is the infinity symbol, not a figure of eight. Combined with my name, it means I am the forever helper and protector of mankind. It has importance in connection with our mission on Earth. However, the mission records were destroyed with our ship. I know not what it was."

"I'm not sure about helping mankind, but whatever you did sure helped me put the boot to the bullies."

"I must determine why you remembered. This is a serious breach that must be rectified. You may have to remain for a few days until we correct the error."

"Sure, Alex. Whatever." He pondered for a few steps. "But what about my mom and sister and schoolwork and stuff?"

"We will return you to the point in time right after you defeated your rivals, but without memory of this place."

"Without memory of this place? Never. How could I forget something that gave me back my hearing and my confidence and the stuff with the fists?"

And there was something about Alex. Eddie really liked the friendly alien, even if he didn't believe the BS about memory and time.

Eddie looked at his knuckles, remembering how it felt to pummel Zack and Bronson. "So, how'd you get here?"

"I have been in this valley for over 180 years. My parents were killed when our ship crashed."

Eddie pointed to the other occupants of the dome. "But aren't those your parents?"

"Alas, no. They are machines, automatons. I constructed them to keep me company. From vid files."

"You mean they're droids?"

"Droids must be the modern word. Our research was conducted before we came to Earth."

"You mean you haven't had anyone to keep you company except these droids for almost two centuries?"

"That is correct."

"I'm sorry about your folks, dude. My dad died in an accident too. A car accident." His face froze for a heartbeat with a sudden memory of the day six years ago when he lost his father and his hearing. He sighed. "You must be lonely. You should come and stay with me and my mom and sister. Mom's a great cook. Piper's okay, for a girl. And I kinda like you. If you weren't a bro, I'd, well, you know."

"I do not know. Please explain." Alex's face twisted with amusement.

"You trying to embarrass me? I mean, if you were a girl, I'd try to make a move on you."

"A move?"

"I'd try to kiss you, stupid, and other stuff. You know. The stuff that comes after kissing."

"Such as?"

"Like touching your boobs and your butt and all that."

"Boobs? Butt?"

"Breasts and um, buttocks, you know. And I'd try to get a home run."

"Home run?"

Eddie lowered his voice. "I'd try to have sex with you."

"Oh, I believe you are referring to copulation. We have that on Alpha-Xonisis too. I understand it is quite a delightful pastime."

"Yeah, well, I haven't tried it. I will someday. But you're a bro, and I'm not into bros. Um, that means boys. So forget about everything I just said. But if you come to stay with us, I'll really have to teach you a lot."

"It sounds intriguing. Perhaps your sister could teach me about kissing and home run, the way it is performed on Earth."

Eddie shoved Alex's shoulder. "My sister's too old for you. Um, maybe not. I guess you're almost 200. I mean, she's too old for a teenager, and that's what you look like. But I could tell you about things, and you could watch movies and go on the Internet and read books."

"It appears that humans rely on sight for much of their attraction to the opposite sex. On Alpha-Xonisis we depend more on senses such as smell, as well as a mental connection, for interaction between males and females."

"What's your planet like?"

Alex appeared as though he were about to cry. "I was very young when we came here. I have minimal memory of my world, except for what I have watched on the vid-screens."

Eddie gestured toward the passage. "Why don't you come home with me?"

"I cannot leave. My people will find me someday." Alex's voice had become flat, monotone. "I must stay close to where the ship went down. As interesting as your proposal sounds, soon you must leave, and forget, and then I will be alone with these droids again." He stared into the distance.

~*~

The sun rose and set many times during Eddie's stay.

Early one morning, Alex had a private conversation with the droids. Then he turned to Eddie. "It is time. The unit recalibration is complete."

Eddie snickered. "Unit?"

"Why are you laughing?"

"Unit, Johnson, penis. Get it?"

Alex's cheeks flushed with a crimson tinge, and his honey scent grew more intense. "I do not understand the connection. My unit will transport you and clear your memory. I will miss you, Edward Duval."

"You got no sense of humor, dude. A unit is ... never mind. You wouldn't understand." Eddie assumed that penis talk was embarrassing to aliens.

Alex led him to the unit and pressed a button. Eddie watched the infinity tattoo fade.

~*~

He was in the cave again. Zack and Bronson were hightailing it down the hill. And Eddie's memory was still intact. He smirked. "You don't get rid of me that easy, Alex."

~*~

He slipped out of the passage onto the hillside.

Alex was sitting cross-legged next to the creek, as though he had anticipated Eddie's return. "It did not work, did it?"

"Nope. I'm here. I'm in one piece, the bullies are gone, and I have all my memories. That machine of yours doesn't work. It's a piece of crap."

Alex grinned. "I am glad to see you. But I believe my unit just requires a small adjustment. And then the portal must be closed. Follow me."

Eddie snickered. *His unit needs adjustment.* He put his hands in his pockets. Whistled. Sauntered with a confidence he hadn't felt since before the accident.

Alex chatted as they walked. "The men of your race. They still wear trousers and hats, and they open doors for females?"

"Blue jeans, not trousers. No hats. And doors? Well, sometimes. I hold them open, but a lotta guys don't."

"The females of your race. What makes them so different from the males?"

"Well, it's like they're from another planet or somethin' … no offense. And they get all moody. Not all the time. Just some of the time. They like to put nail polish on their nails. Most of them have hair longer than mine, and they like to wear clothes that make their boobs look bigger."

The dark flecks in Alex's amber eyes seemed to dance. "Strange customs. And do your females still wear long dresses with petticoats?"

"Nuh-uh. Unless they're at a prom or a wedding or some big black-tie affair. They wear blue jeans like these ones I got on, only sexier, for girls, you know, and sometimes they rip holes in their jeans, and lots of girls wear T-shirts like this, only with low necklines, so you can almost see their boobs. And some girls are real catfish."

"Catfish?"

"Yeah. They wear so much makeup and mascara and padding you can't tell what's real and what's fake. I like real girls. The ones who look like girls. Like my sister. She's a beaut."

"I see."

"Why are you asking me all this stuff?"

"Well, perhaps I might change my mind someday. I might go to visit you and your family. I should be aware of how to behave."

Alex seemed preoccupied as they neared the unit. He twisted a dial and pressed numerous buttons. "There. I believe that should solve the problem." He extended his hand to Eddie. "I believe this is the custom on Earth when greeting or departing?"

Eddie cocked his head. "We're buds, man. Come here." He grabbed Alex to hug him. The infinity tattoo faded as Alex dissolved in his arms.

~*~

He was back in the cave. Zack and Bronson were hightailing it down the hill, and Eddie's memory was still intact. He chuckled. "Here we go again."

He worked his way through the passage, but there was no daylight near the end. He squeezed as far forward as possible, only to discover huge rocks blocking his exit. "Crap." *Backing out of this tunnel isn't gonna be easy.*

By the time he found a spot where he could turn around, his wet T-shirt had bunched up around his armpits, and his midriff was pocked with little bits of sand and gravel. He reached the pool after a strenuous crawl, and he looked up. *I can do this.*

However, he stood for several panting breaths before trying. He thought about the other side. About how much he was going to miss his new friend. *I'll never see him again. Never again. No droids. No weird discussions. No strange food.*

He squared his shoulders and began the arduous process of trying to find finger- and toeholds. On his fourth attempt, he pulled himself over the top and collapsed, gasping, onto a rock.

Eddie groaned to his feet and supported himself against the damp wall of the cave. He didn't feel like going back yet. Even though his mom and Piper would be happy to see him, things would be different now. He could hear again. The bullies would stop pestering him. But ... A stifled sob lodged in his throat.

He slouched as he plodded to the cave entrance and peered out over the valley.

A soft rustle on the right diverted his attention. There, straightening her clothes, stood a girl in tight blue jeans. She was wearing a T-shirt with the neckline ripped low. She had boobs. Nice boobs. Long, curly, brown hair. Eyes of amber with dark flecks. And an infinity tattoo on the left side of her neck.

Eddie blinked. *What a rocket!*

She stepped so close he could smell her honey sweetness. With a mischievous smile, she placed her arms around his neck. "Hello, Eddie. I am Alex. Of Alpha-Xonisis. I am not a bro. Alex is the diminutive of Alexandra."

Her scent coiled around him: an invisible cocoon that made him feel safe, warm. He inhaled a long, deep breath that filled him with strange longings and desires.

She pulled his head closer and gazed into his eyes. "Could you teach me a few Earth customs? I believe I would like to start with the one you call kissing."

No Sense

Kathy Steinemann

This drabble was published by Postcard Shorts in July of 2014.

Harry slammed the front door and flung his *Billy-Bob's Car Repair* cap onto the kitchen table. "It don't make sense. No sense at all."

His wife frowned. "What makes no sense?"

"I been havin' problems with a couple cars in the shop. I keep hearin' strange engine noises when I take 'em out for a test drive after they're repaired. I run 'em back to the service department for another inspection, but the guys there don't never find nothin'. The boss said he'd take care of it. Then he up and fires me."

"Why?"

"He hired a deaf service manager."

Regrets

A. L. Kaplan

Have you ever had regrets that haunted you for years? Danny's
might surprise you.

Regrets? Of course Danny had regrets, most of them about that hamburger he never got to eat. He could still picture it when he closed his eyes. Hot, glistening juices soaked into the sesame-topped bun. Perfectly seared meat, elegantly adorned with a slice of cheddar and two crisp bacon strips. The scent filled Danny's nostrils, making his mouth water. Sweet, greasy onion rings piled generously on the plate completed the image. It was art, pure and simple. Something Danny didn't expect to find in a small roadside diner, especially one named Sanitary. It sounded more like a hospital than a food establishment.

It had been a long time since that exquisite burger. Before Danny could take his first bite, that idiot kid in the next booth had thrown his milkshake across the room. Half-frozen chocolate glop contaminated his perfect hamburger. The kid deserved to have his neck broke. So did the parents that were supposed to be watching him. The rest of the patrons and the pretty waitress with the pink stripe in her hair, well ... they laughed. The only one he let live was the artist who created that burger.

Twelve years and multiple trials and appeals later, Danny still longed for that flawless burger. If only they could have found that cook for his last meal. Saliva ran down his throat as they strapped him down and jabbed a needle into his arm. Only the memory remained. Food ... perfection ... and then, nothing.

Ominous Warning

Kathy Steinemann

Why would a respected professor of archaeology commit murder?
Is Bradley Wilson about to become one of his victims?

"Freeze!" A gravelly voice barked its ominous warning from behind me and echoed through the depths of the cave. Recognizing the authoritative tone of Professor Hamilton, otherwise known as Prof Creepo, I raised my quivering hands and tried not to look at the body near my feet.

Our last dig of the semester. Newly discovered documents revealed that this chamber concealed hidden treasure in a northeast corner. One of Hamilton's archaeological students, Yves Turgeon, had disappeared three years ago. The police questioned the professor, but nobody ever found a body or evidence of murder.

Until now.

"What's the matter, Professor Hamilton? Do you intend to kill me because I know your secret? You're the one who murdered Yves. Perfect place to conceal the body: a cave in an old dig that's already been combed through."

The professor's shadow grew longer as he shuffled closer. "Don't move."

I cursed and wondered what kind of weapon he might have. Pistol? Stun gun? Knife?

My classmates remained silent. Why didn't they come to my rescue? I could hear them breathing and rustling. One of the girls was even close enough for me to smell her lavender shampoo.

I tried to sound calm, even though my legs felt like they were about to give way, as I gazed at the remains splayed face-down before me. School ring on one finger. Tattered clothes that looked like they had been gnawed through by rodents. A cobweb-covered flashlight several meters away. "How did you do it? The police classified it as a missing-persons case, yet here he is, with a huge hole in his head."

"Mr. Turgeon died quickly, and you're about to join him unless you listen very carefully to what I say."

"Why me? You figure you'll get rid of me the way you did him? This time you have witnesses. You can't kill us all."

"You haven't paid attention to details, Mr. Wilson."

"That's your reason for killing me? Because I'm a lousy student? You'll get the needle for this."

Someone hissed, "Shut up and keep still."

Finally one of my supposed friends speaks up.

I focused on the professor's voice. He spoke in a somber tone. "Don't move a muscle. Be quiet and look down. Very slowly."

I scanned the cave floor. The toes of my right foot were almost touching something that looked like a corroded metallic disc, barely visible under its coating of dirt. "I see it."

"Now look up."

My knees trembled. *What has he done? Is he really going to kill me? Kill us?*

Suspended from the roof of the cave was a series of spikes, poised to impale anyone who activated what I now realized was an ancient trip mechanism at my feet.

The Professor's voice wavered. "If you had taken one more step, you'd be dead. Just like Mr. Turgeon, who obviously didn't detect this trap. Did you really think I'd murder him and then lead the class to his body? Unlike you, he was one of my best students."

I felt a warm trickle wend its way down one leg. I covered the wet spot in my pants with both hands and decided to give up archaeology for something safer.

Like skydiving.

Private Property

Kathy Steinemann

A photographer spends the afternoon capturing wildlife and scenery with her camera. Her latest photos are of a moose. As she finishes her shoot, she realizes she's being watched.

A deep male voice penetrated Ramona's concentration. "Ma'am, this is private property."

The young woman gasped and spun around, almost onto the toes of the stranger who had been watching her. His face radiated a timeless strength, as though he had been sculpted from the trunk of an ancient tree. She stepped back a pace. "I'm sorry. I didn't know."

He scrutinized her for a moment. "Who are you? And what are you doing here?"

A nervous thrill tingled through her body, the way she felt just before slipping into the water for a deep-sea dive. She extended her hand. "I'm Ramona Young, wildlife photographer. I was …"

The stranger bowed and kissed her fingers. "I'm Marcos Ingram."

Her hand tingled from the brief contact with his soft, dark whiskers. She shivered. "Is this your land? It's beautiful with the river and woods and all the animals. I was just shooting the moose over there." She pointed, but the moose had disappeared.

His serious expression brightened. "Shooting without a rifle, fortunately. This property has been in my family for generations. And its beauty is eclipsed by yours." His voice resonated with a quiet smoothness that reminded Ramona of Harry Connick Jr.

Her face glowed pink. *How delightfully old-fashioned and charming he is. If I weren't already married ...* "I'll pack up my equipment and leave. Sorry to intrude."

Marcos helped with her gear. "Have you heard the legend of the moose?"

"No."

"Aboriginal lore says that moose are magic, with the power to bestow long life and stimulate fertility."

"Stimulate fertility?"

His chocolate eyes sparkled as though they had been sprinkled with fairy dust. "Yes, among other things."

"My husband and I have been trying to have kids. D'you suppose we should invite a moose into the bedroom?" She giggled.

As they continued to chat, the smiling sparkle in Marcos's eyes intensified.

He loaded the tripod into her truck, and they trudged up the hill for one last look at the river. The wind whispered through the treetops, carrying a light scent of pine and wild roses. Tiny songbirds twittered. The sunset sparkled off the water, bestowing a mystical quality to the scene.

She turned. "Bye, Mr.—" Marcos was gone.

Her gaze shifted to the river, where the moose had reappeared. She squinted. *I swear he has chocolate-colored eyes. And he's smiling at me.*

Nine months later, she delivered a baby girl.

Tropical Getaway

Kathy Steinemann

A disgruntled employee robs the boss's embezzled funds and attempts to escape. Will he succeed? Or will his getaway plans be as lackluster as his work performance has been over the last few years?

I elbowed through crowds and public washrooms. I tried to keep an eye on my carry-on while I bought a sandwich that cost a small fortune.

I hated every second of it.

Now if I could slip through airport security without getting caught, my tropical getaway would be guaranteed: a distant island with sandy beaches, ocean breezes, and whispering palm trees.

No more performance reviews.

No more long hours in a hot cubicle.

No more bootlicking and jumping every time Pixley barked.

Cleaning out his safe had been easy. Old codger used his date of birth for the combination. You'd think a boss bright enough to embezzle from the company for thirty-eight years would be smarter about his combo code, never mind keeping his stash of coke in there: good stuff, the best.

I smiled as I reminisced. Then, I remembered where I was.

Keep calm. Don't look suspicious.

A voice boomed behind me. "Sir, step over here, please."

My fake ID and passport were perfect, and my carry-on should have cleared the scanner. I had put the bills in hollowed out books so they'd be undetectable to all except the closest scrutiny.

Pixley was too stupid to have put an electronic tracker in the cash … wasn't he?

I grinned and attempted to conceal the nervous tremor in my hands. "Anything wrong, officer?"

The officious jerk didn't reply. Instead, he dragged me and my suitcase aside.

I protested, "Hey, watch it, buster. You hurt my arm."

His face clouded with a scowl. A K-9 sniffer came out of nowhere. Another officer cut off the suitcase lock. I cringed and hoped they wouldn't try to open any of the books. My gaze roamed everywhere except my suitcase.

I tried to look nonchalant when a couple of flight attendants stopped to lean in and stare. Someone's overpowering body spray made me sneeze. The K-9 barked. My insides knotted like a hangman's noose, and hot beads of sweat trickled down my nose.

One of the officers chortled. "Look at all the little blue pills. I s'ppose he intended to make some girl happy. And what's this? A firearm? Tsk. Tsk."

I gasped as I gawked at the porn magazines, leather chaps, and handcuffs. "That's not my stuff, honest." My voice squeaked like a little girl's. "Someone must have switched suitcases with me."

"Hmph. Likely story."

As they marched me away, I spotted Pixley clearing security. He wore a smirk wide enough to swallow his face.

And he was towing my carry-on.

Schud Justice

Kathy Steinemann

Sometimes justice lurks in the hands of a jilted woman. Just ask
Fronn Husten.

"Halt. Now!"

"Stop, or we'll shoot."

The demands of two deep voices accompanied the drum of determined footsteps.

The target of the voices, a spindly, thin-lipped alien, tossed a stolen purse. "You have to catch me firssst."

He scrabbled into an alleyway before his pursuers could shoot or stun him.

They searched and probed every corner.

A beefy man with a humongous wart on his nose sighed. "Guess he got away." He returned his laser blaster to its holster. "Don't know how. It's a dead end. Stupid Schud should stay where he belongs: in a swamp."

His scrawny partner with the bug eyes snickered at the *shood shood* remark. Then he looked up. "You'd have to be an arachnibot to reach those windows."

Fronn Husten crouched in the garbage bin. Flies nibbled at the sweat on his forehead. He held a hand over his nose until the men left. Then he sneezed … and sneezed … and sneezed. He swore with a sibilant hiss. "Ssuffering croakers. Chocolate. There's chocolate ssomewhere in here. Sstupid Earthlings and their candies." He hoisted himself out of the bin and horked into a Freshnnex tissue.

Then he strode east, with focused resolve, sneezing every few steps. He had memorized the address of the woman who owned the purse. She had what he wanted, and he intended to get it.

Now.

~*~

Oceane Kozmire finished applying her makeup and stepped away from the mirror to admire the results. That should do it. She approved of the honey-beige lipstick. Mmm. Even tasted like honey. With a hint of chocolate. She wanted at least a couple more tubes. Whenever she found a color she liked on one of these primitive planets, the manufacturer discontinued it. "No time like the present," she whispered.

Although she had other reasons besides lipstick for leaving her condopodium.

~*~

Fronn Husten trailed Oceane, but any passersby who bothered to look would have seen a female instead of a male. A study in dull: androgynous outfit and hairstyle; thin, frog-like lips; sensible shoes. Hives covered his face, and bouts of sneezing still wracked the little alien's frame. He used up a complete pack of Freshnnex before he started to dry his nose on his sleeve.

Oceane picked up her pace. Her heels clicked faster and faster on the sidewalk.

Fronn waited for just the right moment. Then he forced her into an alley and waved a blaster in her face. "Not a ssound, or I'll use this. Achoo! Achoo!"

For a microsecond, she seemed to grin. No, maybe not. A vein throbbed in her neck as she raised her hands.

His gawk glued itself to her purse. "How many purses you got? This isn't the one you had before."

"What's it to you?"

He shoved her and rifled through the purse's contents. "Where is it?"

"Where's what?"

"The CashCard you used this afternoon at Yasmine's Boutique."

"At home, I suppose."

"Then we'll just go get it. Right now." He turned her toward the street, with the blaster in his pocket aimed at her back. "Get moving."

When onlookers saw Oceane walking home followed by a diminutive woman in beige a half step behind her, they paid no attention. They were too busy listening to their audio devices, watching holovids on their glasses, and playing games on their wrist consoles.

Ten minutes later, Fronn forced Oceane to open the front door of her condopod. He glanced around with wary eyes to make sure nobody in the street was paying any attention to them. *Like Earthlings would notice anything except their gadgets. They're a dumb lot.* He pushed her onto the sofa. Bound and gagged her.

Then he sorted through the items on the kitchen counter. Ah, there it was. His counterfeit Intergalactic CashCard. He removed it and replaced it with the one in his wallet. *Our cards must have got mixed up at Yasmine's. I've gotta give up my fondness for women's underwear. But the silk feels so good.* He emptied the dirty tissues from his pockets and grabbed a full pack of Freshnnex as he headed toward the exit.

His head felt woozy. He leaned against a wall for a moment and closed his eyes.

The wooziness disappeared. And so did his sneezing.

~*~

Fronn slipped into his secret love nest and switched on the computer.

He waited for his specialized software to load, glowering and drumming a solo with his fingertips. After several seconds, he inserted the fake CashCard into an adapter and left the computer running while he brewed fresh coffee. Earth computational systems were slow and inefficient. The process would take several hours.

In the meantime, he planned to put up his feet and watch the news on the holovid. He had a hopeless fan crush on the anchorperson: a human woman with sexy eyes and a mesmerizing voice. *I bet she wears silk underwear.*

Monday night. The best night to catch up on intergalactic updates. He cocked his head. *Hmm. No more sneezing or hives. Remarkable recovery.* Usually it took at least a day to get back to normal after he'd been exposed to chocolate. He shrugged and leaned toward the holovid.

"It is now Tuesday, 1800 hours. Time for the Intergalactic News Report …"

He swiped to pause the live feed. Frowned. Restarted at the beginning of the broadcast.

"It is now Tuesday, 1800 hours. Time for the Intergalactic News Report …"

He looked at his computer calendar and cursed. "Ssuffering croakers. I've lost a day. A whole day. Sson of a sspace ssow. Felizitas will never forgive me." He grimaced and squinted, trying to determine what had caused his memory lapse.

~*~

Oceane touched her earlobe communicator. "Initial phase of mission accomplished. Please advise Felizitas Husten that the assignment is proceeding as planned."

She glanced at one of the holovids in her living room. "It was easy to implant a camera in Fronn's visual cortex after he inhaled through the specially prepared Freshnnex. It took me several hours longer than expected to install and test. Schud eyes are always a challenge. But the observation feed is working

164

flawlessly. We can see everything he sees. He'll be disoriented at first, although I'm sure he'll adjust. Agent 3.111-238 out."

She smiled at the beefy agent with the humongous wart on his nose and nodded to the scrawny operative with the bug eyes. "Good idea chasing the Schud into a trash bin. Too bad you had to let him escape. Trash. That's where every Schud should be."

~*~

Fronn rewound the holovid several times. *Exactly twenty-four hours. I've lost twenty-four hours. But that's impossible. I must be confused. Yesterday was Monday and today is Tuesday.* He scowled. *Of course. I'm just a bit confused.*

He slouched into the soft curvature of the sofa. *So relaxing. So tired.* He scratched several times out of habit, even though he wasn't itchy. Then he drifted off to sleep.

Oceane's observation feed turned dark.

~*~

Felizitas Husten swatted at screen after screen of photos. Fronn with an Earth woman. Fronn with another Earth strumpet. Fronn with a Schudalian lush. Fronn with an Erpisonnian streetwalker. "Son of a frog. You won't get away with this, you miserable little snake of a cheater, you."

She continued to review Oceane's evidence.

Fronn, a typical Schudalian, wasn't the smartest alien in the cosmos. Schudalians, called Schuds by most in the Intergalactic Alliance, weren't the most attractive of aliens either. Their thin lips and skinny legs were reminiscent of Earth frogs: creatures that had died out centuries previously due to widespread droughts.

But a male Schudalian's skill in the bedroom, augmented by saliva with aphrodisiac properties, intoxicated his lovers. Enamored females paid no attention to the repulsiveness of the knobby, groping fingers and snake-like tongues.

These ugly aliens were detested for their elaborate swindles and scams; for their trickery and deception. To be called a Schud was considered the ultimate insult on many planets.

Schuds liked Earth. There was hardly any chocolate on the planet since the blight that had wiped out the Theobroma cacao trees in the twenty-third century. Fronn's species was horribly allergic to the stuff. The slightest exposure, even to a chocolate wrapper, caused itchy hives and sneezing. However, few humans bought chocolate anymore. Nowadays it was produced on the planet Erpisonn. The prohibitive shipping cost made it unaffordable for most people.

Felizitas reached the last photo.

The look she gave the walls would have shattered blaster-proof glass. "How could I have joined with a Schudalian? Me, an Earth woman, joining with a Schud? Was I stupid?"

Felizitas glared at her screen. "I was in love with you, Fronn. But not anymore. You'll be sorry. I'll see that you wind up where every Schud should be: in prison."

~*~

Midnight. Fronn woke with a start. *I wonder if the computer's finished.* Yes, there it was. Line after line after line. The largest phishing database in the universe. Credit card numbers, financial information, dark secrets that could be used for blackmail. A Schud's dream. He swiped at his screen.

Whose number should I use first? Doesn't matter.

> "Sspiffy, sspoofy, find a schmo.
> Phish a man with lotsssa dough.
> If limit's high, make him pay
> Heaps of credits every day."

He intended to indulge in every one of his expensive tastes and fetishes, and maybe some new ones.

~*~

Fronn Husten didn't return to Felizitas. He bought fine silk underwear from the most expensive suppliers. He rented the services of a high-class escort, who accompanied him wherever he went in his new aerolimo. He frequented exclusive roof-top restaurants and private spas, and purchased jewelry made of rare gems set in platinum. In fact, he lived like an emperor for one day short of one terrestrial month.

Then Earth police beat down his door and arrested him.

~*~

Oceane touched her earlobe communicator. "Ready to beam up in five minutes."

She dismantled her holovid equipment as she spoke to her fellow agents. "Pity to leave Earth. I've enjoyed it here. Poor Fronn. Guess he didn't appreciate The Agency filling his phony card with the financial information of every intelligence official and CEO on the planet. I'm sure the final straw, so the Earthlings say, was his fraudulent access to the Intergalactic CashCard CEO's account."

She chortled.

~*~

And what became of Fronn?

The judge who presided over his trial had a warped sense of humor. She sentenced him to ten years of hard labor in a factory. On Erpisonn. Good climate. No computers. Billions of Theobroma cacao trees and thousands of chocolate factories.

Felizitas Husten hired The Agency for one more assignment: to locate all of Fronn's secret bank accounts.

When she filed for official unjoining, she liquidated the considerable assets she received as settlement. Then she bought the chocolate factory where Fronn worked, and took over as manager.

Revenge was sweeter than the finest chocolate.

Hot Coffee

Kathy Steinemann

This drabble was published by Postcard Shorts in August of 2014.

Ellie Mae splashed coffee on her customer.

He shoved his chair back from the crumb-covered table. "Damn, that's hot!"

She blushed. "Let me—"

"I can wipe my own lap. And you ain't gettin' no tip. How long you been waitressing, anyway?"

Ellie Mae stared over his head through the dingy blinds. "Let's see. Was it when Billy Bob got married? That was five years ago. No, it was even before that. When Jimmy got his new shotgun? Yeah."

Her eyes widened. "That was ten years ago." She untied her stained apron and threw it on the table. "I quit!"

Atrocity

Kathy Steinemann

*A beta version of this piece won the "Indies Unlimited Flash
Fiction Challenge" of October 12, 2013.*

*A remote bridge on a road used by moonshiners in the old days is
the scene of three recent murders. Old-timers say it happened back
in '31 as well. That's when they discovered Jack Keeley, or at least
most of him. Locals believe these murders are related. Do you
suppose they could be right?*

Detective Seamus Roper flinched when the medical
examiner peeled away the sheet that covered the remains of their
latest John Doe. *Three bodies in less than two months.*

The ME apologized. "I haven't found anything new since
the last time you visited. Poor slob was alive when the person or
creature that committed this atrocity ate the guy's face and internal
organs."

Seamus's expression soured, and he cursed. "It's been four
weeks. Vic and I will watch the bridge tonight. If a serial killer did
this, he's sticking to a schedule. Maybe we'll catch him trying to
dump another body."

Daylight turned to dusk. The two detectives crunched
through frozen underbrush until they found an outcropping with an
unobstructed view of the bridge. The October air smelled frosty,
hinting at an early snowfall.

They waited. And they shivered.

A coyote yelped from across the creek. Wind rustled the
few fragile leaves still clinging to nearby trees. A noisy car spewed

the pungent stink of burning oil as it sputtered over the bridge. It dissolved into the darkness. An owl hooted.

Vic checked his iPhone and cursed. "No reception here. If anything happens, we're on our own."

Seamus's brow knit in a deep grimace. "My stomach hurts. I must have eaten something for supper that didn't agree with me." He leaned toward his partner. "I think ..." He inhaled Vic's intoxicating scent. *Prey. Must eat. Now!*

He succumbed to his instinct.

And his pain disappeared.

Seamus flexed his bloody claws. He gaped at the full moon through glowing, yellow orbs. Then he yowled.

The Donjon of Bones

Kathy Steinemann

There is a sufficiency in the world for man's need but not for man's greed. ~ Mahatma Gandhi

In a bygone century, Marino Payo is imprisoned in an inescapable fortress protected by ghosts. At least, that's what the legends claim. But Marino doesn't believe in ghosts or inescapable fortresses. He intends to prove the legends wrong.

Sparks flashed in the night. Prisoners outnumbered the guards, who were still foggy from sleep.

Iron on flesh. Iron on bone. Iron on stone.

Shouts bellowed above the sounds of battle.

"Unhand me thou son of a sow."

"Thy head is mine."

"Thy mother was a—"

"Thou cur!"

"Escape is impossible."

"Nay. We have a way."

"The exit is barred."

"But we have the keys."

Soon the last moan faded into the silence of death. The prisoners were free. Free to steal the gold. Free to unbar the exit. Free to flee from the dreaded prison dubbed The Donjon of Bones.

Their leader, Marino Payo, had been sentenced to life for stealing the jewels of a wealthy woman who rejected him.

Now, for the rest of his days, he was doomed to waste away in a fortress on a remote island. An inescapable fortress with a cache of pirate's gold protected by ghosts who rode fierce dragons.

Ghosts with fangs as long as their fingers. Fangs that dripped the blood of their victims over the backs of their dragons. Blood that flowed through the air, a shower of red, as the ghosts soared across the night sky.

Or so the legends said.

Marino didn't believe in such preposterous superstitions, and he did not wish to spend the rest of his years without fine wine and women, in this abominable pit of filth.

Gold stitched into his breeches had bribed a guard's silence and purchased a map with the escape route. Verily, the thunder of gold vanquished the whispers of ghosts.

Three months of inciting cellmates, conspiring, waiting.

Until tonight.

Marino guided the bedraggled band of convicts through torch-lit passages. Bats flapped and squeaked from hidden crevices. The stench of their dung mingled with the stink of mold and decomposing rats. The men swiped at spider webs and chanted as they marched:

To the gold, thou slaves,
Thy fortune to follow!
To the gold, thou knaves,
Thy riches to stow.

After they filled their sacks with as much treasure as they could carry, Marino led them toward the only egress from the island.

The footbridge across the ravine swayed in the salty breeze blowing off the ocean: a breeze promising freedom, fair tides, and fine maidens.

They peered back at the fortress that had been their dungeon for so long. Silhouetted against the sky, it was indeed a sinister sight to behold.

Pointed spires. Unyielding stone. A lone watchtower piercing the stars.

But no ghosts. No dragons.

Marino shouldered his sack. "I suppose that's it, then. We should forge onward without delay. Our fortunes and women await us."

Lewd comments and laughter erupted. The men turned their attention to their crossing. With cautious steps, they crept across the bridge.

It shivered. It groaned beneath the weight. It collapsed.

Screams of terror and surprise echoed against the rocks as the prisoners plunged into the chasm below.

Gold on flesh. Gold on bone. Gold on stone.

The grotesque grins of the skulls in the gorge taunted the men's dying cries. The convicts' crumpled bodies reddened the white skeletons that had cushioned their fall. Every man relinquished his treasure and his life, joining the multitude of previous inmates who had attempted to escape: inmates now powerless to appreciate the delights of wine, women, and wealth.

Within the fortress, the guards reawakened to resume their posts. Injured flesh healed. Uniforms mended. Weapons repaired themselves.

The gold vanished from the gorge and rematerialized in the treasury.

A glowing sunrise of red, yellow, and orange peeked through the trees to illuminate a freshly formed footbridge.

And The Donjon of Bones waited for the next greedy fools who dared to doubt the legends.

Traffic Violation

Kathy Steinemann

Have you ever been stopped by a police officer for a moving-traffic violation?

Flashing lights. The yelp of a siren. Motorists craning their necks.

Quentin Parsons frowned and squinted at the police car in the rearview mirror as he slowed to a stop. He rolled down the window and waited with white-knuckled fists on the steering wheel. "What's the problem, officer?"

The cop looked young, probably fresh out of training, and although her square jaw emoted determination, the softness of her Bambi eyes and a nervous tug at an earlobe spoiled the resolute impression. She spoke with a tremor in her voice. "Driver's license and registration, please."

"But officer, I—"

"Now!" She kept her hand on her holster while he rifled through the papers in the glove compartment.

He loosened his tie and sized her up as he perused her name tag. "Here, Officer Kenise. I think you'll find everything in order."

She paused to listen to her personal radio. Her face paled, and she stuffed his documentation into a pocket. "Out of the car and down on the ground."

"But—"

"NOW!"

No matter how righteous a person's case, you don't argue with a loaded gun. Quentin's face greeted the pavement with a haste he hadn't mustered since his last college-football touchdown.

Even as he tried not to wreck his well-worn navy suit, he suspected that both knees would now betray their encounter with the asphalt.

Officer Kenise called for backup.

Squad cars appeared from both directions and squealed to a stop. Police personnel piled out. Three hulks thudded closer, hands on their weapons, and conferred with Kenise.

The sound of honking horns filled the afternoon air, and the stench of burnt rubber wafted over from one of the police cars. Quentin hoped they wouldn't pop his trunk.

They did.

Blood-stained sheets. Shovel. Vials containing a viscous, red liquid.

"You're under arrest." Kenise handcuffed him and read him his rights.

"But I can explain."

"Explain it to the judge."

"I was on my way to—"

"No matter where you *were* going, *now* you're on your way to lockup."

~*~

Quentin spent two hours sharing a holding cell with a pair of cockroaches. Seconds seemed like days as the pressure in his bladder increased. But he couldn't force himself to use the dirty-looking toilet in plain view of anyone who happened to walk by.

Finally, Officer Kenise returned. She forced her face into an awkward smile. "Mr. Parsons, your paperwork checks out. I've been ordered to apologize. Something about keeping you happy so you don't sue us for false arrest."

She scratched her chin. "But I'd like to explain why I arrested you. You matched the description of someone who's wanted for murder, and the evidence in your trunk certainly seemed incriminating at first. Why were you carrying vials of cranberry juice, and sheets stained with pigs' blood?"

Quentin shrugged. "As I attempted to tell you, I was on my way to a wedding. The bride and groom are into this zombie-apocalypse thing, and they have a reception arranged for after the service. The stuff in my trunk was for props."

Kenise laughed. "That explains it. And I suppose it's going to be a *dead* reception full of *stiffs*, with people *dying* to get in."

He grinned. "Funny lady."

Her smile disappeared. "Sarge practically chewed me a new …" Her face reddened.

"Don't worry about me suing the police department. But if I were you, I *would* worry about what the Chief might do when your sergeant fills him in on the details."

"He'll be in a good mood, because his son got married this afternoon."

Quentin smirked. "I don't think so. I'm the minister."

Case Closed

Kathy Steinemann

No one does anything from a single motive. ~ Samuel Taylor Coleridge

Cyclical squeaking noises. The odor of cleaning supplies. Howard held his breath and hugged his knees to maintain his fetal position inside the cramped space of the stuffy supply cupboard.

I can't let them find me.

~*~

Detectives Donna Scharfblick and Rhonda Bluthund inspected a ransom note: large white letters stenciled on a magazine cover. Probably made with a can of spray paint.

They searched Howard's room.

Dresser drawers. Piles of clothing. Boxes under the bed.

Rhonda slid open the door to the closet. She smiled, unveiling a toothy overbite, and beckoned to her partner. Her dark eyes crinkled behind her glasses as though she were gloating over a private joke. "I think I can tell you who the UNSUB is. Look here."

Donna peered inside. Her bright red hair stood out like a beacon against Howard's black clothing.

Stencils. Old magazines. A faint aroma of fresh paint.

The stencil letters matched the characters on the ransom note. One of the magazines was missing its cover.

Donna picked up a sock and sniffed. The splash of freckles on the bridge of her nose squished together as though they were protesting the obnoxious odor. "What's the kid up to?"

"Do you think maybe he's unhappy at home?"

"But the window was forced open from outside."

Rhonda checked the floor near the window, and pushed her short coffee-colored hair behind her ears. "I suppose he could have done that on purpose to cover his tracks, right?"

"Unlikely. Why leave evidence in plain sight?"

"Crime of opportunity? Some guy plans to rob the place and decides to escalate it into a kidnapping? Everyone knows his dad is loaded."

Donna pulled a paperback off a shelf. "Look at all the detective novels, eh. Maybe he copied a plot from one of these books."

"Hmm. Advanced reading for a twelve-year-old." Rhonda scowled. "We can't read every mystery here. It would take forever."

"Let's keep looking."

~*~

Howard woke to the drone of nearby male voices.

Boxes scraped across the floor. Footsteps moved closer—

Blinding light exploded through the darkness as the door to the cupboard flew open.

~*~

Heathrow Hamilton's colorless complexion made him look as though he had spent the night with a vampire. "I'll get in touch with Gary and tell him to do whatever he can to free up some cash. Heaven knows how much money these people will want for my son."

Donna and Rhonda asked in unison, "Gary?"

"Gary Gillison. My financial advisor."

Mr. Hamilton made his call.

After he hung up, he stared at the floor. "I can't lose Howie. I can't." His rough voice and uneven breathing betrayed an attempt to suppress sobs. "My son is everything to me. Everything."

The detectives waited while Mr. Hamilton shared stories about Howard. About how the boy hated sports and camping. "He's not much into video games either. Likes to pretend he's a detective. Sometimes we go to murder-mystery suppers, and he usually guesses who the murderer is before the adults do. He watches every detective and cop drama on TV. I guess you saw the stacks of books in his room. He's got them loaded on his e-reader as well."

He talked about the death of his wife four years previously when their private jet crashed, and how he flinched every time he heard a plane take off or land at the City Airport a few blocks away. "Cindy and the pilot were both killed. They ruled it pilot error."

When he left to use the washroom, Rhonda remarked, "Hmm. Something about his plane story is off. Did you notice the way he was sweating and rubbing at his nose?"

~*~

A computer tech watched the monitoring equipment as though he could force the phone to ring by sheer willpower. Rhonda and Donna swiped screen after screen across their tablets, searching background information and photos from the Internet.

And the waiting continued.

The call from the kidnappers came in shortly after the cuckoo in the foyer announced one o'clock. Rhonda passed Heathrow a note reminding him of what to say. A purple vein pulsed in his pale temple. "Hamilton speaking."

A computer-synthesized voice spoke in monotone above the squeak of an off-balance ceiling fan. *"We have your son. If you want him returned to you in one piece, take five million in unmarked bills to the address we'll text you later. Have the money by eight. And no police."*

"Let me talk to my son."

180

The line went dead.

Heathrow dropped the phone into his lap and stared, slack-jawed, at the opposite wall.

Rhonda touched his arm. "Sir, that was good."

"But they didn't let me speak to him. Maybe he's already dead. And they said no police."

Donna replied in a gentle tone, "Don't think that way, eh. We have to assume he's still alive. When they text you, insist they send you a photo with Howard holding the afternoon edition of the newspaper. And kidnappers always say no police. But they'll figure we're here. They're arrogant. They think they can outwit us."

A woman burst into the room. Heathrow inclined his head in her direction. "This is Amber Beatty: my personal assistant, butler, and chauffeur all rolled into one."

Donna and Rhonda scrutinized her blonde hair and ample boobs. Then they glanced at each other. An unspoken assumption passed between them. This was the kind of woman who got what she wanted whenever she wiggled her hips.

Amber frowned. "I just got back from my jog. Why are there police cars parked outside the building?" She chewed on a fingernail as she listened to Heathrow's explanation. A tic stuttered in the corner of one eye.

She extended a hand to each detective in turn. The tic disappeared, but the worry lines in her forehead remained.

~*~

Howard's stomach grumbled. *I can remember a long drive and car horns and some sirens. Then up lots of stairs. There's a bunch of mops and cleaning carts. I must be in a janitor's room.*

He had weathered his blindfolded and gagged ride to wherever he was with composure and maturity. He had peed in the large soda bottle his abductors gave him. But now he needed a real toilet. "If you don't let me go to the bathroom, I'm gonna crap myself. C'mon. I won't take off again."

The taller of the two ski-masked men pushed him out of the room. "Fine. But no more tricks. If you run, you're dead, kid."

As the shorter man led him away, Howard noted every detail of his surroundings. *I'll look out the bathroom window. Maybe I'll recognize something outside.*

The narrow hallway had hideous vomit-green walls and well-worn flooring. The drab pattern on the tiles was a chaotic reminiscence of TV static. But a layer of frost covering the tiny bathroom window thwarted Howard's attempt to look outside. *At least they intend to keep me alive, or they wouldn't be wearing masks.*

~*~

The detectives escorted Amber into the kitchen and tag-teamed their questions in such rapid-fire sequence she couldn't keep track of who was talking. But she was forthcoming with snappy responses.

"Where did you go on your run?"

"My normal route. Straight down to the shore, onto the jogging trail, around the lake, and then back here."

"And you didn't stop anywhere?"

"No. Surely you don't think *I* could have done this. I adore Howard."

"With kidnappings, time is our enemy. We have to treat everyone as a suspect. Did anyone see you?"

"I wasn't really paying attention. There was lots of ice, and I had to watch the ground."

"Are you aware of anyone who'd be capable of this, or who'd have a motive for hurting Mr. Hamilton or Howard?"

There was an extended pause. Amber's eyes misted with tears. "No. Everyone likes them. Howie and I get along together like mother and son. If I could have kids, I'd love to have one just like him. But there's Gary Gillison. I've heard him muttering trash about Heath when he thinks nobody can hear him."

Donna's eyes narrowed. "Trash?"

"Yes. Gary complains about all the work he does for what he refers to as chickenfeed. About how Heath doesn't deserve his money or his kid."

"Right. That's all for now. We may need to talk to you again later."

Amber dabbed at her eyes and nodded. Donna and Rhonda returned to the receiving room.

More waiting. Pacing.

Donna pointed to her tablet. A newspaper account of the plane-crash investigation showed a photo of the happy pilot with his two sons the morning of the accident. An aunt had fostered the teenage boys. The story confirmed Mr. Hamilton's report of pilot error as the cause. After an inquest, the media dubbed the accident "suicide by plane".

~*~

Howard hugged himself in the rapidly cooling room. *If I could just look outside. I'm pretty sure I'm in a tall building somewhere in the middle of town. Maybe a warehouse? Or a hotel? An old hotel, though. Or a cheap one. If I go back to the bathroom, I could stand on the seat and open the window.*

~*~

Two thirty. Another call. "Hamilton speaking."

"Sir, Larry from the Hamilton Lakeview. The cleaning staff just notified me they intend to go on strike, and the staff at your other hotels are gonna strike too."

"What do they want?"

"Eight-hour days and a one-hour paid lunch."

183

"Tell them no." Heathrow pulled at his collar. "Who's stirring the pot?"

"It's hard to say, sir. The cowards sent the note via messenger. Words cut out of a magazine and pasted on a legal-sized sheet of paper. No return address."

"Deal with it! And don't call me again unless it's an emergency."

Heathrow slammed the phone back into its charger. His shoulders slumped. Amber brought him a hot chocolate, but the steam had disappeared long before he took his first sip.

And the cuckoo announced three o'clock.

~*~

Muted voices. Wash-buckets wobbling in the hallway. Keys jingling.

Howard waited until his abductors unlocked the storeroom.

"Please can I use the bathroom again? All this worrying and stuff makes me get diarrhea."

The tall man gestured toward the hallway. But this time, he insisted that Howard keep the door open.

~*~

Gary Gillison arrived with a valise full of money. Donna scrutinized him, and Rhonda edged close enough to smell his expensive cologne. He offered his hand to both of the detectives in a confident gesture of greeting, then faced Mr. Hamilton. "Here's the money."

Heathrow reached for the valise. Gary's fingers tightened and resisted as though they had minds of their own: minds unwilling to relinquish the treasure they held. A strained gaze passed between the two men.

Gary relaxed his hold and turned to the detectives. "Strange last names. If I remember my high-school German correctly,

Scharfblick means Donna has a sharp eye and Bluthund means Rhonda has a keen nose."

Donna smiled. "Yup. With my super-duper contact lenses, I can see better than Superman. As a matter of fact, I can see someone sweating with anxiety from a hundred feet away. Are you sweating, Gary?"

Rhonda added, "Mmm hmm. And I can *smell* anxiety. It emanates from the armpits and mouth no matter how much a perp tries to hide it."

Gary raised one elbow to sniff at his armpit. Then he breathed into a cupped palm while he sniffed again. He grinned, but as soon as he did it, his face clouded. "I'm sorry. Under the circumstances, I shouldn't be clowning around with you fine-looking ladies."

Neither of the women acknowledged his feeble compliment. They led him into an adjoining room for interrogation.

Questions. Answers. Explanations.

Gary had an alibi for the last twenty-four hours: a trip overseas. He had just returned. He said he couldn't think of anyone who would hate Mr. Hamilton enough to put him through this kind of pain. Except maybe Amber. She didn't like her employer much.

Rhonda and Donna researched both Amber and Gary on the Internet. Staff at the precinct performed customary checks for criminal records and suspicious activities. Their alibis checked out.

And the waiting continued.

~*~

Amber and Gary were two submissive sycophants who bustled with activity whenever Hamilton barked another order. They entered and left the room multiple times to run various errands.

The annoying little bird cuckooed eight o'clock.

Heathrow's phone buzzed with an incoming text: *Hamilton Park 10 pm. Bench by fountain. No cops.*

He replied: *Have money. Need photo of son with afternoon edition of paper. Or phone call. Prefer phone call.*

Ten minutes later, the telephone rang. "Hamilton speaking."

"Dad, it's me. I'm okay. They haven't hurt me."

An airplane formed a winged silhouette against the moon. The roar of its takeoff drowned out whatever the boy said next.

Hamilton yelled, "I didn't hear that. Could you repeat it?"

"Dad, I'm scared."

"Hang in there, son."

The line clicked. Silence.

The tech announced, "Sorry, not enough time to trace the source. But it's somewhere nearby."

Donna scowled. "You figure?"

"Yeah. The noise from the plane was on the line as well. He's somewhere near the airport."

Heathrow sighed. "But the airport's a big place surrounded by lots of buildings. It could take forever to find Howie, and there's less than two hours until drop-off."

Rhonda and Donna huddled together in a far corner and whispered. Then they nodded, pleased with whatever plan they had spawned.

Donna approached Heathrow. "Could you please stand next to Rhonda?"

He complied.

She tilted her head. "Yup. Should work. You two are about the same height. Rhonda will take your place for the drop."

"No way. I want to be the first person my son sees when he gets out of whatever private purgatory they've made for him. I've got a gun, and it's legal. Besides, if they get suspicious, it might blow the whole deal."

The tech listened to an incoming call on his headphones. "They found the cell phone used to send the text. ... In a dumpster on Aspen Street. ... The abductors left it on. ... It was a burner. ... No prints."

~*~

Howard submitted to the indignity of the blindfold and gag once again, and didn't struggle when they forced him into the trunk.

He felt the movement of the car when it pulled into traffic. Something cold and hard dug into his back as the vehicle sped forward. *Stupid guys didn't tie up my hands. They must be amateurs.*

The trunk release didn't work.

He rummaged around to feel for something, anything to use as a weapon.

Then he waited, curled like a viper ready to strike, with crowbar in hand, swaying from side to side as they sped around corners and up a hill.

The car stopped. He could feel vibrations. *We must be near a subway station.* He waited for the sound of the kidnappers' departure, then pried at the trunk lock.

~*~

The air sparkled with brittle ice crystals. The kidnappers' steps in the crusty snow were tentative, careful, as they neared the bench. They shivered and searched their surroundings for any signs of movement while they whispered.

"The coast is clear."

"Don't take any chances."

"Stop being such a worrywart."

"Shh."

"Don't tell me what to do."

"Shut up."

When they reached the bench, the person holding the valise stood and pulled a gun. A grinning overbite glistened in the headlights of a passing car, and a strong female voice announced, "Police! Down on the ground."

The tall man raised his hands. The short one pulled a small pistol from his pocket. His clumsy fingers were unsure of where to place themselves, and the safety was still on.

Rhonda steadied her Glock. "I wouldn't do that if I were you. Look around."

The streetlamps illuminated several SWAT team members, all with weapons trained on the kidnappers.

Both men dropped to their knees.

The leader of the SWAT team pulled the balaclavas off the perpetrators and cuffed them.

In the streetlights, the short man's masked face looked almost ferret-like. He whined, "Let us go, or you'll never see the kid again. He's trapped in the trunk of a car we stole. We ditched it before we took the subway, and he'll freeze by morning."

Donna smirked. "Unlikely. You forgot to tie up the kid's hands. He pried open the trunk. Then he borrowed a cell phone and called his dad. He's safe and warm, drinking a cup of hot chocolate at home."

Detectives Scharfblick and Bluthund fist-bumped.

The short kidnapper shrugged. The tall one glowered.

Rhonda beamed. "Case closed. I recognize you two from the files we've been poring through all afternoon. You're the sons of the pilot who died in that plane crash. The tall one's Matthew and the short one's Jeffrey, right?"

Frosty silence.

Rhonda returned her Glock to its holster. "Why? Why did you do it?"

Matthew strained at his cuffs. "Because Hamilton's a murderer with lots of money. It wasn't pilot error that killed our dad. Hamilton was too cheap to pay for proper maintenance. He bribed officials to shift the blame so nobody would find out the truth. Or maybe he did it on purpose to kill his wife."

He spit in the snow. "Dad's death was ruled suicide. But he'd never leave us. 'Intentional pilot error,' the reporters said. Because of the suicide part, Dad's new insurance policy was invalid, and we didn't get a dime."

Matthew spit again. "We ended up working for minimum wage as janitors in Hamilton's crummy airport hotel. We just wanted to steal some stuff from his house. Then when we saw the kid, we knew what we had to do. Hamilton's a jerk who doesn't care about anyone except himself."

Donna sighed. "Case not closed after all, partner. Now we have tons of paperwork, and a possible negligent homicide charge to investigate. On days like this, I wish I had a really easy job like um, tightrope walker, writer ..."

A Chance Meeting—Or Not

A. L. Kaplan

Mike's retirement is haunted by a persistent memory. Will he ever be able to let it go?

Retirement was supposed to be relaxing, fun, but since his final night as a fireman, Mike had been anything but relaxed—and he certainly wasn't having fun. He breathed in the fresh, salty air and continued his walk down the beach, trying to forget that last fire. Mike and his beautiful wife of thirty years had moved to Boca eight months ago, but the image of his friend's granddaughter, Jackie, leading him out of the firetrap still haunted him.

Mike gazed down the rock-strewn beach and froze. His chest tightened in shock. Jackie sat on a small boulder in a thin, white cotton dress, windblown hair billowing. Mike rubbed his eyes, but Jackie remained. He walked to her on shaky legs.

"Am I hallucinating again?"

Jackie smiled, but it didn't reach her eyes. "No."

"Did I see you in the fire?" Mike's voice sounded strained.

She turned away and stared at the crashing waves, twirling a strand of her brown hair. "You're not crazy, but if you keep talking about it, people will think you are—or worse, it'll attract the attention of some very bad people."

"Like?"

"Like the ones who wanted to kill the boy you rescued. They set the fire. We saved him and will keep him safe, but that's all I'm permitted to say. Please, enjoy the retirement you've earned, but let it go."

A smile crept across Mike's face for the first time in months as she walked away. He'd stay quiet, but letting it go just wasn't his style.

Sleepless with Susie

Kathy Steinemann

Joe is tired. He hasn't slept well for three nights. Will he call in sick? Or will Susie get her way again?

Extra-strong dark-roast coffee, but it didn't register on Joe's taste buds.

I can't survive another night like this.

He groaned and propped his forehead on his fists while he tried to swallow the cotton coating on his tongue. His mouth tasted and stank like a sewer, and crusty sleep crackled in the corners of his eyelids.

Joe had thought he'd be able to handle a few days with Susie while his wife visited her mother, but …

All night? I need a break.

No matter how he had tried to reposition himself, she had crawled all over him.

Whenever he turned away, she squeezed so close he felt her nose and hot breath on his neck. Susie took up half his pillow and most of the bed. His tiny sliver of sleeping real estate shrank by the hour. When she did surrender to sleep, she kept him awake with her sporadic twitching.

Now it was morning. Early morning. Early work morning.

Streetlights still shone through the window, illuminating the kitchen table in a harsh glow.

Maybe I should call in sick.

Trying not to wake Susie, he remained graveyard quiet while he pulled on a T-shirt, plugged in his ear buds, and listened to the news on his tablet. However, his pursuit of quietude was futile.

Susie slunk through the doorway and stared, a glint of mischief in her eyes.

Joe choked on a mouthful of coffee and spluttered it all over the table.

She padded closer, perched on his knee, and rubbed her face over his morning stubble. He stroked her head.

Then he plodded to the fridge to fetch milk while Susie licked her paws and purred.

Brilliant Beacon

Kathy Steinemann

Satellites. Computers. GPS. What next? Drones?

Old Man Saufer grumbled as he climbed the spiral staircase to the lighthouse lantern room. "Satellites. Computers. GPS. What next? Drones? They can't stand up to the fury of a gal like Hanna."

As if to prove his point, the wind wailed, buffeting the tower with rain and barraging it with plunder wrested from land and sea.

The government had declared lighthouses obsolete, but this newly laid-off keeper didn't care about political shenanigans. He had stayed at his post, even when Hurricane Hanna hit. With lots of beer of course. German lager. The darker the better.

"Stupid fancy pantsies. That newfangled electronic gear don't work when the electricity's out. How they supposed to save that ship out there if the new stuff ain't got juice? Maybe the captain'll see my lantern when I get up top."

Saufer paused halfway up to catch his breath. He peered through the tiny window and the driving rain. His gaze wandered over the treacherous waves until he located the ship. It was sailing dangerously close to the rocks, its lights appearing and disappearing as it navigated over crests and valleys. He wiped his eyes. Wiped them again.

"What the—" The beam of the deactivated beacon pierced through the rain. The familiar bass of the foghorn overpowered the roar of the wind as it vibrated stairs and walls.

"Well, I'll be danged. Gotta see what's makin' the light and make sure it stays on." He wheezed. "Ain't gettin' any younger. This is gonna kill me one of these days."

The light grew brighter as Saufer climbed. He squinted when he reached the last step. His eyes widened. The glare wasn't coming from the lens, but from several lanterns positioned around the outer edge of the room. He stumbled backward and almost lost his footing.

A gnarled hand grabbed his elbow. "Careful, watch your step." A stranger with a Van Dyke beard and a scar above his right eye tipped his hat. "Guy's the name. Guy Wyatt."

Saufer blinked. "I ain't never seen lanterns so dang bright."

"Special lanterns, they are. Brighter than a locomotive light. Suppose we can keep them going until dawn, old boy?"

Saufer leaned against the wall. He pinched himself. Then he pinched Wyatt.

Wyatt grinned. "Flesh and bone, just like you."

"I'm in. Let's save that there ship."

~*~

The two men maintained vigil, swapping tall tales and refilling the lanterns with acetylene, until the sea calmed and the sun broke over the horizon. Saufer succumbed to exhaustion. When he woke, Wyatt and the lanterns were gone.

He descended the stairs and hobbled to the pub, mumbling all the way there about hangovers. "Gotta give up drinkin'." He ordered a soda.

While he sipped, he gazed at the framed photos of previous lighthouse keepers. He set down his glass and shuffled closer. There, in black and white, was a man with a Van Dyke beard and a scar above his right eye. The inscription: *Guy Wyatt. 1858-1932.*

Saufer gulped. "Hey, Nick, gimme a beer!"

The Ancient Busker

Kathy Steinemann

Do you avoid buskers? Suppose they could weave magic melodies.

The busker's straggly hair didn't cover the scars on his sun-weathered face. Nor did his threadbare clothing conceal his emaciated frame. His gaunt fingers shivered as they coaxed music from his battered guitar.

But his voice rang true.

His tunes enticed curious passersby, drawing them ever closer. He wove magical melodies that nobody had ever heard before: bewitching music from the reaches of his ancient soul.

By the end of the day, his cardboard donation box overflowed with bills and coins.

And the enchanted spectators, whose pockets had been picked clean by his cohort, never reported their losses to authorities.

No Return Address

Kathy Steinemann

A mysterious package is delivered to the lab. Could it be a bomb?
Or something even worse?

I suppose I ought to write down how I got into this horrible hole. At least then my pen can talk to the paper. It's not the same as sharing with a real person, but I can't bear this solitude.

In March, the courier service delivered a nondescript parcel to my work station. It was addressed to Donald Forscher, c/o Forderly Laboratory. That's me: Donald. But the package didn't include a return address or identifying information. I decided not to unwrap it. Regulations prohibit us from opening anything unless we know what it contains.

I'm a scientist, but I'm also human. I put my ear to the box and listened. It was silent. Further inspection with a stethoscope revealed no noise coming from within. So I figured it wasn't a bomb. I sniffed it. There was no unusual odor either. I resisted the urge to shake it, and promised myself I'd phone Security as soon as I had my coffee break.

By the time I returned to my experiment, I had filed the memory of the parcel in a recess of my brain, along with my mother's birthday and the location of my car in the parking lot.

Two days later, I reached into the cupboard to retrieve the first-aid kit after cutting my finger. I cursed. I had forgotten to call Security about the package.

They were there within two minutes.

They ordered me out of the room. Then they sent in some strange-looking guy from the bomb squad. I could barely make out his face behind the heavy protective mask, but his grin was evident as he closed the door. I figured if *he* wasn't worried, I shouldn't be either.

The mysterious parcel contained a hula doll for my collection. Obviously, someone knew about my predilection for Hawaiian figurines. I set the doll on a nearby shelf.

The grass-skirted effigy soon started to annoy me. Its sharp glare bored into me no matter where I moved. Its expression seemed to change whenever I looked at it. I should have tossed it into the trash, but I didn't.

After weeks of playing hide-and-seek with the stare of the nasty little creature, I snatched it from the shelf on my way to the bathroom and flushed it down the toilet.

The doll became wedged in a sewer line. Normally such an occurrence wouldn't cause a problem, but that section of the line had a weak spot. The pressure buildup from the clog caused a slow leak, which became larger. As the pressure continued to increase, the pipe burst.

Foul-smelling liquid spewed everywhere. Bitter-tasting pathogens hissed into the climate-control system, contaminating everyone's experiments. I was in the deepest parts of the building when the lockdown alarm sounded, so I secured myself in a deserted wing that the company had closed the week before due to cutbacks.

There, I waited for the all-clear alert that never came.

During the long hours of solitude, I discovered a small television in a dark corner of my prison. There were no reality shows, no dramas, no soaps. Just news coverage of a potent virus spreading throughout the world and creating panic in its wake. The mortality rate was close to 100 percent. Investigators determined that the point of origin was one of Forderly Laboratory's sewer pipes.

I continued to watch as the stations went silent, one by one. Until there was a single remaining channel: a small independent controlled by a young woman named Alice Ronica.

I was lonely. I had enough to eat thanks to deserted refrigerators and unsuccessful GMO experiments. I found several books, along with a pen and a few pieces of paper. But I craved human companionship, so I kept the TV tuned to Ms. Ronica's station. When the channel went into standby mode, I pored through *Lord of the Rings* and several works by Ray Bradbury. But no matter when Alice came on air, I stopped flipping pages and watched her instead.

She reported that as far as she could tell, she was the only person alive on the entire planet. She described the state of the world as the Earth shaking its back to remove lice. She complained of debilitating headaches and episodes of breathing difficulties, followed by bouts of extreme fatigue. She said she was going insane. Sometimes she spat up blood, and when she cut herself, she had difficulty controlling the bleeding.

I shrieked at her. "You're not alone. I'm here. Don't lose hope."

I fell in love with her as the weeks passed and her symptoms worsened. Unanswered questions tormented me. Did I dare leave? If I did, what would I find out there? Rotting corpses or maybe a few survivors who might rob or kill me? But what could be worse than the living death down here?

My mind played games with my ears. I heard voices outside, accompanied by the incessant pounding of poor souls trying to get in. Was it all in my head? I feared that the solitude was driving me mad. I suppose my guilt was as well. I wished, over and over, I had thrown that stupid doll into the trash and not the toilet. I tried to concentrate on reading the novels, but I was consumed with fantasies of meeting Alice Ronica.

I'm running out of paper. I'll try to find more.

~*~

I haven't picked up the pen for a few days. This is the only paper I have, and it's so difficult for me to compose my thoughts.

This morning, I watched Alice. Like I always do. At least I think it was this morning. The passage of time is tenuous down here. She seemed more listless than usual. The whites of her eyes became a combination of yellow and red as the blood pooled in them like tears. She mumbled and held toilet tissue to her nose. She sank to the floor. Her speech slurred, and she lost consciousness. Her hand slipped to her chest. Crimson trickled from every orifice.

I scrutinized the screen and hoped for some sign of life, even though I knew she had breathed her last. Hours later, the station went blank.

Now I sit here, writing out my story. A story that nobody will ever see.

I have one choice left.

~*~

"Myrna Wellingham on the scene for Five-Alive News. I'm standing outside Forderly Laboratory as EMTs load a body into the ambulance. Details are sparse, but initial reports indicate that the male suicide victim, name withheld at present, was reported missing by his family three weeks ago. His body was discovered by a coworker, who says he found it in a closed-off section of the lab. Unconfirmed reports state that the victim kept a delusional, time-distorted record of events. Authorities have seized it for evidence."

"Myrna, sorry. We have to interrupt for another live report from Alice Ronica outside Regal Care Hospital. Alice, go ahead."

"Thanks, Sarafina. An entire floor of the hospital has been quarantined. As you can see behind me, several ambulances are unloading victims, most already deceased. I was able to interview

a nurse off-camera. She ... says some kind of unusual virus has already caused multiple deaths, and everyone is ... taking special precautions to prevent the spread of infection. She seemed irration— ... Sarafina, I should ... I don't feel ... "

The camera angle skewed, pitching over bodies and lifeless ambulance attendants as it tumbled to the pavement.

The Five-Alive News broadcast faded to black.

Pretense

Kathy Steinemann

Please don't take offense, Quebecers. This is a tongue-in-cheek parody.

Phillipé, server in an exclusive Montréal bistro, straightened his tie and brushed a speck of lint off a shoulder as he glowered at the security camera. He mumbled under his breath but forced a smile as the door opened.

His first customer took a small table by the window. "Excuse me, garçon. Can you recommend something from today's menu?"

"Je ne parle pas l'anglais."

"I beg your pardon? I don't speak French."

Phillipé shrugged. Glanced at the security camera. "Je suis désolé, monsieur, mais …"

"Does anyone here speak English?"

Phillipé turned away from the security camera, leaned toward the customer, and murmured, "No. French only." He scrunched his eyes. "Sorry."

The customer gave Phillipé the finger and left without ordering.

More diners dined, chatting in French with Phillipé. He recommended wines and today's pièce de résistance. Coffee cups were refilled. Empty plates were cleared. Complimentary desserts were served.

Diners departed with happy expressions after leaving generous gratuities.

~*~

Around eight p.m., an Anglophone actor from Vancouver entered, chose a table, and sat down. He had heard about anti-English discrimination in Quebec, but he had a plan and a few German lessons behind him.

He raised a hand and beckoned Phillipé. "Entschuldigen Sie! Sprechen Sie Deutsch?"

Phillipé frowned.

The actor spoke again. "Sprechen Sie Englisch?"

Phillipé replied in a BBC accent, his rolling French R's now dropped and almost undetectable. "You come from Germany?"

The actor replied with a pronounced German accent, "Ya. Mein English ist not so goot. Understand you me? I speak no French at all."

"Yes, sir. How may I help you today?"

"Have you a gluten-free menu?"

Phillipé smiled and waited on the man, chatting away in perfect English interspersed with an occasional word of German.

~*~

Slow evening. A few more native Montréalers. Another Anglophone Canadian who left in disgust.

Phillipé finished his shift and gave the security camera a one-fingered salute before he walked home.

~*~

Philip's wife greeted him at the door. "How was your day?"

He replied, "Terrible as usual, I'm afraid. Played the part and kept my employer happy on the CCTV feed by refusing to speak English with Anglophone Canadians."

She hugged him and sighed.

His face turned maple-leaf red. "I didn't train at the best acting academy in London just to come to Canada and perform bit parts in commercials or play rude Frenchmen in cafes. Let's move to Hollywood."

Three Wishes
Kathy Steinemann

Be careful what you wish for. Sometimes wishes come true.

Charley Kalinski held the pistol to his head. His sweaty fingers slipped on the grip and threatened to discharge the weapon before he was ready. He laid it in his lap.

It was all my fault.

His eyes focused on the ceiling while he agonized over what had brought him to this dark decision.

~*~

The clock above the bar read 1:06. He still had enough time for one more beer. Rachel and her crapola jaunt around the lake. *When I asked her to marry me, I didn't sign up for hiking in the dead of winter.*

He squinted at the big-screen television in the far corner. *I told her I wanted to watch the hockey game this afternoon. Serve her right if I was late. I wish she'd stop nagging.*

The beer in his stein disappeared. He ordered another. Then another.

The bartender frowned. "That's enough. I'll call you a taxi."

Charley mumbled something unintelligible, resting his cheek in a pool of slobber while he waited.

The bartender helped him into the cab and paid for the fare. "You owe me, Chuck." He slammed the door.

Charley spluttered his address to the cabbie around an uncooperative tongue. "No, thash not right. Not home. I need ta go … ta go ta Moose Meadows Lake." He leaned his head against the seat and drooled a string of sloppy saliva down his jacket as the driver started the meter.

Charley leaned forward. "I chan-changed my mind. Lemme out."

He staggered to his convertible in the nearby parking lot and sat behind the wheel for a slobber or two. Then he fumbled his key into the ignition, stepped on the accelerator, and pulled out into traffic. His car zigzagged down the street, barely missing a parked minivan and several oncoming vehicles.

As he veered into the main approach to Moose Meadows Lake, his head bobbed, his chin sank to his chest, and he snored.

He didn't hear the sickening crunch of metal on metal. Didn't feel the impact that propelled his car into a tree. Didn't smell the pungent fumes of burnt plastic and rubber.

~*~

Twilight.

Gas fumes. Indistinct figures. Faraway voices. An apparatus around his nose and mouth.

Darkness.

~*~

Rachel watched the clock above the mantel in their cabin by the lake. She tapped her fingers on the table. Glowered at the romantic candles. Scowled as she sniffed the aroma of garlic in Charley's favorite casserole, which was slowly turning dry and inedible in the oven. She wondered what was keeping him. He was over an hour late. *I want it to be so special when I tell him the news.*

A tiny tear rolled down to her chin. She glared at the Christmas wreath on the door. He was drinking again. She knew it. How could he?

Her jaw jutted forward, and she beat her fist on the table.

Charley was in the bar. He was always in the bar. *I wish he would stop drinking.*

How many times did she have to haul him out? *I guess I'd better go get him. Again.*

She slammed the car door and sped out onto the road, driving far too fast for the icy winter conditions.

Slipping. Sliding. Metal on metal.

Blackness.

~*~

Charley came to with a throbbing headache. A nurse tapped the line on his IV. It hurt to breathe. It hurt to open his eyes. Every cell and pore in his body protested. He whispered through a partially numb throat that felt as though it had been reamed out by a plumber's snake. "What happened?"

"Another driver hit your car. You're hurt, but you'll be okay."

Twilight.

~*~

The firm squeeze of a large hand brought Charley back to consciousness. "Dad? Is that you? Where's Rachel?"

"You're going to be all right, son."

Even through Charley's analgesic daze, he could see the tears in his father's eyes. "What aren't you telling me?"

"I don't know how to— I can't … Rachel didn't make it."

"What do you mean?"

"The car that hit you. It was hers. She broadsided you when you went around the corner." His shoulders heaved as he continued a broken account of the accident. "Her car went up in flames. There … there wasn't enough time for them to rescue her. I know it's not any consolation, but they figure the crash probably killed her, not the fire."

Charley punched his pillow. His ragged breathing and violent sobs drove daggers of pain through his chest. The nurse touched the panel on a machine attached to his IV, and the pain subsided. He floated on a wavy, narcotic sea that dulled his anguish and made his stomach roll.

His dad studied the floor. "You've been here four days. Drugged up, not very lucid. You missed Christmas. Funeral's tomorrow. You have a broken right arm and three cracked ribs. They had to intubate you for a few hours, but everything looks good." A sob silenced his report.

Charley wept.

His dad's chin quivered. "You're supposed to make a full recovery. They plan to discharge you this afternoon. Blasted medical system. Kick 'em out as soon as possible."

Charley gazed across the hall at the blipping machines with their blinking lights in the Intensive Care Unit. "It was my fault. It was my fault! I'll never take another drink. Never."

~*~

Dad's house.

How long had it been? Long enough that everything seemed unfamiliar. His old bedroom was missing the posters, trophies, and greasy car parts. And it smelled too clean. No stinky socks, half-eaten tuna sandwiches, or sour glasses of milk. He downed several painkillers before he went to bed.

Yet sleep remained elusive. Memories and pain and dreams haunted every heartbeat, every breath, every sob. Shortly before dawn, he fell into a deep slumber, but the pain reminded him that he was still alive, that he still had important duties to perform.

~*~

The church was full. Standing room only.

Charley didn't recognize most of the guests at the funeral. Rachel had been well-liked, but he wasn't prepared for the hundreds of unfamiliar faces. People pumped his hand and mouthed condolences. They all sounded the same. They all looked the same.

He tried to ignore the overheard whispers.

"Poor girl. Such a tragedy."

"Her parents blame Charley."

"He didn't deserve her."

"I can't believe she's gone. She was so young and vibrant."

"I feel sorry for her mom and dad. Look at them."

"I heard she was pregnant."

All Charley could think about was how he had screwed up. How he was about to begin a new year without his soul mate. But this year he intended to keep the resolution he'd made countless times already. *Not another drink. Ever.*

He refused his dad's offer of company after the service. "I'll be fine. Just take me to our … to my place. Please. I need privacy and a few hours to think."

~*~

The teddy bear on the sofa: Charley's surprise gift to Rachel after they'd had a fight about his drinking. He held the soft fuzz to his nose and inhaled the subtle fragrance that was Rachel.

Photos on the fridge: Rachel with binoculars, peering into the marsh on the west end of Moose Meadows Lake; Rachel sitting on his Harley; Rachel blowing him a kiss.

Rachel!

He collapsed to the floor. His right arm throbbed. He wanted to break it out of the cast and pound it on the tiles until he smashed the arm to smithereens. His skin crawled with invisible insects that tortured him with itchy, burning bites.

I need to see her.

He hailed a cab and returned to the cemetery, where he sat on a bench next to her grave. He prayed. He pleaded. "I wish you could give her back to me. Just for an hour. Just so I could apologize and tell her how much I love her. How could I have thought hockey was more important than her?"

The moon seemed to grow larger and brighter with every breath he took. A corona of iridescence glowed around it, transforming it into an all-seeing eye within an orb. A distant siren wailed in the wind. The fresh heaps of dirt on Rachel's grave glowed in the moonlight. Her soft fragrance emanated from somewhere. Charley inhaled it. *Ah. Sweet Rachel.*

Scratching. Shrieking. Moaning.

He stumbled to the grave, pressed one ear against the dirt, and listened. *No. No. No! Rachel.* Too far to fetch anyone. Not enough time. He clawed with his left hand. He broke his fingernails on rocks. He panted. Groaned. He dug faster. Faster. Faster.

Hurry. Hurry.

The ghastly scratching grew louder. The shrieks and moans were hers; he knew it. He dug. He perspired. He continued to dig.

His exhaustion deepened as the hole grew, inch by excruciating inch.

"Rachel, I'm sorry. I'm so, so sorry. I love you. I'll save you."

The scratching stopped.

The air turned silent, still.

The hour was over.

Charley screamed at the sky. "Why? Why would you grant such a stupid wish?"

~*~

Charley Kalinski held the pistol to his head.

Darkness.

210

Sorcery or Strategy?

Kathy Steinemann

The old wizard promised the General favorable weather, but now men were freezing, horses were dying, and the General's most trusted advisor was dubious.

"Lord Reynold, a bolt of lightning has struck the ridge, and the black stones are burning." The young messenger lost his grip on his spear, struggled to catch it, then bowed before me. "The Wizard's spell worked."

The Captain nodded, stroking his beard. "The Fates have looked upon us with favor. They have blessed us with heat so we can defeat the Thrax."

My glare remained steadfast until he averted his eyes, and then I rebuked him. "Your supposition is incorrect. The rocks are coal. The gods and sorcery had nothing to do with this. The Wizard promised us favorable weather, and he failed."

The Captain squinted. "Lightning this late in the season? And warmth exactly when we need it? I, for one, intend to thaw my bones. I care not whether gods or happenstance brought us this unexpected good fortune. Now we can save the horses."

His attitude angered me, but my voice remained calm. "You will order the men to set fire to all the coal they can find. They must melt snow and fill the water kegs. Every man will sleep with his horse tonight. You and I will meet with the General and the commanders to discuss tactics."

Gods! They do not exist. Sorcery? By all the Truths! Magic does not exist either. When will these people learn?

I stomped away from the tent and surveyed our camp: burnt remains of funeral pyres; a dead horse hacked into pieces and roasting over several fires; one of my men moaning, belt in his teeth, as the Healer severed his frost-bitten fingers to save his life.

Even in the bitter cold, I smelled fear. It carried on the breeze, mingling with the stench of sweat and urine and foul breath.

Violent shivers seized me, piercing to my deepest innards with the icy knives of an early winter worse than any I had ever experienced. With my fur cloak pressed to my chin, I hastened toward the tent of the General.

Once we had forged our plans, our watchers stood guard, silhouetted against the red waves of heat, as we enjoyed our first comfortable slumber in weeks. The coal continued to burn and glow through the darkness, alerting the Thrax to our position.

~*~

Thrax soldiers attacked the following night after we had extinguished our fires, and the moon shone high in a heaven bedecked with stars. The enemy crept forward, their bulky shadows bent low, goatskin armor silent, with spears and hammers in hand. They stabbed and pummeled every cloak-covered figure in the camp.

But the shock on their faces was overshadowed by the terror in their screams as our warriors came out of hiding, and the Thrax realized they had besieged bodies of snow rather than flesh.

I surveyed the slaughter. A radiance covered the carnage: a radiance that did not come from the coal. Clinks and laughs sounded from all directions as my men relieved the corpses of valuables and weapons. An unearthly hum vibrated in my bones.

Sorcery or strategy? Perhaps only the gods know.

212

Always, Bro
Kathy Steinemann

*When the Man waked up he said, "What is Wild Dog doing here?"
And the Woman said, "His name is not Wild Dog any more, but the
First Friend, because he will be our friend for always and always
and always." ~ Rudyard Kipling*

Chris stirred.

Where was he?

He tried to remember. …

Skidding. Crashing through the guardrail. The sickening sound of bushes and trees beating on metal after his car veered off the mountain highway. Pain.

He groaned, and his eyes flickered open. His car rested upright, hood crumpled against a large tree. His fingers explored. The seatbelt still imprisoned him in the driver's seat. His ears pulsed and pounded. Another groan escaped his throat. *That's the last time I trust a GPS in a snowstorm.*

He released the buckle. Checked his extremities. Felt his head for blood. *All things considered, stupid, you seem to be okay.*

What now? Should he wait for help? He had read somewhere that you're supposed to stay put if you run off the road. But the biting cold gnawed at his limbs. Staying in the car wasn't an option.

Violent shivers shook him as he checked his cell phone. The battery was dead.

He wrenched the door handle and pushed with his shoulder, but the door wouldn't budge. "Crap that hurt! Feels like a freight train ran over me."

He squeezed through the passenger window and surveyed the damage. The car looked like something out of a wrecking yard. He'd never drive this beast again.

Chris stumbled backward. "I'm lucky to be alive! *Am I alive?*"

If he were dead, he'd feel strange and his body would still be in the driver's seat. He checked behind the steering wheel for reassurance.

"Guess when I don't show up at Rusty's funeral, they'll come looking for me," he whispered, tears stinging his eyes.

He squinted uphill in the deepening dusk, but couldn't see the guardrails at the top of the cliff or hear any traffic noise. He wondered how far above him the highway was. The embankment looked too steep to climb. Maybe someone would see where he went off the road. "Oh, Rusty, I wish you were here to give me some advice. You'd be chewing my ear off. Do this. Do that. Do something else."

Chris sighed. "I miss you. I'll always miss you, Bro. Can you hear me?"

He pulled his scarf closer to his face and clicked the button on his key fob to open the trunk. Nothing. He clicked again. And again. Wiggled the key in the lock. Twisted it. The trunk creaked open a few inches. *Good thing I have a survival kit.*

The kit was new, never opened. He had no idea what it contained, but he pulled it out along with the folding shovel. "Damn, my ribs hurt." He snaked his fingers under his coat and prodded at his chest. "Ouch. What would *you* do, Rusty?" A slight shower of snow sprinkled into the air from a nearby tree. "Right. Build a shelter."

His ribs protested with every ball of snow rolled onto his crude igloo. His breathing became more labored. Was it caused by the cold or his injuries? *I'd better be quick.*

When he was finished, he stepped back to scrutinize his work. "That's as good as it's going to get, Rusty. Ribs hurt too much to do any more. Wish this parka wasn't so thin."

Chris dragged himself into the igloo, which was more a cave than anything else, and opened the survival kit. Flashlight. Toe warmers. "Right on. Wish I'd found these sooner." Solar blanket. First-aid supplies. Jumper cables. Bottled water.

Nothing to eat.

He stuffed toe warmers into his boots. Then he threw the solar blanket onto the trampled snow and wrapped as much of it as he could around his body. *Suppose I ought to look at my chest.* He uncovered just enough to examine his torso. Lots of bruises. Worse than the time Rusty had spiked the volleyball into his ribs. He chuckled. "Ow, that hurts. Good thing it's winter. No beach volleyball for a while. Sorry, Rusty. I shouldn't have laughed. G'night."

Shooting pains disrupted his sleep. The night pressed in on him, shadowy and silent and endless … until a furry muzzle sniffed at his face. Chris flinched. Through the darkness and disorientation, he could make out the shape of an animal. A bear or a dog or—

A friendly bark erased all doubt. "Hello. Where did *you* come from?" The dog whined. It licked his chin and snuggled close. Chris pulled it into the blanket. They fell asleep, sharing body heat and snores.

Daybreak.

Chris was colder than he could ever remember. In the dim light, he could see the dog's long coat. It felt smooth and tangle-free. Was it dark brown? Red, maybe?

The friendly pooch radiated warmth, and its fur smelled of pot roast and onions. He scratched its head. "Hey, what's going on with your ear? Get it caught in a bear trap, maybe? Looks kinda wonky." He rubbed the dog's hindquarters. "Are you a girl or a boy? You're obviously someone's pet. Maybe you can lead me outta here."

A warm tongue curled around his nose.

"Doggie kisses." He snickered. Then he moaned. "Shouldn't laugh. Hurts too much. How can I laugh when Rusty's lying in a cold coffin? No jokes, okay?" Tears filled his eyes.

The dog pawed at his knee.

"What should I call you? Dawg? Pooch? Yeah. Pooch. That's a good name for a dog."

"Woof."

"Good. Now that's settled, let's break outta here and see where you came from."

He gathered everything that might be useful and loaded it into the pockets of his parka. "Guess I was stupid not to pack any food in the car, right, Pooch?"

"Rawr."

"You're right. Rusty would've packed food. You ready to go?"

"Woof."

Man and dog made their way outside, both using trees to relieve themselves.

"Guess that removes all doubt, boy. You look like an Irish setter. A well-fed Irish setter. You know where there's anything to eat?"

"Woof. Woof."

He scanned again for a way up the cliff. There wasn't one. "You came from somewhere nearby. You must have an owner and a house. Lead on, Pooch."

The dog plowed through the snow toward the east. Chris followed, grunting with the exertion, but the pain wasn't as bad as it had been during the night.

"Not so fast!"

Pooch stopped, tail wagging, then scooped a muzzle-full of snow into the air while he waited.

Chris scratched Pooch's good ear. "I was on my way to my brother's funeral. He was just twenty-eight. His name's Rusty. Was Rusty. Well, that's what we called him, 'cause his hair was the color of a rusty nail. Sorta like your fur. His real name was Russell."

They trudged onward. "He was killed on his way to the ski hill. Some stupid guy reached into the back seat of a car and didn't watch where he was going out on Dead Man's Curve."

He blinked back tears. "Rusty was my big brother, and he still had his whole life to live. Just twenty-eight. Guess I already said that. He always knew the right way to do stuff. I never got the chance to say good-bye or tell him how much I loved him. Hard to tell another guy how you feel."

"Woof."

"You're right. I guess he knew. ... Knows. I'm hungry, Pooch. Any good pizza joints around here? No? Just get me to the nearest warm place, and I'll buy you a whole bunch of your favorite dog food."

"Woof."

They slogged on in an endless, icy torture as the sun moved higher over the trees. The bottles of water in Chris's inside pockets pressed against his bruised ribs. "Crap. I figured body heat would be the best way to keep the water drinkable, but it hurts too much."

He transferred both bottles to his hood and pulled the drawstring tight. Intense shivers aggravated his ribs even more than the water bottles had. "I'm gonna upchuck." He supported himself against a tree with one palm.

The nausea passed. He walked. Staggered. Slumped into the snow. "Gotta lie down, Pooch. Just for a minute."

Whiskers brushed his closed eyelids. "Just want to sleep. Go away. Let me be. So cold. ... Can't feel my toes anymore." Pooch pawed at his shoulder.

Chris's tongue felt about as responsive as a block of ice. His speech came out in slurred bursts. "Don't. Don't do that." He struggled to sit. "Go away."

"Woof."

"Yeah, you're right. I'm stupid. If I don't get moving, I'm a goner." He grunted to a standing position and pressed forward. Pooch led the way, always a few steps ahead, always waiting for Chris to catch up.

The sun remained ruthless in its blinding brilliance, but it didn't do anything to warm the subzero air. Chris stumbled. "Damn, I'm tired. And my ribs hurt."

"Rawr."

"Yeah, yeah, quit your nagging. I'm coming."

A few more steps. A stagger. Another stumble.

"Can't do it. Can't ... do it." He slumped into the snow, his eyelids fluttering shut. ...

Chris drifted in a dream world of warmth: a sandy beach with a volleyball net. Multiple balls spiked at him faster than he could react. *Rusty. I see you. I'm coming. ... No! Don't push me away.*

Something wet prodded at his nose. He flinched. "Go away. Get out of here. You're always nagging." *Rusty, where are you? I can't see you anymore. Come back.*

I'll sleep. Feels good. So good.

~*~

Vibrations tormented the agony in Chris's ribs. He forced his eyes open.

Moving treetops. Sunshine. Snowbanks scrolling by in slow motion.

Darkness. Falling. Drifting.

~*~

He woke in a dim room with a crackling fireplace and the delicious smell of pot roast and onions. Prickles of pain shot up his legs. An old geezer sat across from him in a rickety rocking chair.

The geezer cackled. "Yer alive. Thought I lost you back there on the trail. Ambulance is on its way, sonny."

"Where am I?"

"Up the butthole of nowhere. Found you on the edge of my property and brought you here in the toboggan."

"Where's Pooch?"

"Pooch?"

"The Irish setter. He kept me going whenever I wanted to give up."

The geezer's eyes grew wide: two mirrors reflecting the flames from the fireplace. He leaned forward in his chair. "Irish setter?"

Chris nodded. "Yeah. Nice dog. Long reddish fur and a wonky left ear. Really friendly."

"Couldn't be. You musta been hallucinatin'. I didn't see no dog or dog tracks, and that Irish setter's been dead well-nigh twenty-eight years. Good dog, that Rusty. Killed by a guy who didn't look where he was goin' out on Dead Man's Curve."

Ultimate Compulsion

Kathy Steinemann

This is a reprint of my drabble that appeared in Boston Literary
Magazine on June 15, 2015

An eternity of drifting. Floating. Disorientation.

Where am I? How long have I been in this strange place?

Muffled sounds filled his universe. Laughing voices.
Beeps. Whirrs.

He was attached. He was warm. He was nourished.

Then why did he feel the compulsion to leave?

He stretched. He pushed. He strained.

But he was trapped.

Not yet. Conserve your strength.

He slept.

Pressure. Panic. Pain.

Now is the time.

His heart raced. He clawed his way through the ribcage of
his host. The cold air assaulted his lungs. He screamed.

A salivating xenomorph comforted him, hissed in his ear.

Mama.

The Last Three-Horn

Kathy Steinemann

Here is a tale about the ancient past. Will you recognize the event?

The Healer bowed low before the King. "My Lord, your child has the wasting sickness. She is dying. All that can save her now is the yolk of a three-horn's egg."

King Ichik frowned at the Healer's report, and his weathered countenance moistened with tears. "I do not understand."

"I partook of the dream potion and prayed to the Unseens for guidance. They revealed all to me in a vision. The healing power in a three-horn's egg is Kisa's only hope."

"Then go and search for such an egg. I will plead to the Unseens for a successful quest."

The monarch peered out of his lofty palace at his vast domain: a great expanse of verdant jungle stretching into distant mist that met the sparkling waters of the ocean beyond. *All this is mine. My enemies fear me. The surrounding kingdoms dare not attack me. They deem me wise and powerful. But without my daughter, all is nothing. I am nothing.*

Kisa sobbed from her bed. "Father, do not worry. If I must leave you, my essence will fly free with the creatures in the clouds, and I will always watch over you."

"No! Your foolish words fall on deaf ears. I will not allow death to claim you. I will not allow it as long as there is breath within me. I will not even speak death's name. You are the sun of my existence, the delight of my dreams."

His daughter joined him at the window. They watched the Healer as he organized a search party and pack animals. Soon, men and beasts disappeared into the green blanket of trees at the foot of the mountain.

"Father, I was so little when Mother's essence departed. Please tell me about her again. It makes me happy and helps me forget my pain."

"Noonsa was more beautiful than moonlight on the ocean or the flowers in the forest. She was kind and clever, and she loved you more than words can say. The day her essence left us to soar in the sky was the saddest day of my life. But she gave me you. You are the best gift I could ever desire."

His sad eyes studied her ashen face. "Whenever you gaze into the still waters, you see your mother. She bestowed all her beauty upon you."

Kisa leaned on his shoulder and contemplated the sky where it joined the sea. "Sometimes I feel her presence. I feel her love and warmth, as though she is still watching over me."

~*~

The sun rose and set thirteen times before the search party returned.

The Healer knelt before the King. "My Lord, we were unable to find a three-horn. I have gathered all the hunters in the countryside. We will begin another search when the darkness leaves the heavens."

"So be it."

Kisa lay on her bed. Her hair absorbed her tears, and its earthen colors shimmered in the sunshine. King Ichik held her thin hand. "You are the most beloved daughter in the land. No father or king could ever possess as much pride for a child as I do for you."

"I love you also, Father. But my pain grows with every hour, and I know my essence will join Mother soon."

"No! I could not live without you. Our essences will join her together someday." His brow tightened. *I watched my wife wilt into a faded wisp of wind. I will not, I cannot, allow another loved one to be stolen out of my grasp by the claws of death.*

He stroked Kisa's hands and rained his sadness onto her bed. *Why is the Healer taking so long? Kisa is frail. She needs the medicine. Oh please, Unseens of the heavens and hills, save my daughter. I am selfish. I want her to stay with me forever.*

~*~

King Ichik's voice was somber. "What news do you bring, Healer of the People?"

The Healer threw himself on the floor. "My Lord and Master, we must report our defeat. We found a three-horn guarding her nest. A giant-head attacked and killed her mate, but the three-horn fought bravely and vanquished her foe. The Unseens told me there is only one three-horn left. If we kill her to take her eggs, there will never be another, and many of us will die from Kisa's affliction."

"Leave me. Return in the morning and be prepared to journey."

The Healer backed out of the chamber.

The King raised his palms to the stars in silent supplication. *He already has the weakness and wasting. He will die, and Kisa will die, unless we take the three-horn's eggs. Great Unseens, please guide me. I need wisdom. Please help me to be the king the People need and the father my daughter supposes me to be.*

Kisa whispered from her bed. "Father, you know what you must do. I willingly sacrifice my shell, so the People can survive."

Ichik did not answer.

A night of fervent prayer left the King weary. But he was awake and waiting when the Healer requested an audience while the dew still dampened the flowers.

Ichik touched the Healer's shoulder. "You must send warriors to guard the three-horn from the giant-heads. I cannot be selfish. Someday the beast's young will produce more eggs. And *you* must stay here to care for Kisa. You will both sacrifice your shells and fly from this chamber when the Unseens demand your presence. Or perhaps they will look upon the People with favor because of your kindness, and perhaps they will permit us to live until there are more eggs."

~*~

Ichik wiped the tears from Kisa's countenance. The last thing she saw before she departed from her shell was the love in his eyes.

She was buried next to Noonsa.

The King could not be comforted. *The People will be safe, but I cannot endure this pain. Oh, Kisa, I am so alone. Why? Why could it not have been me instead?*

The wise ruler peered out of his lofty palace at his vast domain: a great expanse of verdant jungle stretching into distant mist that met the sparkling waters of the ocean beyond.

And he wept.

~*~

A hissing comet crossed the sky. Ichik watched as the thunderous fiend devoured mountains and trees. The ground shook. It groaned. A deafening explosion spewed clouds of ash, molten boulders, and steam high into the heavens. Boiling waters submerged most of the jungle. Flames consumed the remaining trees. The sun darkened. The scalding air smote the King, thrust him off his feet, and crushed the walls of the palace.

Gone were the three-horn and her hatchlings. Gone were the giant-heads. Gone was Ichik's vast domain.

He moaned as the blazing inferno approached. *Soon my essence will fly to you and your mother, my darling Kisa. Your sacrifice was for nothing. All is nothing. I am nothing.*

Sciatic Symphony

Kathy Steinemann

This piece might seem improbable. However, it's based on a true story. A writer never knows where the muse might lurk.

"My best idea ever."

Amy's fingers flew over the keyboard: no longer a computer-input device, but an instrument of creation. Her body swayed. She composed her story during a symphony of clicks and pauses, batoned by an occasional "Aha" or "Yes, that's it."

Only one interruption hushed the music of her muse: a short break to brew a pot of coffee. *Ah. Delicious.*

She returned to her composition. It serenaded. It harmonized.

However, the drumming throb in her back forced her to repeatedly adjust her laptop desk between standing and sitting positions.

Three productive hours later, she remembered the clock. *Darn. I'd better hurry if I want to get to the chiropractor on time.* She limped to the garage, massaging her lower spine to relieve the sciatic pain darting down her leg.

~*~

Amy returned home with a tango in her step. *Maybe I'll actually get some shuteye tonight. Twelve days ... I should have seen the bone cracker sooner.*

Her symphony burst into a crescendo of musical phrases.

She slept well that night. Ten wonderful, pain-free hours of sweet repose, filled with dreams of dancing princes and flitting fairies.

The next morning, her ideas began to fade. Hour upon hour, try as she might, she could only compose a few hackneyed sentences. She slumped in front of the computer while staring out the window. She googled for ideas; brainstormed with other authors.

The screen taunted her. The concerto from her keyboard had become a halting, staccato melody filled with vacant pauses.

After a week of false starts and stale phrases, Amy closed the lid of her laptop with a resounding slam: a slam that sounded like the discordant clash of cymbals announcing the death of her genius.

She pulled on her winter boots and donned her warmest parka. Then she slogged along a footpath until her cheeks stung, until she lost the feeling in the tip of her nose. She continued to walk until her toes burned, until her lungs complained about the onslaught of sub-zero air. *I suppose I won't accomplish anything by freezing to death. I'll never be able to pay the electric bill this way.*

Amy headed home, gazing at birds, trees, and passersby, hoping that inspiration would come from somewhere, anywhere.

She didn't notice the icy patch in the walkway. She slipped. She pirouetted. And her pain returned.

~*~

Three days later, the ideas sang to her, and the story almost wrote itself. However, she winced whenever a throbbing spasm shot down her leg.

Amy studied her fingernails. With her mind in creative overdrive, the solution was obvious.

She visited the chiropractor.

Then, she drove to the local animal shelter and adopted two kittens to share her bed at night.

Pup 'O Lantern

A. L. Kaplan

Sometimes fate surprises us with its capricious nature, as J. P. Pish is about to discover.

Damn that witch. Like it's my fault her field had the best pumpkins in town. How was I supposed to know it was hers? Not that it mattered. Hey, in my hood, if you want something, you take it and be dammed everyone else. It's called survival, and I was at the top of the food chain. Of course I took the biggest pumpkin. Nothing but the best for J. P. Pish. That's Mr. Pish to you. At least I was at the top before she caught me taking her prize pumpkin. I would have knocked out the old hag. Really I would have, but something tripped me up.

Now I'm in this ridiculous, four-legged form. Big, tough guy like me, you'd think a nice big Rottweiler or even a Doberman. But no, she had to turn me into a wimpy, little, fluff-covered yap machine. If that wasn't bad enough, I'm stuck in a goofy pumpkin costume. I'm so humiliated. She said I owed her for losing the pumpkin prize at the fair. I have to get first prize for cutest dog at the Halloween masquerade, or she'll never turn me back into a human. I swear, one more person rubs my head and says how cute I look, I'll bite their hand off.

Oh God, here comes another. Wait a minute, she's hot. Man, this one can pet me all she wants. Come closer, honey. Mr. Pish has some kisses for you.

Double Your Normal Fee

Kathy Steinemann

Two truckers and a woman who's dispatching a trunk. Nothing unusual, right?

Ken smirked. "What d'ya have in the trunk, a body?"

Jill avoided meeting his gaze. Her eyes shifted momentarily to the huge wooden trunk with its metal hasp and hefty padlock. Then she frowned. "Official disposal. Here's the Wissen Labs incinerator authorization."

"Milton Movers charges extra for transporting dope, counterfeit cash, and corpses. Especially if they're carcasses of dead boyfriends."

"I-I assure you, it's nothing like that. Just medical waste. But I'll pay extra if you get it there on time."

"How much extra?"

She glowered at him. "Double your normal fee."

"Ya sure it's not illegal cargo? The boss'll have my hide if we get searched and the cops find anything suspicious."

"You want to look inside? Here." She dangled a key in her unsteady hand.

Syd took it. "Come on. Quit kidding with the poor girl. She might think we're not legit."

Ken grabbed the key and handed it back to Jill. "Nah. He's right. We gotta get going. We'll take your word for it. Let's load it up, Syd."

Syd whispered out the side of his mouth. "Bet she'd be hot in bed."

Ken glared at him.

Syd gulped and bent over to grab his end of the trunk. He groaned. "Crap, this thing's heavy. We should have used the lift."

They secured the cargo.

When they were ready to roll, Syd tipped his baseball cap to Jill. "Nice to meet you, ma'am."

She nodded at Syd, smiled at Ken, and blushed. Then her gaze darted toward the truck.

~*~

The semi rumbled away, and Ken's grip tightened on the wheel. He watched Jill's curvaceous body grow smaller in the rearview mirrors as he massaged the stitched-up gash on his nose. A delicious shudder ran down his back and into his crotch. He licked his lips. When she finally disappeared from sight, he took a second to admire his profile. Jill said he looked like Matthew McConaughey. He stroked his chin. *Maybe she's right.*

Syd inhaled a few deep breaths through the half-open window and sighed. "Fresh air. You don't get that in the cities. I enjoy these small towns in the mountains with their friendly people and simple living. Wouldn't mind settling here. Little house with a white picket fence and a loving wife to jump my bones every night. You know the dream."

Ken checked the speedometer. "Yeah, you're always telling me about it. But ya forgot about the sporadic cell phone signals and crappy Internet service."

"I suppose I could live without a few bells and whistles."

Ken sneered. "You'd get tired of it in less than a month."

"Guess I'll never find out." Syd shrugged. "You okay to drive while I snooze?"

"Sure. But take off your boots and stinky socks. Last time I climbed into the sleeper after ya used it, it smelled like something died back there. And no farting."

Syd grunted as he climbed into the back of the cab, and he was asleep within seconds, snoring so loudly that Ken had to adjust the volume on the radio.

Hours passed. The radio faded in and out.

"Storm warning for the east ... Winds up to ... Roads closed near ... body of suspected murder victim still missing. Officials have no leads. ... Wissen Lab officials are searching for ... that disappeared on ... [Buzz] ... top-secret government projects ... unidentified source claims ... cloning ... [Hiss] ... [Pop]"

A low-frequency hum filled the cab. Ken checked the mirrors. Was it his imagination? Or maybe one of the tires? With Syd sawing logs in the sleeper, it was hard to hear what was going on. A strange feeling of lethargy clouded his senses.

I need to do something to keep awake.

He pressed buttons and twisted knobs. No service on AM or FM. What about satellite-radio? Nothing. He pounded on the dash. Silence. *Dammit!* They couldn't stop to fix anything if they were going to get there on time. They only had a one-hour window to use the incinerator. He decided to sing.

After a few minutes, he realized he hadn't heard anything on the CB for at least a hundred miles. Several turns of the dial produced nothing but fuzzy pops and whirrs. He yawned and blinked a few times.

Jill sure had acted nervous. Almost blew it. Their little performance probably did the trick, though. Once he got rid of the old boyfriend's body, it would be clear sailing for them. Feisty little twerp hadn't wanted to die. It would take weeks for the scratches on Ken's chest to heal. An image of the man groping and gasping for air flashed through his brain. He shivered.

Syd doesn't suspect how I got this slash on my nose. Not the brightest bulb on the Christmas tree.

He drove for a few more miles and frowned into the emptiness, wondering what Jill was doing. Why did he feel so damn sleepy? The lines on the pavement blurred …

He jolted awake. Too late. The semi veered over the shoulder and forged a trail of furrows in the mud and gravel, knocking down bushes and bouncing over rocks. "Hey, Syd, you awake?"

"Of course I'm awake. What the hell happened?"

"What do ya *think* happened? We're in the ditch." He checked his phone. "No cell service, and the CB's busted." He flung open the cab door. "Let's take a look. Maybe we can drive out if we do it right."

Both men climbed down and strode to the rear of the trailer. Ken's eyes bulged. "Would ya look at that!"

Broken containers and cargo lay in disarray among rocks and trees. But Ken's finger pointed toward Jill's trunk. A bright laser-blue light streamed through the crack under the lid, and a sound like a swarm of buzzing insects grew more intense as they listened.

Syd covered his ears. "It sounds like, like a giant beehive or something. Every hair on my body's standing up."

Ken swore and chucked his cap at the trunk. He swore again. Then he yelled, "Maybe we should pry it open and try to turn off whatever's inside."

Syd grimaced. "You're nutso, man. You do whatever you want, but I'm outta here." He scrambled up the embankment and disappeared out of sight.

Ken was captivated by the mysterious light, mesmerized by the buzzing. He tiptoed toward the trunk. The sound abated slightly. He edged closer. His spine tingled, and his face grew warm.

His fears danced to the front of his brain. Then the happy experiences of his life flitted into view. The holographic images seemed so real that he reached out to touch them. They wiggled and wavered: memories of his past and world events.

He wondered if he was going batty. He tried to turn away. But his feet seemed to move of their own volition, inch by inch, toward the light. He vomited. Stuck one boot toe in the gravel to wipe it clean. *Man, I haven't felt this awful since I got drunk in Vegas.*

He moved closer. Closer. Now he was within arm's length. *Do I dare open the blasted thing?*

Determined not to surrender to nausea and dread, he picked up a heavy rock and smashed at the partially sheared-off hasp. Then he lifted the lid and peered inside. He froze, silent, awestruck by the inexplicable.

He was looking at … looking at … himself!

"Hello, Ken. Memory transfer complete. Do ya think Jill will like me? Excellent replication, I think."

"But how—"

"I'm the Wissen Labs SmartClone 250. I was Jill's boyfriend. Ya know, the one ya tried to kill. Now I'm *you*, her *new* boyfriend, Ken."

Ken dropped to his knees.

His look-alike laughed. "The small DNA sample from your nose was enough for me to reassemble in this form. Jill will never suspect. I'm just as human as you, only better. And I have emotions like you. I feel love, jealousy, pain, and passion." He rubbed at his nose. "Like the passion for revenge."

Old Ken stumbled backward as New Ken's fingertips discharged brilliant bolts of blue light. "Good-bye, Ken. I wish I could say it was nice to know ya."

Geist Investigations Inc.

Kathy Steinemann

You can kill the body but not the spirit. ~ Robert Louis Stevenson

I don't know which was wetter in that graveyard: the woman's tears or the pouring rain.

Lightning flashed between the dark clouds beyond the dripping tombstone, illuminating the marker's final reminder of a departed soul. The rapidly ensuing thunderclap exploded like a bomb in my ears.

As the woman pounded on the freshly laid sod, her form seemed to waver and flicker in the deluge. I wiped my eyes, hoping it would help me see her better. A persistent feeling that I'd met her before poked at my sensibilities. But her memory eluded me, just on the edge of my awareness.

I'm Gardi Gespenst, of Geist Investigations Inc. I'm a paranormal investigator. Some people call me a ghost hunter. I search for poltergeists, ghosts, ghouls, or whatever else you might want to call them.

I wracked my brain for a clue to her identity as I pressed forward and stood next to her. Long, dark hair clung to her face. A heart-shaped freckle nestled just below her left ear lobe. Bottomless eyes the color of the sapphire in my signet ring swam in limpid pools.

Ah yes, the woman behind the counter at the gas station. Gardi, you've done it again! But why didn't you recognize her straightaway?

I couldn't recall seeing an announcement anywhere. Keeping track of death notices and obits is part of my job, and I'd had a crush on the woman for as long as I could remember. I usually filled up with gas when I was only down a quarter of a tank. I had begun to hope she felt the same way about me. Sometimes I'm pretty dense, but I know when a woman's trying to flirt.

Strange. I can't remember her name.

I imagined her on a picnic blanket, reaching out to accept an engagement ring with a tiny diamond that sparkled in the afternoon sunlight.

Ah, the vagaries of life and death. Why didn't I tell her how I felt? I might have been able to save her.

The image of her on the picnic blanket returned.

Warbling birds in the trees. The fragrance of freshly mown grass intermingled with a sweet perfume wafting from her long neck. Gazing into her happy eyes as she accepted the marriage proposal.

Unease enveloped me. The lightning flashes and rumbling of thunder faded from my consciousness. Minutiae. Unimportant. My mind became a whirl of images and thoughts and memories, all leading to … her.

I realized that my imaginings were real.

Even though I knew it was impossible to make contact, I fixated on the woman and reached out to console her. Of course, my hand went right through her shoulder. It always does with ghosts.

Gardi, you silly dolt.

Then my attention strayed to the tombstone, and I recoiled.

Gardi Gespenst

1971 - 2015

Gone to Glory

The Dip and the Diamond

Kathy Steinemann

The accomplice is trained, the victim is targeted, and then the mark's wallet disappears. Our pickpocket has everything figured out.

Larry hung a freshly painted notice near a busy intersection:

CAUTION!
Thieves operate
in this area

He stepped back and admired his bright yellow-on-black handiwork: a perfect forgery of the official alerts the police department had posted in other parts of the city.

Every man who spotted the sign touched a pocket to make sure his wallet was secure. Once Larry knew where the wallet was, his scantily clad female accomplice went to work. The heads of most men whipped in her direction as she paraded by: tight mini-skirt, spike heels, low-cut blouse made from a semi-transparent fabric.

Ingrid would drop her purse, revealing her cleavage as she bent to retrieve it. Or she'd sidle up to the man and compliment him on his best feature. Sometimes she'd bat her mascara-heavy eyelashes and ask for directions to a nearby sports bar.

Ingrid's cool voice, hot body, and enticing perfume created the perfect diversion. When the victim wasn't paying attention, Larry dipped into the man's pocket, relieving him of his wallet. It always worked. Even priests fell for the ruse.

But that sultry afternoon in June took an unexpected turn.

A red-haired mark smirked when Ingrid approached him. He groped her, pulling her blouse off her shoulders. Then he pushed her against the wall. She struggled and tried to remove the pepper spray from her purse. Unsuccessfully. She pressed her lips into a firm line of determination and kneed him in the groin.

The redhead stumbled away, grinning.

Larry puzzled over the man's attitude. Was someone on to their scheme? He gazed at passersby. Some rushed down the street, massaging their phones with their thumbs. Others hurried to unknown destinations, jostling with their elbows to push through pedestrians. A blind man tapped by with his service dog.

Guess it wasn't a police sting.

He frowned and placed his hand on Ingrid's shoulder. "You okay?"

"Yeah. No big deal. I got rid of the creep before he could hurt me. You get his wallet?"

"No wallet, but I cleaned out his pockets. Let's knock off for today." He slipped her a fistful of bills. "Here."

Ingrid straightened her disheveled clothing, grabbed the cash, and slid it into her purse. "Pretty good afternoon, considering."

"Yeah, but we need to find another corner. That guy might be back. I'll text you later with a new location."

"Sure. Whatever. I gotta get home to my kid, anyway."

Larry watched her wiggle toward the bus stop, the clicking rhythm of her sexy stilettos fading into the din of traffic. He sighed and opened the plastic box he'd lifted from the redhead's pocket.

His pupils dilated.

The box contained a huge blue gem. *Looks like a diamond.*

His eyes closed while he dreamed of cruises, hot women, and a penthouse suite.

Could it be genuine? *If anyone can spot the real thing, it's Jakob.*

~*~

The pawn-shop door clattered shut behind Larry. The seedy joint was empty right now, but he could still smell the sweat from the last guy who had tried to weasel money for some trinket or other.

Jakob, well-known fence and fixer, raised his gaze from his computer tablet. "Whatcha got for me today? The crown jewels?"

Larry shrugged. "Maybe." He opened his fist to reveal the treasure in his palm.

Jakob took the gem in hand. He squinted with blue-grey eyes. They widened. He pushed his glasses higher on his nose, grabbed a monocular from under the counter, and held the sparkling object a hand's breadth from his face. "Where'd you get this?"

"You really wanna know?"

Jakob swore. "It's real."

"Then why do you look so mad?"

"You been watching the news?"

Larry snickered. "Me? News? I was watching a movie marathon last night. What's so important about the news?"

"This is the Glasklar Diamond. It was stolen from the Kristall Collection last night. I can't fence this."

"Why not? It looks like it's worth a heap of dough."

"It is. That's part of the problem. But it's too well-known. And it's also cursed."

Larry snorted a laugh of derision. "Oooooooh. Jakob believes in ghosts and magic and weird things that go bump in the night." A burst of wind pushed the door open for a heartbeat. Larry flinched. "You need to get that fixed. Might let in some scary monsters."

Jakob ignored the sarcasm. "The legend says that if this gem is stolen, the thief will be punished with a fate worse than death."

"Oooooooh. Now I'm cursed and my teeth are gonna fall on the floor before I drop dead with a heart attack."

"I said a fate worse than death."

Larry huffed. "Like a lifetime with my ex-wife?"

Jakob continued to study the gem, nostrils flared, fingers twitching. "If I believed every crappy rumor about cursed jewels, I'd be poor and on the street."

Larry cocked his head. "Yeah. And you could have invented the whole thing just to knock down what you're gonna pay me. What does the legend say about getting rid of the curse?"

"If the thief returns the diamond to its owner, or another person willingly takes it from him before the sun sets, he'll be spared." Jakob pursed his lips. "This was stolen during the night and the sun is about to …"

Larry's ears couldn't process whatever Jakob said next. A wave of nausea consumed him. He squeezed his eyes shut and hugged his stomach.

Unfamiliar voices floated toward him: pleading murmurs uttering prayers of repentance.

The nausea passed, only to be replaced with an icy pain that radiated to pore and bone. Glassy planes of brilliance reflected giant blue-grey eyes peering at him from every direction.

Jakob's voice boomed, reverberated, amplified. "Larry? Larry, where are you?"

Larry peered out from his faceted prison of glittering blue inside the diamond. He screamed. His scream boomed, reverberated, amplified. It mingled with the melody of despair from the other thieves who had dared to covet the jewel.

~*~

Jakob continued to stare at the gem. He had waited a lifetime for something like this: unequalled clarity and color, like a faceted planet filled with countless universes waiting to be explored and conquered. His eyes closed while he dreamed of cruises, hot women, and a penthouse suite.

He gazed around the shop, muttering as he wondered what had happened to Larry. He shrugged. "Guess I must have lost track of time while I was looking at this."

He stowed the diamond in his safe. "Finders keepers."

Martian

Kathy Steinemann

Have you ever met a Martian? Would you realize if you had?

Willie drained his last mouthful of beer. "I tell you, I saw it with my own two eyes. It was a Martian. I swear. A real, honest-to-goodness, red-haired, red-skinned Martian with red peepers and two antennas. Antennae. Whatever." He banged his glass onto the bar and burped. "Gimme another one."

Bob smirked. "C'mon. You've had too much to drink. Everyone knows Martians have glowing peepers, green skin, and three antennas." He refilled Willie's beer glass and dried his hands on his apron.

Willie stared at the grinning jack-o'-lantern perched at the end of the bar. "First beer I've had all day. You know me. I can hold my liquor. Takes a lot more than one to get me drunk. It was a Martian. They're gonna infiltrate us and take over the world."

Bob flicked a fly off the peanuts. "And where did you meet this so-called Martian?"

"I was lookin' up at the new billboard on Twenty-Fifth Street. The one with the chick advertising that new perfume they got on all the commercials. You know, the brunette with the low-cut leopard skin dress? Then I heard this clickin', and the next thing I know, this guy's standin' next to me. Only it wasn't a guy. It was a Martian. A real one. From outer space."

"Right. And I have an oil well I can sell you. Cheap."

"I'm not kiddin'. He knew all about Mars and said the women on his planet have three boobs."

A snicker was Bob's response.

Willie continued, seemingly unaware of the bartender's reaction. "I asked him why he was on Earth. He said because of the view. When I jabbed him in the ribs, he swore he was a 100 percent Martian with a passport and a spaceship just around the corner, and he sounded funny, like he was under water or somethin'."

Bob slapped the counter and laughed, tears at the corners of his eyes. "You mean like the guy sneaking up behind you?"

Willie turned.

A Martian tiptoed toward him, snapping its fingers as it crept forward. Its hand reached up to peel off a rubbery mask pockmarked with acne-like bumps. "Trick or treat. You ready for the costume party? I really had you goin', didn't I?"

Ralph. It was only Ralph, burbling through a straw.

Willie smacked Ralph on the shoulder. "I forgot all about the stupid party. Hey, Bob, s'ppose I could buy one of those tablecloths off you? I wanna make a ghost costume."

"Sure. Take the one from the corner table over there. No charge. It has a few cigarette burns in it. Here's a pair of scissors."

Willie grabbed the scissors and worked a little magic, cutting holes for eyes and mouth. "What about you, Bob? You got a costume for tonight?"

"As a matter of fact, I do. Walmart had a big sale."

Willie chuckled. "Heh heh. Don't eat too much candy."

Ghost and Martian staggered out of the bar, Willie tripping over the edge of the tablecloth several times as he leaned on Ralph's shoulder.

Bob turned to the barmaid. "Slow night. I've worked late all week. Think you can manage by yourself? I got a party to crash."

"Sure. Happy Halloween."

He headed toward the storeroom. "Happy Halloween."

His face contorted into a grimace. *Red-haired, red-skinned, two antennas. What was Willie thinking?*

He removed the blue contact lenses from his purple eyes and detached the hairpiece that held down his single antenna.

Perfect.

No Execution, No Payment

Kathy Steinemann

The affairs of this world are so shifting and depend on so many accidents, that it is hard to form any judgment concerning the future; nay, we see from experience that the forecasts even of the wise almost always turn out false. ~ Francesco Guicciardini

Gillian Wilkins stumbled over a rock as she exited her car. She covered her head to protect it while she fell. The gravel crunched beneath her back, grinding into her shoulder blades.

She moaned. Something sniffed at her nose, whined, and pawed at her shoulder. She blinked.

The stench of burning rubber, steam, and antifreeze overpowered the odor of dog. She brushed at the tiny Yorkie peering into her face. "Hello, puppy. Where did you come from?"

The dog barked.

Gillian pulled her cell phone out of her pocket. *There should be enough juice to make at least one call.* She stood and keyed in her boyfriend's number. "Freddie, my radiator blew, and I need you to come get me."

"Where are you?"

"I'm not sure. I was following my GPS on a new route to the lake. I'll have to walk a bit and see if I can find a landmark or a sign." The screen blanked. "Dammit. A fight with Freddie. A broken-down car. No cell phone. Can anything else go wrong today?"

The Yorkie stood on his hind feet and whimpered. Then he danced a lively little jig, with paws held high and stumpy tail wagging.

"Hey, puppy. That's a pretty good trick." Gillian grabbed a crooked stick and threw it. The Yorkie fetched the stick and dropped it at her feet. She tossed it a few more times. When he seemed to have had enough, she laughed and put it in her jacket pocket. "We'll play some more later."

She scrutinized the damage. "Just like me to get lost and stuck in the middle of nowhere. I suppose I should've paid attention to the check-engine light."

A movement in the bushes flickered in her peripheral vision. A black tom-cat stopped to spray a stump, skulked toward her and the dog, then laid his ears flat and hissed. The Yorkie sat and extended one foot. The cat stopped short. Both animals went into stare-down mode.

After a few seconds, the Yorkie surrendered, lay on his belly, whimpered, and covered his nose with both front paws. The cat pranced with his tail in the air and rubbed his cheek against Gillian's ankle as he purred.

"Well, now that you two are sort of friends, I have to find some help." She felt her head. "Guess I was lucky to get by with just a little bump."

She leaned against a tree. Something glinted in the late-morning sun. She stepped closer and picked it up. "I'm no bomb expert, but this certainly looks like a detonator I saw on a TV cop show. ... Nah. Can't be."

She stuffed it into her other pocket.

~*~

Freddie Ferguson cursed. Three attempts to contact Gillian had gone to voice mail. "That senile old man. He screwed everything up." He jabbed at the screen on his cell phone as he headed toward his car.

~*~

244

Harold Niesen responded to his *Wedding March* ringtone when Freddie's call ID showed on his screen. "Phase one completed."

"Negative. She just called me."

Harold adjusted his hearing aid. "What?"

"You heard. No execution, no payment. You screwed everything up." The line went dead.

Harold kicked up a cloud of dirt and paced beside his car. He got behind the steering wheel and turned the key in the ignition. Click-click-click-click-click

"Crap-crap-crap-crap-crap!"

~*~

Old Norm Ritter called from the front porch. "Yokie. Here, Yokie. Here, boy. Here, boy." He whistled. "Darn dog. Where's he off to now?"

Sadie Ledige called out over the fence. "Devil's taken off again too. They're prob'ly out and about playing their silly little power games. Shall we go look for them?"

Norm slipped into his shoes and mumbled under his breath. "I know what that ol' spinster's up to. Whenever she lets Devil out, supposedly by accident, Yokie chases after him, and we have to go look for them. Horny ol' broad's been trying to jump my bones for months." He turned sideways to hide his grin.

He usually led the way, but today he let Sadie take point while he ogled her derriere and continued his quiet muttering. "Nice caboose for an ol' broad. Dagnabbit, little Norm, control yourself. Down boy." He lagged behind by several steps.

Sadie stopped and looked back. Her glance darted for a microsecond to his jeans zipper. The dark valleys in her hastily applied lipstick disappeared as she smiled and blushed even deeper than the ample rouge on her cheeks. The amusement and twinkle in her eyes grew. She pirouetted to her previous position and slowed her pace. "There's a blue car up ahead. Maybe the driver's seen them."

Norm's gaze stayed riveted to her backside. As much as he didn't want to admit it, he enjoyed their little chats and jaunts in the country. He'd even considered asking the big question. After so many years, he was lonely, and having her in his bed would be better than fantasizing.

~*~

Gillian walked along the edge of the road, hoping a kind motorist would happen by and offer her a ride. The Yorkie and black cat followed as though they had known her forever. "You two should go home. But if you want to come with me, I don't mind. I enjoy the company. I just had to get out of the house this morning. Boyfriend troubles, you know? ... I guess you wouldn't."

She sighed and continued her one-sided conversation. "Freddie and I have been together for five years, and he *still* hasn't proposed. I keep on hinting, but he doesn't bite. Guess if I want him to marry me, I'll have to do the asking."

She stopped midstep. "Maybe I should think twice about that, though. We had a huge fight this morning. I could almost swear he started it on purpose."

A blue vehicle became visible as she neared the crest of a hill. The driver kicked the left-front tire. "That man looks like he's having a bad day. Wonder if he's got car trouble too."

When she reached Harold, suspicion scraped at her sensibilities like fingernails on a blackboard. Internet reports of scams to attract women and then rob or rape them forced their way to the front of her mind. After her initial hesitation, she decided she was being paranoid. An old guy with a hearing aid was probably harmless. "Hi. Car troubles?"

He sneezed. "Yeah. Probably the battery. Or maybe the starter. Never was very good with vehicles. Could you keep them critters away? I'm allergic. I sneeze at the sight of 'em."

She shrugged. "I'm unlucky with cars too. Mine's kaput. I don't usually travel in the boonies, but I had a fight with my boyfriend and took a drive in the country to cool off. Big mistake. Do you have a cell phone? My battery's dead." *Shoot. I've got to stop running off at the mouth when I'm nervous.*

"Pardon?" He adjusted his hearing aid.

"DO YOU HAVE A CELL PHONE?"

"No need to yell, Miss Wilkins." He fumbled in his pocket and took out his phone. Pressed a few buttons. "Just need to clear some stuff. ... There. All done." Harold passed it to her.

Her fingers shook. *He knows my name.* She retreated several paces and called Freddie again. "Can you come get me? My car's toast. I'm at ... uh ... just a sec." She asked Harold for their location.

He gave directions while she relayed them to Freddie. After she disconnected the call, she returned Harold's phone with outstretched arm, not getting any closer than necessary.

"Thank you, Mr. ..."

"Niesen. The name's Harold Niesen."

Behind her she heard feet scraping over rocks, accompanied by raspy breathing. She turned.

The old man coming out of the woods looked at Mr. Niesen. Recognition sparked in his eyes. His curt nod was followed by a businesslike greeting: "Harry."

Niesen responded, "Norm. Sadie."

Gillian's heart raced. She hid her shaking hands behind her back to keep everyone from seeing them. *Norm, whoever he is, knows Niesen. And the woman. She looks like she has something going with Norm. What the heck are these people up to?*

She scrutinized everyone.

Norm: He could be anyone under all that hair. Shaggy beard with streaks of grey. How many scars could that bush be hiding?

The woman: Could be Bonnie from Bonnie and Clyde for all Gillian knew. Except Bonnie was dead.

And Harry: Looked like a bumbling fool with those bent glasses and mismatched socks, but there was more to him than that. She was sure of it. These people might be old, but they could be dangerous.

In the few seconds she had taken to make her appraisal, Norm and the woman picked up the dog and cat. Both animals seemed happy to be reunited with their owners, and Harry was ecstatic that the furry, sneeze-inciting bundles were nowhere near him.

Norm coughed. "Miss, would you mind holding onto Yokie for me? I'd like to jaw with Harry in private. If that's okay with you, Sadie?"

Sadie shrugged.

Gillian extended her arms and pulled Yokie close. He licked her nose. Norm and Harry shuffled toward a clump of dense bush. Sadie's stare followed Norm. Gillian tried to eavesdrop on the men as Sadie chatted away like an excited magpie, but all she caught were occasional snatches of their conversation from behind the wall of leaves and branches.

"… Had to do something. Ran out of money."

"You're too old for this."

"Can't pull out now. Rep's on the line. …"

The wind whipped up dust from the edge of the road, and its howl masked the rest of their discussion.

Gillian's focus shifted. She bounced Yokie as though he were a baby needing a burp while she felt for the crooked stick in her pocket. *It's shaped kinda like a gun. If I had to, I could try to bluff my way out of here.*

Norm and Harry returned from behind the bushes as Freddie's car appeared over a hilltop. It rocketed down the road, spewing up gravel and grit, and skidded to a stop. The driver's door flew open. Freddie stomped toward the two men. Then he glowered at Harry. "You screwed it up."

Gillian threw Yokie into Harry's face and grabbed Sadie. "Nobody move, or she pays the price. I have a gun."

Harry sneezed and fell against his car. He rubbed at his eyes. Norm and Freddie raised their hands, and so did Sadie.

Freddie paled. "G-Gillian. Sweetheart. Wh-what's gotten into you?"

She glared. "I know all about your plan. I found the detonator." She tossed it at his feet.

His eyes widened. "Detonator?"

"Yeah. Detonator."

"It's not— I hired—"

"Yeah. You hired Harry. The hitman. I know."

Freddy smiled. "Honey, you got Harry pegged all wrong. His company is Passionate Proposals. Tell her, Harry."

Harry grimaced. "Can I put my hands down?"

Gillian shook her head. "No. You explain everything, or I shoot Sadie."

"Freddie hired me. I set an activator, not a detonator, to hack your GPS. It was supposed to lead you to a park on the east side of the lake."

Beads of sweat formed on his brow. "I was gonna dress up like a clown and deliver flowers and balloons. Look in the rear seat of my car and see for yourself. Then Freddie was gonna pop out of the bushes, propose, and take you away to a romantic bed and breakfast for the night."

Gillian released her hold on Sadie. She peered into Harry's car and then gazed at Freddie's loveable cowlick and apologetic expression. Her nausea abated, the familiar tenderness for his goofy antics resurfaced, and tears of relief flooded her face. "You were going to propose?"

Freddie grinned. "You drove away in such a snit this morning I couldn't keep up with you. I went to where you were supposed to be, but you weren't there." He knelt in the gravel at her feet and popped open a ring box. "Gillian Wilkins, will you marry me and put up with all my future pranks and schemes?"

She pursed her lips and glowered at him while she made her best attempt to look angry. "I swear, Freddie, if you ever do anything like this again, I'll …" She tousled his hair. "It'd serve you right if I said no. But I love you. Yes, you goofy nut. I'll marry you." She pulled him up and kissed him. "Let's get out of here."

As they left, she heard Norm whisper to Harry, "Hey, I've got a job for you."

Tropical Daydream

Kathy Steinemann

Are you a careful driver? Do you exercise the same vigilance in the water?

Kara waded into the waves, mesmerized by the sun reflecting off the ocean. She floated on her back and drifted past rope-connected buoys.

Her earplugs shut out the world, and her closed eyes intensified the isolation. She enjoyed this feeling of solitude, this oneness with the universe.

Ahhhh. The rocking lulled her to sleep.

"Ma'am?"

Kara fought her way back from unconsciousness. She ached. Everywhere. A handsome stranger cradled her bruised body. "Ma'am? My boat hit you. Why were you swimming past the buoys?"

She gazed at his face, mesmerized by the ocean reflected in his eyes. She murmured, "Fate?"

Suppose
Kathy Steinemann

Suppose your life were in jeopardy. What would you decide?

"Remove your sandals, Initiate, and kneel before me."

"Yes, Master."

"Suppose, my son, that you could alter the fate of many with a single word. However in doing so, you would cease to exist. Would you say it?"

"I know not, Master. It would depend on the circumstances."

"You would save lives."

"How many lives would I save?"

"Is the number important?"

"Yes, Master. If I could save a million lives, I would gladly surrender my own existence."

"Suppose you could save a thousand lives. Would you still say the word?"

"Yes, I would."

"Would you do so for a hundred lives?"

"If they were good people."

"And if they were evil?"

"Perhaps the world would be a better place without the evil people. Perhaps I would let them die and preserve my own life."

"You consider yourself good?"

"Yes, Master. I treat others with respect. I do not curse. I pray. I give to the poor. I help the elderly and infirm."

"Yet you would permit a hundred people to perish in order to save your own life. Does that not make you evil?"

"No!"

"Is it not evil to knowingly allow the deaths of others?"

"Yes, Master. But I am confused."

"Why? You know the Seventh Tenet: Thou shalt not allow the unlawful killing of the innocent."

"I would not be killing the innocent. I would be saving my life, a good life. I would be protecting the world from the evil those people would commit."

"But who is to say those people are truly evil? Who has the wisdom or the right to judge them? And if they are evil, do you not suppose they could change their lives and become good?"

"Yes, Master."

"Then you are evil for condemning them to death."

"No ... I ... Yes, wise Master."

"Now is the time, my son. You must choose. You have admitted that you are evil. What must you do?"

"I must say the word."

"Then you must turn your back to me. Your inner spirit will reveal the word. You must say it. You must willingly submit to your fate."

"Yes, Master. I see the arrows of the archers pointed at my evil heart. I bow my head in sorrow, but I obey. ... Fire!"

"The archers will not launch their arrows, Initiate. You have proved your worthiness. Your heart is pure. You may now enter into the Hallowed Hall of the Acolytes."

The Lamb

Kathy Steinemann

Since the beginning of time, children have struggled to understand adult rules. And sometimes they contrive ways to evade them.

Miriam skittered down the cliff. "Don't be scared, Abel. I'll rescue you!" Her favorite lamb wriggled and thrashed in a myrtle bush. His plaintive bleating echoed from the opposite shore of the great lake.

Miriam clambered, scraped her fingers, and spilled into the bush. Abel's nose flicked a leaf from her face. She cuddled him while she caught her breath, and her thoughts wandered like a dream in the daytime with bright colors and moving pictures.

Abel's pregnant mother bleated in pain, wedged between two trees. Miriam pushed the ewe free and helped her give birth to her first lamb: white and without blemish. She felt an immediate fondness for him that she had never felt for any farm animal, and she named him Abel.

Abel wiggled.

"Keep still. I'll get you out." She slung him around her shoulders and clawed up the cliff. He followed her home. Sometimes he ran ahead, bouncing into the air, throwing up tiny puffs of dust. Miriam giggled.

~*~

Mama's face turned red. Then, she sobbed. "I was so worried about you. Why did you take the lamb out of the fold? Put him back before your father finds out. This lamb is the firstborn, and he belongs to God."

"But I love Abel."

"What am I going to do with you, child? You are eight summers old now: old enough to know better." Mama pointed. "Go."

"Yes, Mama." Miriam plodded to the sheepfold and watched Abel as he frolicked. *It's not fair. I won't let them sacrifice him.*

Papa sent her to bed early. She fidgeted and fussed, trying not to wake her older sister Martha, until she finally fell asleep.

A dusty, hot trip to the temple in the faraway city. The death twitches of doves, lambs, goats, and calves. The nauseating stench of blood and smoke.

She woke. And wept.

An eternity passed before the house was finally whispering with the sounds of sleep.

Miriam crept to the fold. She led Abel far away, and bound three of his legs together. She seized a huge stone. Hesitated … bit her lip. Then, with all her strength, she smashed the stone down onto his free leg. He made a horrible noise that sounded like a scream as he struggled to break free.

Tears formed channels down her cheeks. She crouched beside the mewling bundle of wool and tried to pet him, but he shrank from her touch. She bowed her head. "I'm sorry, Abel. So, so sorry. I'm sorry, God."

She ripped a piece off the hem of her mantle to make a bandage for his injured leg, and carried him back to the fold, where she slept beside him all night.

~*~

Papa found them at dawn. He yelled and shook his finger. "What did you do? Now he's useless. We'll have to substitute another one." He grabbed a knife. "Young lamb makes good stew."

Miriam shrieked. "No. I'll take care of him and shear him and feed him and everything. Please don't kill him."

That horrible look on Papa's face was something she would remember forever. His expression was so stern. But then, it softened. She would always remember that, too. "As punishment, you have to do double your chores for an entire year. He's your responsibility now."

She stared at her toes while she attempted to hide the tears in her eyes and the happiness tugging at the corners of her mouth. "Yes, Papa."

~*~

Abel's leg mended, but he hobbled with a pronounced limp. Miriam was sad for his pain, for his lameness, for her guilt. *But he's alive.* Every night, exhausted after her chores, she apologized to God and prayed for Abel's pain to go away. After her prayers, she fell asleep within seconds.

One morning while she was working in the barley field, she saw a boy walking toward her. He smiled. Miriam stared, captivated by his presence. The sun shone behind him as he neared, transforming him into a silhouette surrounded by a halo of light.

Her eyes protested against the brilliance, and she squeezed them shut. When she reopened them, he was standing directly in front of her. He touched her shoulder. "You don't understand, do you, Miriam?"

She shook her head.

"Someday you will. It's not time yet." He stroked Abel. "You love your lamb, don't you?"

"Yes. But I had to hurt him to save him."

"Sometimes pain and suffering are necessary."

She blinked—and he was gone. *I must have imagined him.*

But no, there was the path through the barley.

A tingly feeling crept from her neck to her toes.

~*~

Miriam was pensive during supper, and at bedtime, sleep eluded her. *I'll go to the fold and stay with Abel.*

A deep slumber soothed her tired, aching body.

The boy walked toward her in the barley field. He pressed his palm to her forehead. His smile filled her with awe, with love. "I am the Lamb of God. Your lamb will be made whole. All you have to do is believe in me."

She felt strange—light and energized. She reached her hand to touch his sleeve. "I believe."

~*~

Miriam stretched in the damp chill of morning. Abel stood and pranced a few confident steps. "Abel! Your leg is better. But you're not white anymore, and you have spots."

She beamed.

I wonder if I'll ever see the boy again.

Serial Slayer

Kathy Steinemann

A serial killer has already murdered four civilians and a cop.
Always with a .45. Always during a snowstorm. Looks like the
Iceman is at it again.

Two blood-soaked bodies slumped in the front seat of a car, their faces frozen in terror. A bullet hole peered from the center of each forehead, like a crimson eye socket. Two corpses: no longer men, but grotesque monsters with black pockmarks and singed hair.

The car's motor still idled, its wheels stuck in the deep snow on the shoulder. A downed power line snaked across the road a short distance away, its end buried in the snow.

State Trooper Della Redmond cursed. *Guess I gotta stop.* Her fingers gripped the steering wheel in a white-knuckled embrace. *I can't ignore a front seat full of DBs.* An involuntary shudder sent heat to her ears and neck, even though the rolled-down window had cooled the air to below freezing. A fist of fear seized her stomach in its frosty grip.

The Iceman had already murdered four civilians and a cop. Always with a .45, close-range, between the eyes. Always with cigarette burns and blackened hair. Always during a snowstorm.

She radioed for help and cursed again. *It's gonna be dark soon.* She scrutinized the power line. *Better be careful. Wouldn't want to step on the danged thing.*

Rather than chance driving forward and getting stuck, she put the squad car in reverse for a few feet. Then she angled it so the headlights illuminated the lifeless vehicle. This left the driver's door tight against a snowbank.

Deep into that darkness peering, long I stood there, wondering, fearing, doubting, dreaming dreams no mortal ever dared to dream before. The Poe quote slithered into Redmond's thoughts. A flush of adrenaline bathed her in sweat.

She clambered over a pile of library books, squeezed out the passenger door, and waded through the snow, snapping photos with her cell phone as she neared the victims. Her ears burned. Ice crystals frosted her eyebrows.

Click. Click. Click. [CLICK]

Redmond knew the click of her camera. She also knew the click of a cocking .45. She dropped into the deep snow and drew her SIG. She waited, quivering and nauseated. None of the Iceman's victims had ever lived long enough to identify him. Would she be another one of his playthings, tortured and discarded like a dead mouse?

Her mind raced as she struggled to formulate a plan. She was alone. How long would it take for backup to arrive? How long could she stay out of—

A voice whispered from somewhere nearby. "Nothing's as dangerous as resting when you're walking in the snow. You doze off and die in your sleep."

Redmond recognized the Wittgenstein quote. And something about the voice seemed vaguely familiar. A moment seemed like hours as she tried to figure out where she'd heard the man before.

She twisted toward him and replied, "We build statues out of snow and weep to see them melt."

Footsteps crunched closer. "Hmph. A Walter Scott lover. A scared little, namby-pamby, *girl-cop* Walter Scott lover. You think you're going to melt me with your heater, cop? I see your tracks, but you can't see me."

The voice edged even closer as it mouthed another quote. "Those who cannot understand how to put their thoughts on ice should not enter into the heat of debate."

Redmond heard an intense buzzing sound. Saw a dazzling flash of light. Smelled the nauseating reek of electrocuted flesh. *The power line?*

She shivered while she waited and listened.

Silence. Cold. Darkness.

When she heard the whine of approaching sirens, she stood and shone her flashlight at the heap in the snow. *So the Iceman is the town librarian. Wonder if he was murdering book borrowers with overdue fines.*

She lowered her SIG. "Paradise was made for tender hearts; hell, for loveless Icemen. Voltaire and Redmond, 2015."

She cursed.

Reward or Punishment?

Kathy Steinemann

If people are good only because they fear punishment and hope for reward, then we are a sorry lot indeed. ~ Albert Einstein

Through the window of his cubicle, Elmer Franks stared at a dizzying array of planets and stars. He massaged between his eyebrows and cursed as he tried to remember how he got here. The last thing he could recall was brushing his teeth and ignoring Maisie's badgering. What was it this time? Throwing his dirty socks on the floor? Leaving the toilet seat up? Forgetting her birthday?

Why was he still with her? She cheated on him. She was a lousy cook. She always had a "headache". He could so much better. There was Lorelei and—

A voice croaked from somewhere nearby. He pivoted, scrutinized the ceiling, and peered at the wall. Where was it coming from?

His head.

It was in his head.

"Prepare for the competition." The words burbled, understandable but alien, like a goldfish speaking through bubbles.

Elmer's perplexed eyes darted in every direction. "Competition?"

"You have been selected as a contestant for the 'Filial Feud Reality Show'. Bow to the audience, please."

He didn't see any cameras, and he seemed to be alone. "Who are you? What's happening to me?"

Everything blackened. Elmer blinked.

Suddenly he stood in a round room with dozens of barely discernable video panels. Beyond, darkness loomed. He sensed the eyes of a multitude. His brain buzzed and hummed as though millions of mites were invading his mind.

On his left and right were two other people. He adjusted to the gloom. No, they weren't people. One was tall with white fur. Muscular. An albino gorilla? But it stood too upright to be a gorilla. The other was pale and handsome. When the pale man snarled, Elmer could see fangs. No. Surely it couldn't be a vampire! They didn't exist.

Elmer forced his hands into fists. Opened them again. Pinched his arm. Was he dreaming?

He sensed laughs from all directions, echoing and cascading like a waterfall. Millions of them. Or maybe billions. Perhaps trillions? He shook his head, but the laughs persisted.

The bubbly voice spoke again. *"This is not a battle to the death. It is purely a test of intellect. The winner will have a choice of two prizes, one valuable beyond measure. The losers will be returned to their former state, minus any recollection of these events. Three contestants: human, yeti, and vampire. Are you ready to play? Are you ready to abide by the rules of the game?"*

The vampire and yeti nodded.

Elmer inhaled a deep breath. *A valuable prize, or a return to my miserable life with trampy Masie and no memory of right now?* He had nothing to lose and maybe a lot to gain.

He nodded as well.

The static in his brain stirred: trillions of beings in uncomfortable, cramped quarters. They yearned for entertainment, for open space.

Their yearning grew silent. The room grew silent. He could hear the worried breaths of the other contestants.

The room flooded with blinding light, and the vampire shrieked. The smell of smoke and burnt flesh filled the air as he shriveled to a pile of ash.

The burbler mused. *"How unfortunate. It would appear that these Earth species are not as robust as we had calculated. However, with only two contestants remaining, the chances of winning have increased by 16.66666667 percent for each of you."*

Trillions of cheers and claps reverberated through Elmer's brain.

His tormenter continued. *"Now human and yeti will compete in a simple race. We will place you on a world that we have chosen. It is not dissimilar to many regions of Earth. You must wait for the signal. Then follow the path to the finish line. The first one to cross will be given a riddle.*

"However, there is as they say on Earth, a catch. The path takes many forks. If you finish first, AND if you solve the riddle presented to you within sixty seconds of Earth time, you will be free to choose your prize. If not, you will be forced to face another contestant."

Fuzziness. Blackness.

Human and yeti found themselves on a strange world with an orange sky and three moons. Several red, rocky spires in the distance towered over a desert-like terrain. Craters pockmarked the rest of the sandy landscape. Before them lay a gravelly path with two forks. A tall thicket of thorny vegetation with crimson leaves obscured the lateral view.

Shimmering force bubbles separated Elmer and the yeti. It took but a tick for him to realize that the temperature was too high to be comfortable. He guessed it was well over one hundred degrees Fahrenheit.

He speculated. Soldiers on Earth marched left-right, left-right. He'd start with the left fork. Without waiting to see what the yeti would do, he raced forward, his force bubble keeping pace.

Within minutes, his lips blistered from the heat. *Water. I need water.* His bubble rained moisture. He stopped and funneled the liquid into his throat with his tongue. On a hunch, he concentrated. *Too hot. Cool to seventy degrees.* The air temperature dropped. Elmer chuckled. *Fast. Go fast.*

He ran.

Fast.

When he reached the next fork, he stopped to recover his breath. He peered from left to right and scanned behind him. There lay the yeti, collapsed on a pile of rocks several yards away.

He ran toward the finish line. Then stopped. Turned.

Elmer couldn't let the yeti die. No prize was worth murder. No prize could quell the guilt he'd feel for ignoring the plight of a being with self-awareness, a being who would suffer as it fried in this horrible heat.

He dashed toward his rival. The creature was still breathing. He moved as close as he could, and the bubbles merged.

He felt the yeti's face. He didn't know beans about yetis, but he was sure this one was too hot. He concentrated. *Cool to sixty degrees. Water.* Satisfied with the results, Elmer squatted and waited.

The yeti's eyes flickered open. Fluttered closed. "Thank you. I figured I was going to end up like the vampire." The voice was feminine. Not an annoying squawk like Maisie's, but a throaty, dulcet tone that reminded Elmer of his high-school sweetheart, Lorelei.

He fell back on his haunches. "You're a female? And you speak English? The aliens must have done something to your brain." He sensed trillions of corroborating cheers.

"My name is Arnaaluk. I come from high in the mountains where it's usually below freezing. I wouldn't have lasted much longer in the heat." She gulped. The fur on her face grew wet with tears. "I owe you my life. I can't think of the right words to thank you."

"Let's do this together. Then we can split the prize. If they'll let us."

The burbler deliberated. *"No one has ever ... I suppose ... I must consult with the competition judges and I— Yes, you may."*

Elmer and Arnaaluk strolled forward. Why rush? There was no need. ...

They reached the finish line. There, on a rock, rested a scroll wrapped in a red ribbon.

Elmer glanced up at Arnaaluk. "Shall we open it together?"

She twisted her features into a grotesque smile.

He read the riddle out loud. "What can be shared over and over again, and once used, never dies. It is more timeless than time. It comes from the soul and speaks without sound. But once it speaks, it can never be silenced. You have sixty seconds to answer the question correctly."

He shouted into the air. "This is unfair. She would never guess the answer."

The fishy voice sounded upset. *"You both agreed to abide by the rules. Every contest is weighted in someone's favor. This is a game show, not reality."*

Elmer protested, "Then why do you call it the *Filial Feud Reality Show*?"

Protracted silence. Trillions of conflicting brainwaves. Disapproval.

Elmer smiled while he waited for the audience to settle. He whispered in Arnaaluk's ear. Then they shouted in unison. "A story. That's the answer."

The alien tut-tutted a disapproving croak.

Stillness. Trillions of approving votes. Another croak. *"The judges and audience have indicated that you are both to be declared winners. However, you must pick and share the same prize."*

Elmer's attention focused on a hologram that appeared before them: two red curtains, each flanked by a fish-like creature with green hair, silver scales, and full lips.

The burbler announced, *"The curtain on the left will return you to your previous life with a guarantee of excellent health for your entire lifespan, and you will have no remembrance of this game. The curtain on the right will transport you to a wondrous place of relaxation with all your needs provided. There, the two of you may share thousands of Earth years. Any one of our citizens would relinquish everything to go to this place."*

Elmer contemplated his unfaithful girlfriend, his monotonous job, and his financial obligations. The yeti was ugly by human standards, but she had a pleasant personality. He conferred with Arnaaluk. Their agreement was immediate. "The curtain on the right."

Blackness. Iridescent swirls. Nausea.

Elmer and Arnaaluk found themselves on a large, desolate asteroid encased within a shimmering force bubble. Their living quarters were well-stocked with food, first-aid supplies, and instruction manuals in poorly translated English for alien equipment with unknown functions.

Human and yeti were the sole occupants.

~*~

Years later, when the first supply ship arrived to restock provisions, Elmer and Arnaaluk learned that the alien race lived on an overpopulated water planet. Squeezed together like sardines, their greatest desire was solitude.

266

The aliens couldn't understand why Elmer and Arnaaluk had wanted to be together.

Vito's Incarceration

Kathy Steinemann

Does the punishment fit the crime?

A cold draft assaulted Vito. The distortion of time made it impossible for him to know how long it had been since he last saw Carmen. Darkness was constant, day and night. Dim shadows and shapes lurked, never revealing their true forms in the murky dampness.

He rattled the bars and tried to breach the door; searched for weaknesses in the cell.

Cold metal blocked every attempt.

Vito hung his head and closed his eyes. He groaned, beset by a chill that shivered through his frail body, a chill as inescapable as this dank dungeon.

Conditions had been good before the transfer. The meals were regular, and Carmen escorted him out of the cell every night for exercise. He enjoyed the interactions with his jailer. Over the months, they developed a rapport. In fact, Vito fell in love with her. Who could resist her soothing voice? Her soft fingers? Her sweet smell? But for some inexplicable reason, she had transferred him to this cement-encased expanse somewhere in the bowels of the earth.

A distant noise. Carmen? It had to be her! He shrieked until his voice grew hoarse. However, after several unsuccessful minutes of desperation, exhausted by his efforts, he slept.

Nearby sounds startled Vito awake. But an eternity passed before Carmen approached and light flooded his surroundings. He called out a cheerful greeting.

She ignored him, her back turned, as she rustled about in a distant corner. The sound of running water and the scent of fresh food tormented his empty stomach.

He ran through his entire vocabulary of English.

Still no response.

Food and water appeared through the slots in his cell.

He yowled. Carmen scowled at him.

Ah, finally some attention! She unlocked his prison and patted him on the head. "That's enough. You be quiet, Vito." The door clanged shut.

He tried every trick he knew and reached through the bars in a plea for mercy.

Carmen flipped the light switch off, and the basement became bleak once more. Her heavy footsteps faded as she climbed the stairs.

The umbrella cockatoo uttered a sad gurgle.

And he plucked another bloody feather from his almost-bare chest.

~*~

Although this piece is fiction, the situation is not. Millions of birds like Vito need care or rescue after their novelty wears off. Many caregivers don't realize how intelligent birds are, and have no idea of their emotional needs. Please support your local bird sanctuary.

Somnus Interruptus

Kathy Steinemann

A use has been found for everything but snoring. ~ Mark Twain

"You were snoring again," Josie mumbled. "Roll over. I need my sleep. Bobby has Tiny-Tots soccer at seven."

"I was not snoring." Vern pulled the covers up to his chin.

"Yes, you were." *I don't know if I can survive another night like this. Why won't he see the doctor?*

Josie's restless dreams teemed with grinding gears, rumbling freight trains, and snarling tigers.

Early in the morning, long before dawn had touched the sky, Bobby climbed into their bed. "Mommy, I'm scared. Could I please sleep with you? My room is too quiet, and Daddy's growling keeps the monsters away."

Tech Support

Kathy Steinemann

When was the last time you called tech support? Did you wait forever on hold? Suppose it sounded something like this.

"Press one for support—" BEEP

"Stupid menus. Where the heck are the people?" …

"Good afternoon. This is Larry. How may I help you?"

"I didn't call the dairy."

"LARRY, ma'am."

"Larry, you've sent the wrong color. Again. I asked for white, but that's not what you shipped."

"We'll fix that. Any other problems?"

"Aside from the flimsy construction?"

"Customer code, please?"

"A-532283."

"I'm sorry, but I can't find you in the system."

"Your telephone support is as rotten as your stocking support."

"Stockings? Ma'am, I think you've called the wrong number. This is Foundation Electronix, not Foundation Sox."

Fluxxatron Malfunction

Kathy Steinemann

Do the seagulls know something Samantha doesn't?

Samantha Fischer pointed to an underwater shadow off the starboard side of the boat. "I think that's a torpedo heading toward us."

Her boyfriend, Jamie, adjusted his binoculars. "Impossible. Where would a torpedo come from in this remote area of the islands?"

Samantha laughed. It was the kind of laugh her mother always made when Samantha did something stupid. "Not a man-made torpedo, doofus, a torpedo stingray. Look. It's dipping and swaying in the water like a ballerina."

A lone seagull circled above the boat. Its high-pitched call sounded like a warning: "Die. Die. Die."

The ray accelerated its approach. The boat lurched and stayed suspended on the crest of a wave as the ray passed beneath it. A buzz filled the air, and electricity arced from metal to metal. Sparks exploded into steaming jets of water. The boat listed.

Samantha's head hit something hard.

~*~

When she came to, the boat and Jamie were gone. The ray swam beneath her, holding her afloat near a lifejacket. She paddled away.

Struggling to keep from swallowing seawater, her eyes frantic, she watched the creature. Two green apertures next to its gill slits glowed like neon lights. She tried to don the lifejacket.

The creature moved closer. Nudged her.

She pushed at it with both hands. "Go away. Leave me alone." Its eyes blinked and widened. She gaped into their crystal depth. And stopped thrashing.

The water drew her down, down. Soon she was floating in a strange place, submerged in a rhythmic sound that might have been music or machinery. She closed her eyes to alleviate the dizziness caused by fluctuating pressure in her ears, and drifted in darkness, with patterns of flickering light lulling her into unconsciousness.

~*~

The sweet sunshine of a sandy beach caressed her body. The rough tongue of a sable Burmese cat lapped the seaweed from her brow. She gazed into its yellow-green eyes and shuddered as she remembered the torpedo ray. A young boy shook her shoulder. "Hey, lady. You okay?"

She mumbled.

He moved closer. "What?"

"Where's Jamie?"

"There's only you, lady. If you're okay, I'll go get my dad and mom."

Samantha nodded, then closed out the world again.

A flock of seagulls swooped and drifted above her. Their cries echoed from the cliffs, becoming fainter as she slipped back into oblivion: "Why? Why? Why?"

~*~

She regained consciousness in a cozy living room with blonde-oak walls and a picture window overlooking the sea. A middle-aged woman offered her tea. "It's chamomile with lots of honey in it. Do you want anything to eat?"

"No. No thanks." Samantha strained to talk further, but her tongue refused to respond. The room turned fuzzy. Nausea welled up in her throat, then subsided. And as hard as she tried, she couldn't stay awake.

~*~

Samantha emerged from a dark tunnel in her mind and willed her eyes to open. She scowled at the brightness of the room. *How did I get to Mom and Dad's house?*

Her head throbbed. The refreshing aroma of mint tea floated from the kitchen.

Involuntary recollections flashed into her mind. Green mint leaves. Teal-green waves. Yellow-green eyes filled with tears. She sobbed.

A familiar voice spoke. "Samantha?" Sweet almond aftershave—

"Dad?" His hair, normally brown, now had grey at the temples. His face hid behind an unfamiliar vista of wrinkles and valleys. She peered closer. Squinted. *Yes. It's really him.*

He grinned with the playful expression that always made her feel safe, and he poked her nose. "You're back again."

"What happened? You look older. Did you find Jamie? How did I get here?"

Mr. Fischer's response seemed tentative, uneasy. "Jamie's boat was wrecked." His chin quivered. "They never found him. All they recovered was a single lifejacket. Someone who lives near the marina discovered you two weeks ago. But you've been missing for ten years."

"Ten years?" Samantha bolted to an upright position on the sofa. She touched the necklace around her throat. *Necklace?* She tugged at it and glanced down. An emerald glistened from a starfish-setting on a soft, intricately woven cord. She stared into the gem. It grew warm in her hand. *I can't remember anything, but somehow I know this necklace is important.* "Ten years?"

"Ten years. We thought you were dead. When the police told me you'd been discovered, I figured they were mistaken, or that maybe someone was playing a cruel joke. But it was you, and you look the same as you did the day you sailed off. You're still my pretty little girl."

She stood to hug him. His outdoorsy smell reawakened images of camping trips, fishing out on the bay, and slow hikes along the shore. "Where's Mom?"

His body grew rigid. "She …" His voice cracked. "She's gone. She had a heart attack two years ago."

Father and daughter swayed in their sadness as sounds of the rising tide swished through the open window.

She broke away. "Mom's gone? Jamie, my job, my friends, my apartment. I'll have to start all over again. Ten years?"

"Ten and a half, actually. You were taken to the hospital after they found you. The police asked you questions, but you didn't have any answers. You kept waking up and asking where you were. We told you. You forgot and went back to sleep. Then it repeated all over again. Other than that, the psychiatrist and doctors say you're okay. I insisted they let me bring you home."

She sank onto the sofa and held her head in her hands. "What happened? Why can't I remember?"

~*~

Samantha's dad suggested that she stay in the guestroom until her recuperation was complete. A week later, they chatted over breakfast before he went to work.

She kissed the top of his head after pouring him a fresh cup of coffee. "I think my short-term memory is back. Living at home must have been the cure."

"You're looking better every day."

"But it's hard. Everything is so different now."

"It'll get easier, Sammie. I thought I'd lose my mind when your mother died, but you know what they say about life. It goes on. Whether we want it to or not."

"What could have happened to me?"

"Whatever it was, it must have been good. You look healthy and well-cared-for." He chuckled. "And you smile in your sleep."

"You watch me sleeping?"

"Sometimes. You're still my little girl, and I worry about you. Things will get better. Give it time."

The weeks crawled by as Samantha mourned her mother and Jamie. She talked to her dad about taking refresher courses so she could return to nursing. But he insisted on waiting. "Why waste money on something you might forget?"

So while he went to work, she moped around the house, learned how to load books onto the e-reader he bought her, and browsed the Internet. But she often sat in silence, staring at nothing, wondering about the elusive missing element in her life.

The emerald necklace never disappeared from her neck. It warmed under her fingertips whenever she stroked it. Glowed when she looked into its depths. It comforted her and stimulated fragmented recollections of the creature with the green eyes.

One day, Samantha strolled along the beach, splashing in wave pools and wiggling her toes in the foam. She caressed the emerald and waded into the ocean. Deep. Deeper. The water covered her shoulders.

With a shuddering gasp, she turned and waded back to shore, fixating on the seaweed washing against the rocks. *Sooner or later, I'll remember. I have to.*

As more weeks dragged on, she dreamt about the creature, waking afterward in a cold sweat. Always the same beginning, always the same end:

Rhythmic pulsations relaxed her. Repeating patterns of light flashed and sparkled: beautiful, expanding patterns. Salty seaweed scents wafted in the wind. A breathy voice called her. The creature beckoned. She drifted to it.

Whenever she woke, it took several seconds for her to reorient, to realize the dream wasn't real.

The darkness was real. The thunder of her dad's snoring in the next bedroom was real. The swish of the surf breaking against the nearby rocks was real.

An increasing number of hours was spent walking on the beach and gazing out to the horizon. She retreated into retrospection, and struggled to ignore the worried look on her dad's face.

On an overcast morning at low tide, she tiptoed into a hollowed-out cave at the water's edge, rested against a smooth rock, and slept.

Rhythmic pulsations relaxed her. Repeating patterns of light flashed and sparkled: beautiful, expanding patterns. Salty seaweed scents wafted in the wind. A breathy voice called her. The creature beckoned. She drifted to it. It changed form and became a being with yellow-green eyes, square jaw, and warm lips.

Kai.

He apologized. "My BioInterFace Fluxxatron malfunctioned. I could not save your friend."

She didn't understand, but she nodded. His breath on her skin caused shivers of anticipation.

He whispered, "Do you trust me? Do you want me?"

She leaned back. Succumbed to the passion of his lips on her neck and breasts. She murmured, "Yes. Oh, yes."

He laid her on a bed of silky softness and undressed her. She yielded. She loved.

She woke.

Samantha's cheeks were awash with tears. She caressed the emerald. *Kai gave this to me. Kai. Oh, Kai. I don't understand.*

She plodded to the house and undressed for a shower, puzzling over her appearance in the mirror. She fluffed her hair. Admired her wrinkle-free complexion. *Ten years?* Her gaze strayed to her stomach. *There. Why didn't I notice them before?*

Almost-invisible stretch marks.

She gasped.

How could she tell her dad? He wouldn't understand. He'd tell her she was imagining things.

~*~

Samantha returned to the cave several times, but always woke after Kai made love to her. Her preoccupation intensified. The desire to know more filled every waking moment, every sleeping moment … until the afternoon she borrowed her dad's boat and navigated to where Jamie's craft had gone down. She turned off the engine and allowed the boat to drift while she listened to the seagulls.

She leaned back against a lifejacket and let the cries of the birds lull her into a floating reverie: "Kai. Kai. Kai."

Her whispering lips replied, "Kai." And she slept.

Kai held a baby. Their baby. Suddenly, he was an eight-year-old boy with a serious expression and green eyes like his daddy. Samantha remembered him. Loved him. She reached …

And woke.

Samantha sobbed into the depths. "Are you there?" She wept into the sky. "Are you there?" She wailed, "Kai! Analu!"

The only response was the slapping of waves against the hull.

278

She peered into the deep azure sea and leaned far forward over the railing. For a fleeting moment, the thought of slipping into the water enticed her. However, she forced herself back and started the engine. *I've got to tell Dad he's a grandfather.*

But she couldn't.

Every day she sailed to the same spot, dreamt the same dream, and wept. *I want to be with my husband and child. But how?*

On the tenth day, she grasped the emerald and held it to her heart. She folded both palms over it and murmured, "Kai, Analu," as she fell asleep.

Kai whispered, "You must choose your path. Your world or our world. Your people or our people. Once you choose, you can never go back. We love you, but the choice must be yours."

~*~

Samantha's father scrutinized her during supper. Her preoccupied silence had become commonplace, but tonight her mood was even quieter than usual. "What's the matter, Sammie?"

"Could you take me to the exact place where they found me?"

"Sure. It's a few hundred yards down the beach. Do you remember something?"

"I think so. I need to go there before I tell you though."

They walked into the wind, and she grabbed his hand. "I love you, Dad."

He grinned. "I love you too. I'm always here for you, Sammie."

They dodged incoming breakers, laughing as the foamy waves filled their shoes with sand and salty water.

He slowed his pace. "See the rock over there that looks like it came from Stonehenge? And the dock? You were here, between them."

Samantha clutched the emerald, looked at her feet, and gazed into the green eyes of a sable Burmese cat.

~*~

"Sammie?" Dad's voice. So far away. "Sammie!"

Sunlight and surf and sand. The cat sat on one side of her, and her dad knelt on the other. She rose to her knees and scratched the cat behind the ears.

It purred.

She hugged her father. "Dad, suppose you were a grandpa, but you might never be able to see your grandson. Would you still want to know?"

"Of course, Sammie, and I'd move planet and stars to see the boy." He held her at arm's length. Studied her face.

She pulled up her shirt and hitched down her shorts a few inches. "You're a grandpa." She endeavored to explain, but his confused expression stabbed at her heart.

He steepled his fingers under his nose. "Let me take you home, Sammie. You've had a hard day. We can talk about this in the morning."

She picked up the cat and kissed its nose. "Soon."

~*~

Breakfast. Small-talk. No mention of the previous day.

Samantha's father frowned at her with an appraising eye. "Are you sure you'll be all right by yourself? I can ask someone to come and stay with you for a few hours."

She poked his belly. "I'm okay. Let's talk about something else—like your paunch. You've been eating too much. Time for a diet, starting tonight." She hugged him. "I love you, Dad. You mean the world to me."

He poked her nose. "The paunch is *your* fault. Too much good cooking."

Another hug. "I love you so much. You have a good day at work and don't worry about li'l ol' me. Go. Now."

"Fine. I'll clear out so you can dance on the ceiling or whatever it is you do when I leave." He winked and walked down the hallway. The back door closed behind him with a gentle click.

Samantha groaned. *He'd have me committed if he knew what I plan to do. Where's that pad of paper he uses for his doodles? There ... Now what do I say?*

She spent over an hour writing, wadding pieces of paper into scrunched balls that landed in the wastebasket, and rewriting. *That's as good as it's going to get.*

~*~

The cat was waiting for her at the spot near the strange stone on the beach. Samantha picked him up and stepped into the pounding surf. The cat purred as the water grew deeper. An undulating shimmer surrounded them, and they disappeared.

~*~

When Mr. Fischer returned home from work, he discovered Samantha's note on the kitchen table. His shoulders sagged lower with every paragraph of her parting words. He sobbed. "Sammie. My poor, poor, Sammie."

He trudged into the living room and entreated her photo above the fireplace, "What do I have left to live for? Your mother is gone. Now, you're gone too."

He scuffed his feet on the carpet. Paced. Threw his head back. Looked out the window at the waves breaking against the shore. "Yes, I believe you, sweetie."

Mr. Fischer walked to the place where Samantha had been found, and he waded into the water, whispering her name into the wind.

~*~

Friends found the note in the kitchen, but they never found the bodies.

Locals claim they can still hear the seagulls cry: "Kai. Kai. Kai." And the surf whispering its reply: "Sammie. Sammie. Sammie."

Not Your Time

Kathy Steinemann

Is Wendell hearing voices in his head? Or is he being watched?

A melodic voice echoed from somewhere behind Wendell. "You must not go. Do not do it!"

Wendell flinched. He scanned the kitchen and searched for someone, anyone, who might have issued the warning. His skin erupted in goosebumps. Could it be his mom talking to him from beyond the grave? But it didn't sound like her.

He squinted. "Who's there?"

No response.

Mom always claimed she had ESP and precognition. I wonder if I could have inherited something from her.

Wendell dropped into a chair and brooded in the silent room.

He picked up his keys to leave; grabbed his suitcase and carry-on; gripped the door handle.

After several deep breaths, he released the handle and called his travel agent to cancel his Bermuda vacation.

As soon as he returned the phone to its cradle, he inspected the kitchen for hidden cameras. Nothing seemed out of place, but the hair on the back of his neck prickled the way it did when he jogged over a forest footpath at night.

What do I do next? Two weeks of mandatory vacation, and now I have nowhere to go.

He switched on the television and flipped through pages of a *National Geographic* magazine while his favorite TV channel blared in the background.

~*~

A noise woke him during the six o'clock news. Was it the voice again? Still in a haze, he rubbed his eyes and tried to go back to sleep. But he bolted upright when he heard the news report:

"*... and the plane, on a flight to Bermuda, caught fire shortly after takeoff. As you can see, the flames are making rescue efforts difficult. However, unnamed sources claim that nobody survived the crash. We'll have more live updates as soon as they become available. Right now we're talking to an eyewitness. Mr. Daniels, can you tell viewers what you saw?*"

Wendell's insides tightened. He concentrated on every detail of the broadcast. That was his flight. If he hadn't listened to the voice, he'd be dead now. His scalp tingled and crawled.

He shuffled to the kitchen and microwaved leftovers for supper. A hiss of steam scalded his fingers when he removed the plastic. A loud expletive exploded from his lips as he ran cold water over his hand.

Wendell frowned. That tingling suspicion of being watched brought a shiver to his spine.

His meal grew cold while he checked every crevice and closet in the house. No secret cameras or hidden wires upstairs or down. Even the basement was clean.

~*~

Sleep. Uneasy sleep. Impossible sleep.

The covers on his bed became a tangled mess as he dreamed. He woke repeatedly, his nightmare images eluding him. They were so close he could almost touch them. His heart hammered as though it were trying to escape his chest. Yet whenever he peered into the gloom, he couldn't remember what had caused his fear.

~*~

The brightness of the morning sun brought a new perspective. Wendell decided it must have been his mind playing

284

tricks on him. He'd been working too hard. But … the plane crash. That wasn't a trick.

He went for a brisk ten-mile walk. Ah, the invigorating scent of fresh air and mowed lawns, the twitter of songbirds, and the soft give of the sandy soil beneath his sneakers. *Inhale. Exhale. That's it. Feel the sunlight. Smell the air.*

He stopped to catch his breath while he relaxed and watched joggers. He laughed at a seagull dive-bombing a kid with a chocolate bar, and he felt envious as his gaze followed two honeymooners who couldn't keep their hands to themselves.

A raven cawed from a nearby branch. Was it watching him? The beady eyes seemed intelligent. Too intelligent. He struggled to shake the foolish thought out of his head.

The drone of distant sirens and the faint sound of traffic reminded him that the city was nearby.

He ignored the hairs bristling on the back of his neck as the large bird swished away. Maybe he'd do some dusting when he got home. Then his sister wouldn't have any excuse to criticize him when she visited on Thursday.

~*~

The dusting didn't take long. He admired his excellent job. Crap. He had missed a spider web. "Outside you go, little fella."

He scooped the spider into the yard and refilled the food and water bowls he had set on the porch for stray neighborhood cats.

Back inside, he opened the fridge and poured a glass of milk. His nose wrinkled.

He laughed and spoke to the walls. "You could have warned me. I don't like sour milk."

The ensuing silence didn't comfort him.

His attempt to read a book left him drowsy, but sleep eluded him when he fell into bed. He flinched at every tiny noise, stared into the blackness of his bedroom, and listened.

When sunlight poked through the crack between the curtains, he was already wide awake.

He performed another search of the house. Then he hunched over the kitchen table while he sipped on coffee and gazed across the room. There, in the corner, was another spider web. *I'm sure I removed that yesterday.* He chuckled. "It can't be the same one, dodo." He scooped the web's owner into a glass. "Off to the great outdoors."

A melodic voice protested, "I prefer the ambience in this room to the moist grass in your yard."

He dropped the glass. Broken shards shot across the floor, but the spider marched away and climbed, unscathed, back up the wall.

Wendell hyperventilated. He fell back against the counter. "Was that you talking? And was that you before?"

No reply from the spider.

His knees felt weak. He wondered if he was going insane.

Just when he was about to assume he had imagined the entire encounter, the spider spoke. "Insanity is often the logic of an accurate mind overtasked. However, I can guarantee that you are quite sane."

Wendell's eyes widened. He ran his fingers through his hair as the blood pounded in his ears, and he grabbed at his chest to massage the sudden heartburn bubble. "Wh-why did you save my life?"

"I have been monitoring you for weeks. I am supposed to observe, not communicate. But it was not your time, so I could not let you perish in that plane crash."

"Not my time? Not my *time?* Either this is a hidden camera joke, or I'm having a doozy of a nightmare. I'm not falling for it. I'm a scientist. I don't believe in supernatural hocus pocus." He laughed a harsh, hollow laugh.

"Yet you thought your mother might be communicating with you from beyond the grave."

Wendell scowled at the unnerving mental image of a colossal tarantula with a turban on its head gazing into a crystal ball and reading his future. *Yes. This is a nightmare.* How could anyone, or any*thing*, know his innermost thoughts? "I'm going for another walk. You keep filming without me in the picture."

~*~

His walk became a slow jog, then a full-out run on a path near the beach. He stopped for a moment near a dense growth of shrubs and admired a spider web, marveling at its size and intricacy. He looked closer. Yes, it seemed real. He poked, and the spider spun away on a gust of wind.

Wendell turned toward the ocean. The salt spray kissed his face, the taste and scent reminding him of a boating trip: a trip where a pair of killer whales had surfaced and splashed the passengers with their blow. He sniffled. That was the last time he saw his parents before the fire that took their lives.

He walked toward the shore. In his effort not to trample on a spider, he stepped the wrong way on a tree root, twisted his ankle, and plowed into the sand with one knee and an elbow. When he straightened his leg, a pain shot up to his thigh. "Damn!"

A disheveled teenage girl with purple hair and holes in her jeans appeared. She stared down at him. "Mister, are you all right?"

"I think so. It hurts, but I'm sure I'll be okay."

She twisted her lip. Her grimy cheeks were streaked with dirty trails that hinted at a recent bout of tears.

Wendell studied her face. "Never mind me. Are *you* all right?"

She shrugged, avoiding his eyes.

"Why aren't you in school?"

Her face drained of color, and she turned to leave.

"Wait. Look, I won't turn you in for playing hooky, if that's what you think. I just want to talk."

She fixated on his leg. "I hurt my ankle last week too. I slept at the church over there for a few hours, and when I woke up, it didn't hurt anymore."

"Why were you sleeping at the church? Where are your parents?"

"I ran away from home."

"What's your name?"

"None of your business. You'll call the cops, and I don't intend go back."

"Why don't you sit here for a moment?" Wendell patted the ground.

She hesitated, with narrowed eyes, and then sat a few feet away. Her shoulders tightened. "Guess you'd never be able to catch me with that bum ankle."

He repositioned his sunglasses. "Nice nose ring."

"Thanks."

He focused on an ant toting the body of a dead fly. "I lost my mother and father when I was about your age. I never had the chance to tell them how much I loved them before they died. An uncle raised my sister and me, but it wasn't the same as having Mom and Dad around. Are your parents mean to you?"

"No. We're having a dispute about my courses."

"Courses?"

She tugged her knees to her chest. "I want to be a scientist, someone who can find better ways to farm and increase crop

288

yields. The world can't sustain our current population growth forever. My parents want me to be a doctor, but I can't stand the sight or smell of blood. They don't understand. I don't like my courses, so I don't study. I'm probably going to fail the year."

"So you're just giving up?" He raised an eyebrow.

"We had a fight. They took away my computer. And cell phone. And grounded me for a month."

Wendell scrutinized her. She seemed familiar. Maybe if her hair were brown …

She picked up a pebble and threw it toward the ocean.

He cleared his throat while he thought about what to say next. "I wouldn't be where I am now if I'd given up. I didn't quit when my mother and father died, or when my fiancée left me. I didn't quit when the work was hard, and I kept at it even when people scoffed at my ideas."

"You're old. Things are different now."

His jaw fell. "I'm only—"

"Uh, what I meant was … I didn't mean to …" Her face reddened. "But guys like you got it made. I bet you have a nice house and a big car. And friends. And a good job."

"Yes, I have a few good friends and, coincidentally, a career as a scientist, even though nobody believes in my latest research."

She held her lips in a thin white line of determined rebellion.

He sighed before he continued. His speech was slow, his breathing strident. "My biggest regret is that I don't have a wife and kids."

Her gaze moved to his face. "I'm sorry about that. I mean, about you not having a wife and kids. But you're not *that* old. It could still happen."

He repositioned his ankle to alleviate the throb. "Thanks for the ambiguous vote of confidence. Yes, it could happen, but we're talking about you. You need to continue your schooling. The doctor stuff is useful for scientists. Every bit of knowledge you cram into your brain is useful."

He pulled several bills and a business card out of his wallet. "Here. You take this cash. Buy yourself something to eat and some new pants, and then go home. Look me up when you get the chance."

She studied the card and stuffed the cash into her pocket. "Thanks, Mr. Oliver, but there's nothing wrong with my jeans. They're *supposed* to have holes in them."

Her tongue played with the piercing in her bottom lip. "Do you want me to stick around long enough to see if you can walk?"

He stood. "Look. I'm just limping a little, and I live close-by." He offered his hand to help her up.

She rubbed at the dirt on her face. "Thanks for everything. I'll return the money as soon as I can." Without another word, she spun on her heel and disappeared into a small grove of trees.

Wendell massaged his leg. *I suppose she could take the money and blow it. But she has an honest face.* He continued to watch the trees while he speculated about where he might have met her before.

The encounter had been a temporary respite from his worries about spider webs and strange voices. But his anxieties returned with the strength of a sledgehammer. He started to shake. His hands grew moist and sticky.

He hobbled through a nearby neighborhood for at least an hour, in no particular direction, making frequent stops to rest his ankle. He eyed every dog, cat, bird, and insect with suspicion, wondering if his feeling of being observed was pure paranoia.

Of course it is.

When the wind turned cold, he headed for home. Then he stood on the welcome mat, squared his jaw, and unlocked the front door.

The voice spoke, loud and strong. "That was a good thing you did."

Wendell leaned against the doorjamb. "Now I'm sure I'm nuts. There's no way anything as small as you could have moved fast enough to follow me."

"I can change form at will. Birds, arachnids, insects … While you wandered about and attempted to find your courage, the girl returned to her parents. They were ecstatic to see her."

"How do you know …?"

"We are many, and we know much. The girl will see your obituary in the newspaper."

"Obituary?"

The spider's eyes glowed yellow-green as it paused. "Your time is coming. Soon."

Indigestion burbled up again in Wendell's chest. He clutched at his shirt. *Blasted heartburn.* He started to perspire, and his breathing became thready.

The voice grew louder. "The girl will idolize you, continue her education, and complete your research, which, I might add, is flawed in its current state. One day she will develop a new food supply that will save your species after our emergency rescue of indigenous creatures. Without your encouragement this morning, that would never happen, and humans would perish."

The spider crawled closer. "Your daughter will never forget you."

"My daughter? That girl was my daughter?"

"You thought she looked familiar, did you not?"

"No, she couldn't be. … Are you sure?"

"Yes. Your ex-fiancée gave the baby up for adoption. Your daughter will attend your funeral. Soon she will learn the truth about her heritage."

Wendell squeezed his eyes closed. Tried to control his breathing. "No! I need more time … more time. Please. Give me a chance to get to know her better."

"We can only act in limited fashion on the timeline. I am sorry. You are having a heart attack. It will be fatal."

Tears streamed down Wendell's cheeks. "But why do I have to die? Save me like you did before."

"That is impossible. Now is your time. You are a mediocre scientist, but like the paintings of an artist who dies prematurely, your ideas will be respected after you are gone. You have commenced a process that your daughter will continue."

An optical disruption that looked like a transparent pool of water opened in the kitchen wall. The fading voice spoke its final warning. "Now is your time. Now is …"

The Rescue

Kathy Steinemann

The way to love anything is to realize that it may be lost. ~ Gilbert K. Chesterton

Ramon stroked the disc hanging from his neck. "We're lost, and we might not get to ERIC in time." His young voice was almost inaudible over the wail of the wind assaulting the mountain.

He frowned and wiggled his bare toes to dislodge a toad from his foot, then watched the warty creature hop away. He yelled again to his invisible companion. "These stones hurt, BIFF. I wish my shoes hadn't come off in the pond."

Darkness fell.

The wind became a whisper, and the forest seemed to transform into a breathing being with moving limbs, glowing eyeballs, and bright flashes followed by loud rumblings. As Ramon trudged forward, the fragrance of pine needles and moldy moss wafted into his nostrils. The overcast sky offered no light from moon or stars, and wet rain squalls soaked him, plastering his hair to his head.

He scrunched through a thicket. Stepped out the other side—

Into empty space. He clutched at branches and roots; grabbed at slippery rocks; dug his fingers into the soil on the side of the cliff to slow his descent. …

An eternity later, his mud-coated body came to an abrupt stop on a rocky ledge. He panted and leaned away from the crevasse. His clothes stuck to his skin, and he shivered in the cold. Mosquitoes clung to him. But as soon as he shut his eyes, he succumbed to a deep slumber.

In the dampness of dawn, the seams of his denim coveralls began to dig into his tender skin. He stirred. A ray of sunshine peeked through a cleft in the mountains. He interrupted his yawn with a giggle. The canyon floor, invisible last night, lay only six feet below.

Ramon scratched at the mosquito bites covering his body, smiling in spite of his discomfort. After searching for the easiest way east, he trekked downhill, taking care not to step on snakes or insects.

A mist rose in the distance. "It's water, BIFF." His nose led him to a rocky bluff that burped intermittent bursts of water. He followed the trickles to a stream.

A raccoon stood in frozen stance, scrutinizing the water from the shadows. One of its forepaws snaked below the surface in a swift, almost-invisible movement. The paw reappeared with a wriggling fish in its grasp. Ramon bowed in a moment of silent meditation, his face moist with tears. "I hope the fish didn't suffer."

He uprooted a few dandelions and washed them in the stream, then munched with a sour face for several minutes before pushing away the bitter leftovers. "It's sure taking a long time. I hope it's not much farther."

~*~

Ramon's youthful legs stumbled more frequently as the day progressed. Sunlight glinted off the disc at his neck, creating a prism of color that sparkled like a halo of fairy dust. The sun punished everything it touched and turned his tender skin redder with every mile. The straight line toward ERIC meant that he had to climb rocky hills and descend through stinging vegetation devoid of nuts or berries.

He complained about his thirst during frequent, one-sided discussions with BIFF, although his swollen tongue made speech difficult. He licked his lips to keep them moist, but that made his mouth crack and bleed. Late in the afternoon, he curled up in the shade to escape the heat.

The wind returned, sweeping dark clouds across the sky. A single droplet of moisture splattered and burst on his nose. A deluge of raindrops ensued. He peered skyward and opened his mouth to drink, but the rain stopped as quickly as it had begun. He pounded his fist against a tree. Two ravens cawed a strident warning from a branch above him.

"Must get to ERIC ... must." He sank into a layer of leaves beneath the tree, his hand on the softly glowing disc, and flinched when the birds defecated on him before they flew away.

Ramon climbed high into the tree and wedged himself against a sturdy fork. There, he searched for liquid on leaves and found barely enough to ease the dryness in his throat.

The gradual onset of a deep sleep spared him from the physical and mental anguish that consumed his juvenile form.

~*~

The woods were still dark the next time he stirred. "BIFF? Yes, I hear it."

He groped toward the faint sound of flowing water, testing the ground before each step to avoid crawling creepers of the night. A spider web brushed his cheek. When he swiped it away, the startled spinner cast off on a silken thread that glistened in the dewy darkness. He shivered. "I hope it's all right. I didn't mean to break its web."

The noisy rush of the river soon overcame the chirping of crickets. He waded into its depths and scooped water into his mouth until he couldn't drink any more.

The violent current whipped at his legs, pulling him off balance and pushing him over a large root. He stumbled; regained his footing; stumbled again. Then he crumpled onto the sandy bank at the water's edge. White bone protruded through the shin of his right leg. He vomited; moaned with pain; closed his eyes.

His life ebbed away with the copious red liquid soaking into the sand.

~*~

The early morning drizzle hugged moss and leaves in its damp embrace, but the moisture stopped within a foot of Ramon's motionless body. His skin was free of injuries, bites, or sunburn. His leg was whole, and his clothes were dry.

A pack of wolves encircled him. Their piercing, yellow stares waited and watched.

He wakened, stretched, and focused on his surroundings. His face showed no fear or worry. The alpha wolf dropped a rabbit at his feet and rolled over into a submissive posture, paws in the air, until he rubbed her belly. She responded by baring her teeth in a silly grin. Ramon shook his head. "I respect the gift and the animal that gave its life, but I can't eat that. You keep it."

He stroked the disc hanging from his neck. It emitted a pulsating, emerald-green glow that gradually transformed into an iridescent rainbow of color.

Ramon held the disc to his lips and spoke. "Thank the Creator you're back, BIFF. Adult form, please." His melodic laugh became a hearty sound that deepened and loudened as his youthful body grew taller and broader. His clothing stretched until it shredded from the strain.

He stroked his muscular chest and scratched at the stubble on his chin. "That's better. When you were damaged after the pod crashed into the pond, I was afraid I'd be trapped in that body forever. Poor choice on my part. I had no idea how vulnerable

Earthling young can be. But surely you could have re-morphed me with a clean-shaven face. These whiskers are itchy."

A metallic voice emanated from his BioInterFace Fluxxatron. "Artificial life-forms are not programmed to have emotions, but I believe I am pleased that my external modulation function has returned. You never should have immersed me in that pond after my casing cracked. It is fortunate this planet has a bright sun and I was able to recharge so quickly. You should have set me on a rock to dry."

"Would you stop prattling and— Never mind. I see you have already provided fresh clothes. Please enter into your databank that the juveniles of this species are poorly equipped for Earth's harsh environment."

"Duly noted."

"Murder. Farming of animals for food. Using them for research and circus performances. A barbaric race."

"Duly noted."

"And the hills. Your altimeter malfunction almost killed me when you sent us over the cliff."

"However, my programming did guide us in the correct direction. Observe."

Ramon scrutinized the glistening optical disruption that had opened nearby. "It appears very similar to where we crashed. Frankly, when I first saw the pond, I thought it was our portal."

"We are just in time."

Ramon scanned the terrain and the vast assemblage of creatures that had gathered. More appeared in tiny whirlwinds of transported atoms that rematerialized as he watched. "The people of this planet don't realize how fortunate they are ... *were* ... to have such diverse fauna. In seconds, the animals will disappear and these savages will have to manage without them."

He strode to the edge of the undulating shimmer and announced, "Portal 9-239-278 standing by."

An authoritative voice spoke from within. "Synchronization complete. ERIC coordinates confirmed from all Earth portals. Emergency Rescue of Indigenous Creatures sequence to initialize in ten, nine, eight …"

Afterword

Just when I think I'm finished, ideas for more short stories coax their way into my imagination. They always come at the most inopportune moments. As Anais Nin said, "My ideas usually come not at my desk writing but in the midst of living."

I'm jotting down most of my inspirations, and even as this book goes to publication, I'm massaging them in my word processor. They'll become new tales in my next anthology.

I'd like to talk to you now about reviews.

Positive comments and ratings help authors earn a living. After you reach the end of this book, I urge you to post a review. If you didn't like what you read, please get in touch and tell me why. I'll try to address your concerns:

Author@KathySteinemann.com

And remember Joseph Addison's observation: "Reading is to the mind what exercise is to the body."

Keep reading.

Contributors

Many thanks to Barbara Galler-Smith for writing the foreword; and to Amber Hayward, A. L. Kaplan, and Donna Milward, who contributed stories for this anthology. It was a pleasure to work with you.

I would also like to thank everyone else who helped this book become what it is today: Alain, Jen, Derek, John, Chrystina, Patti, Nancy, Tricia, Jeroen, and the many Scribophile writers who critiqued my work. I couldn't have done it without your advice and assistance.

Kathy Steinemann, Grandma Birdie to her grandkids, is an award-winning author who lives in the foothills on the Alberta side of the Canadian Rocky Mountains. She has loved words for as long as she can remember.

As a young child, she scribbled poems and stories. During the progression of her love affair with language, she won public-speaking and writing awards, and she contributed to her school newspaper. Then every Monday, rain or shine, she walked home instead of taking the bus so that she could deliver her latest column to the community weekly.

Her career has taken varying directions, including positions as editor of a small-town paper, computer-network administrator, and webmaster. She has also worked on projects in commercial art and cartooning.

Her books include *IBS-IBD Fiber Charts*, *Top Tips for Packing Your Suitcase*, the *Sapphire Brigade* series, and several others.

Kathy's Website
KathySteinemann.com

Barbara Galler-Smith lives in Edmonton, Alberta, Canada.

She's an award-winning short story writer, a long-time member of Edmonton's largest speculative fiction writers group, The Cult of Pain, and co-founder of a group designed for emerging speculative fiction writers. She's also a fiction editor for *On Spec: The Canadian Magazine of the Fantastic*.

Along with U.S. writer, Josh Langston, she's the author of The Druids Saga—an historical fantasy epic trilogy: *Druids* (2009), *Captives* (2011), *Warriors* (2013), and a contemporary romantic comedic fantasy.

She has also committed Costuming at the World Science Fiction Convention Masquerade and won ribbons.

Barbara's Website
GallerSmith.ca

Amber Hayward is the author of a trilogy of speculative fiction novels, the *Children of the Panther* series, released by Edge Press. Her short fiction and poetry have appeared in Canadian and international periodicals, including *Daily Science Fiction*. From May 1, 2011, she wrote a flash fiction piece each day for a year and posted them on her website.

She is one of the owners of the Black Cat Guest Ranch near Jasper, Alberta, and teaches writing workshops there and in the nearby community of Hinton.

Amber's Website
AmberHayward.ca

Amber's Stories
Crying Girl
Dog Diary of an Old Man
Transported

A. L. Kaplan's love of books started at an early age and sparked a creative imagination. Her work has been included in *Indies Unlimited's 2014 Flash Fiction Anthology*, *Dragonfly Arts Magazine* 2014 and 2015, and the *Balticon 49 BSFAN*. She holds an MFA in sculpture from the Maryland Institute College of Art and is the President of the Maryland Writers' Association's Howard County Chapter. When not writing or indulging in her fascination with wolves, A. L. is the props manager for a local theatre. To keep up with A. L.'s writing, visit her blog.

A. L.'s Blog
ALKaplan.Wordpress.com

A. L.'s Stories
A Chance Meeting—or Not
Blood Money
Pup 'O Lantern
Regrets

Donna Milward is a willing cat slave living in Edmonton, Alberta, Canada with her cats Spartacus Jones and Freya, along with her troll, Dan. She's been writing since grade two, but only in recent years has she made a career out of it after an RWA convention in Washington convinced her to go for it. Her first two novels are titled *Thoeba* and *Aphrodite's War*.

Donna is currently working on the first novella in a series called *Her True Name Volume One: Egypt*, as well as her fourth novel, *Elaina's Fate*, about an assassin in a different realm. She is also shopping around her third novel, *Chasing Monsters*, which is about a paranormal investigator who meets a demon with a soul. When not writing, Donna can be found in her garden with her beloved furchildren, or canning beans and tomatoes.

For more information about Donna Milward, please find her at:

Facebook—Donna Milward, Author
Amazon—Donna Milward Author Page
Twitter—@DonnaMilward
Her blog—earthtothoeba.blogspot.ca

She can also be found on Goodreads and Yelp Edmonton YEG.

Thoeba

Darkness has conquered the heavens, forcing Thoeba to flee with the weakened Energy trapped in a crystal. She finds herself on Earth among humans, a race she is not fond of. Evil has followed her, and she has no choice but to ally herself with Peter and his teen-aged children. She will learn about herself, about love and human endurance, but will she save the universe?

Aphrodite's War

Bored gods are dangerous. Aphrodite and Ares are engaged in a contest. Aphrodite must make two humans fall in love, and Ares must stop her. Loser leaves Olympus for 100 years. Simple enough. Too bad humans have minds of their own. Not to mention Ares has his own agenda. And Ares always cheats.

Donna's Stories
How to Tell if Your Human Worships You
The Guardian's Angel

Books by Kathy Steinemann

- Envision: Future Fiction
- Nag Nag Nag: Megan and Emmett Volume I
- Suppose: Drabbles, Flash Fiction, and Short Stories
- The Doctor's Deceit: Sapphire Brigade Book 2
- Vanguard of Hope: Sapphire Brigade Book 1
- The IBS Compass
- Top Tips for Packing Your Suitcase
- IBS-IBD Fiber Charts
- Practical and Effective Tips for Learning Foreign Languages
- Life, Death and Consequences
- Leben, Tod und Konsequenzen (German Edition)
- Matthew and the Pesky Ants
- Matthias und die verflixten Ameisen (German Edition)
- Top Tips for Travel by Air

You have reached the end of the book. Thank you for reading. If you enjoyed it, please recommend it to a friend and review it online.

www.ingramcontent.com/pod-product-compliance
Lightning Source LLC
Chambersburg PA
CBHW071108250626
47159CB00002B/653